THE SONG OF RISING SHADOW

SONG OF THE FALLEN SWORDS
BOOK 3

RYAN KIRK

WATERSTONE
MEDIA

RYAN KIRK

THE SONG OF RISING SHADOW

Copyright © 2024 by Waterstone Media

All rights reserved.

No part of this book may be reproduced in any form or by any electronic or mechanical means, including information storage and retrieval systems, without written permission from the author, except for the use of brief quotations in a book review.

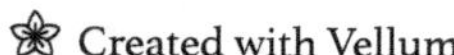 Created with Vellum

For Justin
Not sure I could ask for a better gentleman to go adventuring
with.

THE STORY SO FAR...

Our story opens on Radyn, our primary protagonist, as an older child working the fields on the surface of the floating city of Firestone beside his father. The city is attacked by another floating city while they work. His father, who Radyn had only ever known as a farmer, reveals an impressive martial skill while he defends the city. Thanks in large part to Radyn's father's efforts, Firestone is saved from the attack, but Radyn's father dies in the battle.

In the years following, Radyn joins Firestone's clan, which acts both as the governing force in the city and as the standing army. The Daggers and Swords of the clan are known for their ability to connect with shards from the mighty Engines that rest in the heart of each city, keeping them afloat. Connecting with the shards gives the Manirah increased focus, strength, and speed, and their maniblades, powered by the Engine, can cut through steel.

Radyn begins his training during a tumultuous time. Whitehawk, another floating city, falls from the sky, and even Firestone suffers from an event known as "The Little Fall." There are groups within the city advocating a return to the surface, even though long-term human habitation has so far proven elusive. Whatever dark forces drove the Makers (Radyn's ancestors) to build the cities and take to the sky, they've thus far prevented any return.

Radyn's master is a young but powerful Sword named Elora. She exposes Radyn to the shards far more than the typical master, attempting to forge him into a new type of Sword. As their world becomes more dangerous, she eventually suggests the bold idea of embedding the shards directly within Radyn's flesh. Few Manirah can handle such prolonged exposure, but Radyn takes well to the shards, granting him a hidden strength most aren't aware of.

Eventually, Radyn and Elora's search for truth uncovers a conspiracy that reaches all the way to the 12th Blade of Firestone, the ruler of their city. In coordination with Nightkeep, another floating city, the Blade hopes to land Firestone in an ancient Maker city and attempt to survive on the surface.

Radyn and Elora fight off the surprise attack, but in the process, Elora sacrifices her life singing to the Engine alone, a sacrifice that saves the city.

In the aftermath of the battle, Radyn volunteers to take the blame for both Elora's death and the deaths of both the 12th Blade (a hero among the people) and the Master Singer. This agreement, struck solely with the 13th Blade of Firestone, an honorable man named Jyn, keeps the peace in the city.

Ostracized from his clan, Radyn attempts to live a more peaceful life as a farmer with his wife, Aria. The peace lasts for about a year before Radyn is once again pulled into the affairs of the clan. A brutal set of murders leads to Radyn's arrest, and he must work with a clever Shield named Nikki to uncover the truth. In their journey they discover a conspiracy to kidnap a young woman named Kaya, whose prodigious talent at singing to the Engines makes her a target for both those who want to protect the cities and those who want to destroy them.

In their investigation, Radyn also meets with the soulkeepers, a small group of humans who are making a secret attempt to survive on the surface. Caught between the clans, the dark conspiracy, and the soulkeepers, Radyn eventually saves Kaya and lets her choose her future. Kaya chooses to join the soulkeepers on the surface, and in so doing, guarantees Radyn will never be allowed to live peacefully in Firestone. He and Aria join Kaya and the soulkeepers on the surface, which is where our third story opens.

1

As Radyn lifted today's weapon above his head, he wondered whether he preferred the maniblade or the hoe in his hands. The hoe was a symbol of stability, of a future in which parents didn't worry whether their city would have enough food to feed their children or not. It represented routine, both of the daily variety and of the seasonal, and it was safe. Outside of exhaustion or carelessness, a person with a hoe in their hands was almost certain to return to their family's dinner table as the sun went down.

Maniblades represented chaos and the uncertainty of the future. They were a necessary tool in a world where both monsters and enemies roamed freely. A Manirah had their own daily routine, training body, mind, and spirit to enact the will of the clan. They weren't guaranteed the farmer's evening return, but in exchange they enjoyed honor, privilege, and the knowledge they fought for a future in which hoes far outnumbered maniblades.

Radyn was all too aware of the shortcomings of both hoe and maniblade, having lived both as a farmer and as a

Manirah. Depending on the day, he longed for one or the other, but he knew himself well enough now to know the longing would pass, soon to be replaced by its opposite.

He laughed bitterly to himself. Fortunately, he didn't have to choose anymore. Thanks to his poor choices and Miranda's boundless estimate of his abilities, he served as both farmer and Manirah, laboring in two roles but enjoying the benefits of neither. He would have complained, but it was suitable punishment for failing Firestone and his clan. It didn't matter if he fought with hoe or sword, but he'd do everything in his power to protect Underhill.

He brought the hoe down, breaking up the resilient clump of soil that stood in his way. Then he angled the hoe and dug a furrow he'd soon fill with the seed Miranda had somehow acquired. Seed that rightfully belonged to the cities, but Miranda claimed they wouldn't even notice it was missing.

Having seen firsthand some of what passed for security and logistics within the cities, Radyn guessed she spoke truthfully, which only frustrated him more. How much more would the cities be capable of if the people and systems they relied on did as they were supposed to? How many more people would be alive today? He suspected the number was even higher than he would guess.

Another clump of soil broke under his wrath, and something about the act must have caught Jarrod's attention, because the boy asked, "You have a fight with Aria this morning?"

Radyn snapped his head around and stopped the growl before it escaped his throat. Jarrod held up his hands and took a step back. "Didn't mean anything by it. You're just attacking that dirt like it owes you something."

Radyn's knuckles turned white as he gripped the shaft of

the hoe, but only for a moment. After all these years, Elora's training still held, and he breathed out his frustrations and forced himself to observe Jarrod.

Radyn labeled him a boy, but that wasn't accurate or fair to the young man. Jarrod was only a few years younger than Radyn, perhaps about eighteen or nineteen, if he was forced to guess. What separated them wasn't years, but experience. Jarrod and his girlfriend had fled their city six months ago because their parents hadn't wanted them to get married, and in an act of true love that was as reckless as it was stupid, they'd decided to join the soulkeepers on the surface. Radyn still hadn't figured out why someone would rather risk almost certain death instead of a family's disapproving stares, but he was hardly knowledgeable about family affairs. His own hadn't stuck around long enough for him to learn.

Jarrod was an easygoing sort, and one of the few that regularly volunteered to work with Radyn, and Radyn still hadn't figured out if it was some sort of misplaced hero worship or something else. Most days they worked well together, but Jarrod had either never heard of or had completely forgotten what personal privacy meant, and sometimes he pushed too far into Radyn's life.

Today, Radyn's observation bore quick fruit. He and Aria never fought in public and rarely even in private, so it was a strange guess to leap to. But Jarrod's hair, which was usually washed and combed in the morning, was messier than usual, and the lines under his eyes made Radyn think the boy hadn't slept much the night before.

"No, not a fight," Radyn said. He gestured to their field, which was closer in size to a large garden than a true field, but they had to start somewhere. "Just one of those days when I'm frustrated about our slow progress. You and Isabel doing well?"

His answer wasn't entirely truthful, but it wasn't a lie, either, and Jarrod's reaction to Radyn's question convinced him he'd aimed his own guess well. His face fell, as though he'd just gotten the news there'd be no rations for the week.

"Not as well as I wish we were. Both of us expected something different when we came down here, and it's wearing on us. Last night Isabel asked if maybe we'd made a mistake, and I'll confess I didn't take it well."

Radyn grunted. "If the soulkeepers were truly honest when talking to people in the cities, no one would join."

Jarrod chuckled, but only for a moment, his gloom too thick to be pierced by Radyn's halfhearted attempts at humor. "Do *you* think we made a mistake coming here?"

Radyn bit back his first retort. Jarrod and Isabel had arrived with an impressive lack of skills, but both had worked hard to make up for their lack. Yes, it had probably been a mistake for them to move to the surface, but that didn't mean it had to be a mistake to stay.

"You two are really interested in starting a family soon, right?" he asked.

Jarrod nodded. "We've been trying for almost a month."

Radyn flinched, still not used to Jarrod's unguarded openness, then continued. "Then staying down here is for the best. The soulkeepers may have spoken too kindly about daily life on the surface, but they didn't lie about what matters."

Jarrod looked to the sky, as though he expected to find a city floating above his head. "The cities' Engines are failing."

Radyn nodded. "It doesn't seem like it now, but there will come a time when you'll know that coming here early was the best decision you ever made."

Jarrod considered this for a moment, then grinned. "Thanks, Radyn."

"You're welcome."

They hefted their hoes and returned to their labors, but it wasn't long before movement in the distance caught Radyn's eye. He looked up from the field and saw a clump of grass a few hundred paces away moving against the wind. As he watched, he caught the slightest flicker of a tail. He swore softly to himself, then spoke quietly.

"Jarrod, you're going to want to get back to Underhill as quick as you can."

For a moment he feared his warning hadn't been heard, but then he saw that Jarrod had been listening. Instead of running, he was standing tall in the grass, looking for whatever danger had prompted Radyn's orders. Repeating the instruction would do no good, as Jarrod had a stubborn streak when it came to being told what to do, which was probably one of the reasons he was down here in the first place.

"Banti. To the west, about three hundred paces. I can't tell how many, but more than one."

Jarrod paled even as his eyes searched the western grasses. From the way his gaze kept moving, Radyn knew Jarrod hadn't seen them.

The banti had more wisdom than Jarrod, or at least had senses honed enough that they knew when they'd been spotted. A pair burst forward, still not directly visible, but they carved a path through the tall grass that left no doubt as to their location and their destination.

Jarrod froze in place, his feet rooted to the ground more deeply than the wheat they soon hoped to plant. Not that running would have made much of a difference. Radyn didn't think that even he could outrun one of the predators long enough to reach safety.

He dropped his hoe, and his hand went to his side, where Elora's maniblade was clipped to his waist. One practiced motion freed the blade, and with a thought he connected to the shard within. The blade sprang to life, and Radyn tapped into the shards in his body to extend the weapon an extra foot. He stepped between Jarrod and the banti, and his first cut went clean through the nearest predator.

His blade bit into the soil, but he twisted his wrists and cut again, slicing lengthwise across the second banti. It died without a sound, the parts of its corpse coming to a rest only a pace beyond Radyn. He checked both corpses to ensure they were well and truly dead before letting his maniblade vanish.

Banti were nasty creatures, something between a snake and a lizard and with an unpleasant temperament to boot. They preferred to slither along the ground like a snake, and they could move with impressive quickness, as he'd just witnessed. If the need arose, they unfolded their powerful legs and leaped into the air. They weren't that hard to kill, but they sometimes clung stubbornly to life, crawling for several paces even after a lethal blow.

These two were dead, though, so he didn't have to worry about a bite from their poisoned fangs. One nip from them was enough to fell a full-grown man in a matter of minutes.

Jarrod was about to congratulate him, but before he could finish opening his mouth, Radyn held up a hand. Thankfully the brief ambush had successfully convinced Jarrod to pay full attention, and he shut his jaw without a sound.

Banti hunted in packs, and Radyn had never come

across a pack of less than four. Not that such a pack couldn't exist, but Radyn's hairs still stood on end, his body aware of a danger he hadn't yet consciously observed. He reconnected with the shards in his body and slowly turned in a circle, stretching his senses to their limit.

He swore again. Not just a pack, but a large one. They'd been advancing slowly, possibly nearing the two farmers all morning. The two to the west had gotten too eager and moved too quickly. Radyn silently thanked them for the warning. Three approached from the south, two more from the north, and two big ones blocked their retreat to the east.

Alone, Radyn wouldn't have worried much about the pack. He could have rushed the three, then picked off the remaining four without too much trouble. Protecting Jarrod meant he couldn't roam far, though. If the banti pulled him more than a handful of paces away, Jarrod would fall to a poisoned fang within moments. The boy was about as good in a fight as an old dry stick, but once the thought occurred to him, Radyn reconsidered.

He'd rather have the stick by his side.

"Radyn?" Jarrod asked.

"We're surrounded," Radyn said.

Except that wasn't quite true. The west was open, even though it only led them farther away from the meager safety of Underhill. Still, it was better than nothing.

"When I tell you to, I want you to run west as fast as you can. Don't look back, no matter what sounds you hear. Run as fast as you can for as far as you can, and only stop when I call for you."

Jarrod shook his head. "You can't fight seven banti on your own."

"I have a better chance than if I have to protect you too."

He didn't miss the hurt in Jarrod's eyes, but they didn't

have time for kindness. The kid could swing a hoe well enough, but he was nothing except dead weight Radyn had to carry in a fight. It would be all Radyn could do to keep that metaphor from becoming a reality.

He hated Jarrod, then, for being so weak in a place that required strength. Because he couldn't protect himself, he risked both their lives. Radyn breathed out his frustration again. There was no point, and especially not now.

"Can you do that?" he asked.

Jarrod swallowed hard and nodded, and Radyn turned south, connecting with all his shards but letting the maniblade sleep a while longer. The three banti approaching from the south were the closest, and their numbers and distance away made them the obvious first target.

"Run now," Radyn said.

Jarrod only hesitated a moment, but before Radyn could fear he was stuck for good, he took off, feet churning through the tall grass. Radyn launched himself south, and the banti responded instantly. The three south came for him, and the other four chased after Jarrod.

Radyn's maniblade came to life with a hum of power, longer now than before. He cut through the first banti before it came close, the second as it lunged for his lower leg, then snapped the blade up as the third shot out of the grass and aimed for his neck. His cut passed through the banti's scaled flesh with ease, and he stepped to the side to avoid any flying parts. One of its claws, not realizing it was supposed to be dead, reached out for him, but he'd put just enough distance between them, and the sharp claws passed harmlessly by.

He turned before the jumping banti's body hit the ground. Four banti closed on Jarrod, from the north and east, and Radyn joined the chase, the song of the Engine flooding through his muscles. Their relative angles meant Radyn had a chance to save Jarrod, but it would be close.

He intersected the banti chasing Jarrod from the east first, and their attention was so focused on their prey that they didn't notice Radyn's arrival. His maniblade flashed twice, cutting grass and banti alike. He sprinted past without checking to see if they'd died. The cuts only cost him a step, but it was enough to keep Radyn from reaching Jarrod in time.

The banti closest to Jarrod leapt first, but Jarrod either saw or sensed it, for he leaped to the side before its jaws could close around the back of his neck. It ran its sharp claws across his back in revenge, but he didn't cry out. He didn't even turn around. He just kept running, his breath coming in ragged gasps.

The second banti had a better angle and leaped straight at Jarrod. Radyn extended his maniblade even further, stretching it to the limit his will and shards allowed. He was a step too far away to land a killing blow, so he slapped at the banti with the flat of his blade.

The blow landed, though not well. Still, it was enough to knock the banti off its killing line, and its jaws snapped closed on nothing at all.

Then Radyn was between the two banti and Jarrod, and despite their anger, his maniblade cut through scale and spine with ease. They fell still, and he cut each once more to ensure they stayed dead.

Finally he allowed himself a deep breath. "Jarrod! You can stop!"

Jarrod ran a few more paces, then stumbled to a stop. He bent over and put his hands on his knees. Radyn gave him time to recover, and eventually Jarrod shuffled back to him.

The young man was clearly in pain, but he did his best not to show it. Jarrod looked down at the two dead banti, then said, "You got the rest?"

"I did."

"Thanks. I didn't realize you could kill so many banti."

Half a dozen responses warred within Radyn, but he chose the most generous. "I couldn't have gotten them without you. Your running pulled four after you."

Jarrod straightened at that, and some of the color returned to his face.

Radyn tilted his head east, toward the field and Underhill. "Come on. Let's get you home before those cuts get infected."

He let Jarrod set the pace, only pausing to ensure all the banti were good and dead. His maniblade had done its work well, but his spirits fell when they came upon the small field they'd been working. The banti that had worked their way around them had churned up the fields with their claws, and most of Radyn's work would have to be redone tomorrow.

He grunted, but thankfully Jarrod was so focused on walking straight he didn't notice.

He was farmer and Manirah, but as he looked at Jarrod's torn up back and their destroyed field, he couldn't help but think he was failing at both.

2

The knock on the door interrupted Nikki halfway through her set of pushups. She glanced up, then gradually lowered her chest to the ground, paused, and pushed herself up again, each repetition slow and controlled. Two pushups later, the knock repeated, more insistent this time.

Nikki grunted and pushed herself to her feet.

She whipped open the door, almost earning a knuckle to her face as her reward. The Dagger on the other side of her door froze mid-knock, and he stared wide-eyed at her naked, sweat-streaked form.

"What?" she growled.

The Dagger recovered, dropping his hand and bowing deeply. "The Blade requests your presence immediately, ma'am."

Hardly surprising. There weren't many other reasons a Dagger would show up at her door this early in the morning. Hopefully Jyn had something interesting for her. "I'll be there soon."

She turned away and started to close the door behind her, but stopped when the Dagger cleared his throat.

"Is there a problem?" she asked.

The young man's face was so flushed she wondered if he wasn't about to burst into flame. "I'm sorry, it's just that he was very insistent on the 'immediately' part."

Nikki arched an eyebrow. "Whatever it is, I think it can wait long enough for me to get dressed."

She closed the door on his half-hearted objections and shook her head. May the song save her from earnest young Manirah.

SHE WAS HALFWAY surprised to find the Dagger waiting outside her door when she emerged a few minutes later. He breathed a deep sigh of relief, and she wondered how much of it was because she was appropriately dressed and how much of it was because she hadn't made him wait long.

Though she could have found the Blade's study in her sleep, she gestured down the hallway. "Lead the way," she said.

Firestone's hallways were never quite empty. The city couldn't afford to fall completely asleep, and they passed by several bleary-eyed workers returning home from their overnight shifts. Lights, powered by the Engine, burned dimly in these early morning hours. Nikki walked these hallways every day and knew them as intimately as she knew her own body, but their relative emptiness made them feel longer.

Or maybe she was just eager to hear what fresh mystery the Blade had for her. It had been months since he'd requested her, and the monotony of her daily duties as a Shield bored her.

Those few residents they passed stepped to the side, dipping their heads as the Dagger and Nikki walked by. The Dagger didn't acknowledge the signs of respect, accepting it as his due. Nikki, though, bowed in return.

"Do you have any idea what this is about?" she asked.

The Dagger shook his head. "None, but whatever's happening has caused a commotion like I haven't seen since becoming a Dagger."

Given his age, that probably wasn't that long, but Nikki kept the thought to herself.

He led her straight to the academy, where the guards admitted them without question. Nikki noticed the shift in atmosphere as soon as she stepped through the gates. Students filled the hallway, trading significant looks with one another as though they knew what was happening. Instructors prowled among the students, eager to punish any minor infraction of the clan's rules. The Dagger navigated the maze of hallways, ignoring the students as though they were no more than debris. Manirah like him were the reason Nikki was sometimes glad she'd failed out of the clan's training. Too easy by far for the power and respect to fill a head with delusions of grandeur.

A small crowd of Swords had gathered outside the Blade's private study. Magni, the giant Sword who served as the Blade's chief aide and principal guard, towered over all of them, looking like a vaguely displeased instructor. When he saw Nikki, he offered the smallest of bows, which she returned.

She liked Magni. The giant gave off an impression of being a muscle-bound fool, but he was smart and surprisingly kind once he dropped his guard. He'd married a Singer almost a year ago, and Nikki swore the glow hadn't worn off him yet. Magni cleared the Swords away from the door, allowing her to walk through the crowd.

She ignored the pointed glares shot her way, the Swords sickened by a mere Shield wandering their hallowed territory. She rapped quickly on the door, and a deep voice on the other side bade her to enter. She obeyed, pleased to put the stares of the Swords behind her.

Jyn, the 13th Blade of Firestone, looked like he'd just woken from a long nap, had a slow, filling breakfast, and enjoyed a quiet morning. Knowing none of that was even close to true made Nikki respect him all the more. It was a facade, but one that never dropped. For Jyn, duty to Firestone came before all else.

The light behind his eyes, which normally shone like the light from the Engine, was dim, though.

"Thanks for coming so quickly," he said, as if she'd had any choice in the matter.

"Of course, sir. What's the problem?"

"We think there's been a murder."

Nikki nodded, then noted Jyn's phrasing. He was a man who spoke carefully, so each of his words carried weight.

"You think?"

Jyn grimaced. "I haven't seen it for myself yet, but I've been led to believe that there's no trace of a body."

Nikki frowned. It was too early in the morning, and her mind struggled to keep up. "A murder with no body?"

The Blade nodded. "If it made sense, I wouldn't have called you. But now that you're here, we can investigate together."

～

MAGNI and another Sword escorted them away from the academy. They were met by a Singer as they neared the heart of the city. The white-robed figure bowed deeply toward the Blade and led them deeper into the bowels of Firestone. They stopped before a thick blast door. Before the door stood two Daggers, who paled when they saw their Blade approaching.

The Blade didn't even have to ask. Both dropped to their knees and pressed their foreheads against the metal deck. "We don't know what happened, sir," the woman on their left said.

Her partner chimed in. "We were both alert, sir, and then the next moment we were being woken up by a Singer."

"How much time did you lose?" Jyn asked.

"About two hours, sir," the woman said.

Others might not have noticed, but Nikki heard Jyn's controlled inhale, and she imagined one of the equatorial volcanoes breathing deeply in before exploding. Once his iron-clad control had settled back upon him, he said, "We'll send replacements soon. I want both of you to head straight to the academy healers for a full exam."

"Yes, sir." They replied in unison, sounding like they had just been spared an execution.

Which, Nikki thought, might not have been far from the truth. A missing body was mystery enough, but the only space ahead of them was the Engine, restricted to Singers alone. Allowing a murder here while on duty was unforgiveable. It put the entire city at risk.

Jyn wasn't as stern as his public persona, but he wasn't particularly forgiving, either.

"And of course, not a word of this to anyone until we've figured out what happened," Jyn said.

"Yes, sir."

Nikki kept the corner of her lips from turning up in a smile, but barely. Jyn had just bought the loyalty of these two Daggers for the rest of his life. She would have been impressed if she hadn't already seen him do it so many times.

The Singer stepped toward a post next to the blast door and placed her hand upon the sphere which rested on top of it. She closed her eyes and a moment later, the blast doors opened with a rumble.

Nikki glanced down at the two Daggers. Hard to sleep through that.

"Is there anyone besides the Singers who can open this door?" she asked.

The Singer shook her head. "It's a newer level of security we implemented a few years ago. The only people with the skill to open it are the Singers. Not even the Blade, for all his strength, could do so."

Jyn didn't disagree, so Nikki assumed the statement was true.

"Aria developed the technology before she left," Jyn added.

"The theory, at least. Getting it working took us several months," the Singer corrected.

Nikki once again held back her smile. The Singers must still be smarting that someone who couldn't even become a Dagger had figured out new ways to utilize the song. She wondered, not for the first time, what Firestone would be like if Aria and Radyn hadn't chosen exile.

Of course, they'd probably be dead by now, so maybe not all that different.

They continued deeper into the city, and Nikki's pangs of

unease grew. Initially she chalked it up to being so close to the Engine, but it wasn't the effect of the song on her crude senses.

A minute later, they came to another door with another post, and Nikki swore to herself.

Jyn had been waiting for her reaction. "Did I forget to mention the murder happened in the Engine room?"

Nikki fixed him with a hard stare that did nothing but bring a hint of a smile to his face. Her stare lost its heat, and her eyes darted away from his gaze. It wasn't much help, but she was glad she could put a dent in the tension that threatened to consume him. "Must have slipped your mind," she said.

His grin widened. "Must have."

The Singer turned to Magni. "Only the Blade and the Shield may enter with me. You are welcome to stand guard outside the door."

Magni's eyes went to Jyn, to see if the Blade would challenge the Singer's decision, but the Blade said nothing, and Magni accepted the order.

The Singer placed her hand on the post, and after a moment of concentration, the door to the Engine room opened. She gave Jyn a concerned look but said nothing as he strode through the open door.

Nikki didn't know how powerfully the Song tormented the Blade. The song of the Engine affected all Manirah, and this much proximity was deadly to most. Even Nikki, who only had the crudest senses, felt sick this close to the Engine. But if Jyn suffered, it didn't show on his face.

She followed Jyn. Though she'd lived her entire life in cities, she'd never been to an Engine room. The sight of it froze her in place.

The Engine itself looked like a crystal, a clear stone that glowed with a soft blue light. It floated in the middle of a perfectly spherical room, connected to the city via a set of cables that hung from a hole in the ceiling. A catwalk ran around the inner diameter of the spherical room, with a balcony that reached closer to the Engine every thirty paces or so.

"It amazes me every time I step in here," the Singer said, adoration in her voice.

Nikki nodded, unable to form a coherent sentence. Here was the Engine, the heart of the city, the mysterious source of power that was all that kept them from an early grave. Shrouded in layers of myth, mystery, and rumor, Nikki couldn't say how much humanity actually understood about the Engines. The Makers had known, but their knowledge had been lost long ago.

Jyn brought her attention back to the present. "It happened on the first balcony."

They followed the catwalk to the first balcony. Nikki looked toward the Engine to see if she could see any evidence of a body, but all looked normal. Jyn grunted and pointed toward the wall. Nikki turned and followed his finger.

It was as though something had painted a silhouette on the wall, or the opposite of one. The metal of the spherical wall looked like an otherworldly heat had scorched it, except for the clean wall where a human body appeared to have absorbed the deadly flames first. The silhouette's arms were spread open wide, as though the victim had tried to embrace the Engine.

Nikki slowly moved closer. Now that she was looking for it, she could see some of the grating beneath her feet was scorched, too. The catwalk still supported her weight without a problem, so the heat hadn't lasted long enough to weaken the structure.

Nikki looked back to the Engine, then to Jyn. "Can the Engine do that?"

"I've never heard of anything like this, but it has the strength to do anything," the Blade said.

Nikki ran her hand across the scorched metal, confirming it wasn't paint or soot. She peered down through the grates of the catwalk, searching for any sign of the human that had stood here, but the Engine room was perfectly clean besides the scorching. Every shred and fragment of the body had been destroyed.

"Do we have any idea who this was?" Nikki asked.

Jyn shook his head. "We'll have to do a citizen check to be sure."

Nikki groaned. That would take days and would result in dozens of leads.

"We know it's a Singer, though. We're the only ones who can access the Engine Room," the Singer said.

"No. A Singer was only needed to reach the Engine Room. That doesn't mean it was a Singer who died here," Nikki said.

"Still, it's a good place to start. Go to your quarters and take a count," Jyn ordered the Singer. "It shouldn't take long."

"I can't leave you here alone," the Singer said.

Jyn's flat glare quickly changed the Singer's mind, and soon the Blade and Nikki were alone.

"What do you think?" Jyn asked.

"I'm not sure I have an opinion yet. Are you sure it was a murder and not a Singer messing with the Engine?"

"I'm not sure of anything, but it sets me on edge. I suspect there were at least two people involved."

Nikki had thought the same. "One who could put the guards to sleep, and a Singer. It's possible it was only one person, but unlikely."

Jyn gestured to the closed door. "Those doors don't just open to all Singers, either. A certain level of skill is required."

"And the technique of rendering Manirah unconscious?"

"Very few are officially taught it. The technique is difficult to perform correctly and takes time."

"Unofficially?"

Jyn shrugged. "Knowledge wants to be free. Sometimes, the more we try to keep it contained, the faster it escapes."

"You're running the whole city, and you still find time for philosophy?"

"Sometimes it's forced on us whether we like it or not."

She sensed he didn't want to be disturbed, so she turned her attention back to the potential crime scene. He took a seated position on a separate balcony and slipped into some sort of meditative trance.

Nikki walked the whole catwalk, letting her eyes wander around the room. Being so close to both Jyn and the Engine made focus difficult, but fortunately the Engine room was as barren a crime scene as she'd ever come across. The Singers kept it meticulously clean, and beyond the scorch marks, there was nothing to see.

The door opened sooner than she expected, and the Singer returned. Nikki stood up straighter. From her expression, it was clear she'd discovered something.

She made sure the door was shut before turning to Jyn. "There's only one Singer unaccounted for. All others are within the neighborhood."

"Who?" Jyn asked.

The Singer swallowed hard. "Rebecca, sir."

Jyn's face lost some of its color, and Nikki's eyes darted toward the closed door. She knew that name, as did almost everyone in the city.

Rebecca wasn't just a pillar of Firestone's community. She was also Magni's new wife, and one of the strongest Singers of their generation.

3

Radyn escorted Jarrod all the way to the infirmary, then waited by his side while Pardin, Underhill's healer, examined the young man. The wounds were in danger of infection, but Pardin was up to the task. He treated the cuts with a homemade poultice, made of various plants Radyn picked when he patrolled the surrounding areas. Jarrod winced as Pardin coated the wounds, and Radyn sympathized. He'd suffered under the same poultice several times, and though it smelled terrible and stung even worse, it worked. Despite numerous cuts, Radyn had never suffered an infection since living under Pardin's care.

Pardin settled Jarrod comfortably on his stomach, then shooed Radyn out of the room so Jarrod could rest while the poultice did its work.

Once the door was closed behind them, Radyn said, "Those are deep cuts."

Pardin answered the unspoken question. "I'll be able to close them up. There will be scars, but they shouldn't bother him. I'm impressed he was able to walk in on his own two feet."

Radyn's thoughts flashed back to the chase through the prairie, and how Jarrod kept running even after his back had been sliced open. That uncommon display of courage had likely saved his life. Had he even slowed, it might have given the banti time to finish what it started. Radyn grunted, more to himself than to Pardin. The healer shot him a questioning look, and Radyn said, "He's impressed me more than once today."

Pardin arched a skeptical eyebrow. "Are you sure *you* didn't get poisoned? Or have you spent too much time in the sun?"

Radyn didn't take offense. Pardin had more than earned the right to mock him. "It surprised me, too."

Pardin looked as though there was more that he wanted to say, but he saw something in Radyn's expression that gave him pause. Then he said, "Well, barring any unforeseen complications, Jarrod will be fine. You should get some rest. How many banti did you have to fight?"

"There were nine in the pack."

Pardin paled as though he'd seen them himself. "*Nine?*"

When Radyn didn't elaborate, he said, "You're going to tell Miranda?"

"Now that I know Jarrod's in good hands, yes."

Pardin slowed and allowed him to walk on ahead. Before Radyn got too far, he called out, and Radyn turned back to the healer.

"I would hope you know we all feel this way, but it probably doesn't get said enough. Thank you for being here. This would be a lot harder without you."

Radyn looked at Pardin for a moment, then nodded once and continued deeper into Underhill.

Today the lanterns hung at regular intervals along the hallway burned bright, transforming the incredible energies of their Engine into a warm light that banished the darkness. The Engine ran well today, as it had the day before and the day before that, which was an incredible feat in its own right. There were still days when the lights flickered or went out completely, but they were growing fewer and farther between.

Perhaps it was the lights, or maybe it was Miranda, or maybe it was something else completely, but Radyn sensed a subtle shift in the attitudes of the few neighbors he passed. It wasn't any one thing he observed, but a group of impressions. A carpenter with a confident step, a cook with a smile on her face, and another farmer with an easy greeting.

They were starting to believe. Last winter hadn't been pleasant. There'd been too many nights without heat, huddling behind doors as monsters sought a way into the ruin. The end of the season had been hard on stomachs as their food supplies ran low.

And yet, Radyn and Tanwen had been able to hunt enough game to keep everyone full enough, and they'd survived to see the days lengthen and the prairie flowers bloom. Once they had a more secure perimeter, they'd get sheep and cows from another of the soulkeeper settlements, and then food would no longer be an issue.

Still, their success made them proud, and Radyn saw it reflected in the faces of those he passed. If they survived another year, he probably wouldn't be able to tell the difference between walking through Underhill and Firestone.

The thought lasted until he passed out of the inhabited areas and into the abandoned ruins. Underhill possessed far more space than the small number of people living here needed, but most tended to have apartments in the same neighborhoods, as though they weren't comfortable if they weren't surrounded by people. Some areas, like the hallways where Pardin's healing rooms could be found, were crowded, while others were nearly devoid of life.

The lanterns still burned, though, patiently waiting for the day they could light the way for new settlers.

Radyn stopped by Miranda's rooms first, but when he knocked on her door there was no answer. He walked to the nearest square, once again passing into a neighborhood full of people, but she wasn't patronizing any of her usual haunts, so Radyn wandered deeper into the center of Underhill.

Underhill's precious Engine was protected by nothing more than a steel door, little different than any of the others that separated sections of the city. He'd successfully convinced Miranda to at least put a lock on the door, but as he approached, he saw that it was currently unlocked and open. He shook his head as he walked through.

A couple of turns brought him close to the Engine room proper, and he disconnected as completely from his shards as he could. Despite the training he'd undergone under Kaya, he wasn't a Singer, and it would be all too easy to lose himself in the song of the Engine for good.

He opened the last door and looked inside. Here, more than anywhere else in the ruin, he felt the difference between Firestone and Underhill. Firestone's Engine room had been a perfect sphere, with the Engine suspended from the ceiling. Here, the Engine rested in a socket, the wires and tubes that connected the Engine to the city hidden under thin sheets of the same metal that the Makers had used to build the hallways, doors, and furniture of their protective cities.

The sight of the Engine, humming along contentedly in its cradle, made him wish he understood the Makers better. How had they built so much and still fallen to the monsters that roamed the land? How had they constructed cities that lasted hundreds of years after their knowledge was gone?

The two women standing in front of the Engine were nowhere near as content as the Engine. Though they had been alone until a moment ago, they leaned close and spoke in hushed whispers, as if they were trying to keep a secret from the Engine.

Though she'd only been here a year, Kaya had grown from a girl into a young woman. It wasn't just the height she'd added, but the way she held herself, like there was nothing in the world that frightened her anymore. She'd come so far from the scared child Radyn had first met that it was almost as if they were two different people. He wasn't sure how much of it was her impossibly intimate relationship with the song and how much was having to grow up after everything she knew was ripped away from her, but he respected her as much as Miranda, if not more.

Miranda glanced sharply up at Radyn, but everything about her was sharp. Underhill wouldn't have succeeded under anyone else's leadership, but sometimes she went too far. Underhill's success had become everything to her, and no sacrifice, either from the willing or unwilling, was too great. They generally got along well enough, but when they didn't, the other citizens of Underhill ran away as fast as their feet would carry them.

"What do you want?" Miranda snapped.

"To bask in the pleasure of your company."

Kaya rolled her eyes and took a step away, clearly

expecting an argument, but in a surprising twist of fate, Miranda backed down first. She made a sound in the back of her throat that was as close to an apology as Radyn was likely to get, then said, without preamble, "I'm worried about Maker's Mound. We were supposed to receive a dragon from them several days ago, but there's been no word. I was just asking Kaya if she could learn anything about them."

The flash of frustration in Kaya's eyes told Radyn everything he needed to know. "You weren't about to ask her to travel between Engines, were you?"

The expression on Miranda's face made it clear she'd been considering just that, but she shook her head and Kaya didn't contradict her. "Of course not, I just wanted her to search the song. If something happened to their Engine, she'd feel it, wouldn't she?"

Radyn didn't want to answer for Kaya, so he said nothing.

"Not necessarily," Kaya said. "I can sometimes distinguish between different songs, but I've never been able to identify any specifically except for Nightkeep's, and that's only because I grew up with it."

"You could try," Miranda said.

Kaya glanced at Radyn, who shrugged. She was old enough to make her own choice, and she hardly needed his permission. She considered for a moment, then said, "Fine, but I'd like Radyn with me."

Miranda didn't bother asking Radyn his opinion. "Then get it done."

Radyn's stomach twisted at the thought of diving into the song with so little preparation, but Kaya had requested him for a reason, and if it helped protect Underhill, it was worth it.

"Before we do, there's something else you should know," Radyn told her.

"What?"

"While Jarrod and I were out, we were attacked by banti. Nine of them, and they encircled us."

That sufficiently distracted Miranda from her preoccupation with Maker's Mound. She turned her full attention toward him. If he were anyone else, he was certain she'd have quizzed him endlessly, but she knew him well enough to know he wasn't one to be deceived by a gust of wind. If he told her there were nine banti, there were nine banti. Instead she asked, "What do you make of it?"

"Not sure. I don't like it, though. I've never seen banti plan an ambush like that. If anyone else had been out there, you'd be down two farmers."

Underhill couldn't spare farmers. They were short enough as it was.

"What would you have me do about it?"

He hated the answer before he gave it, but it was the only one. "I think you need Manirah protecting the farmers, at least until we know what's happening."

"It'll be done," Miranda assured him. "I'll talk to everyone tonight. The fields?"

Radyn shook his head, and she clenched her jaw.

With nothing more to be said, he walked over to where Kaya waited. She'd sat cross-legged on the steel grating, close to the Engine. He sat across from her.

"It'll be just like we trained, except we're going to go deeper into the song. For now, follow my lead, and if I ask for your strength, please don't hesitate. I won't ask for more than I need."

Radyn clenched his hands, then shook them out and nodded. Kaya gestured for him to go first, so he connected with the shards embedded underneath his skin, and it felt as though he'd stepped under a waterfall. The powerful energies of the Engine, which he'd kept his body from while speaking with Kaya and Miranda, poured into him, erasing the aches and pains of the day and giving him the strength to bend the Maker's steel.

He breathed the energy in, then breathed it out, releasing instead of holding. His spirit slipped into the current of energy, and he let it drag him along. The process of surrender reminded him of flying on Tanwen, bound to a power he couldn't comprehend. The song drew him deeper, a soft melody that revealed the structure of reality.

Philosophers, Manirah, and farmers alike debated the nature of the song, and Aria spent most of her waking hours obsessed with uncovering the mysteries that surrounded it. Once, Radyn had been much the same, but his experience as a Manirah and his time with Kaya had shifted his perspective. Any explanation of the song was destined to fall short, and any description would be woefully inaccurate. Over the past year he'd worked on letting go of his desire to explain it.

Instead, he sought to understand it, not with words or logic but with intuition and awareness. Aria had at first thought him mad, but his training made him even more sensitive to the song than before, and she couldn't deny the progress he'd made as he let go of rationalizations. His new way would never be hers, but she'd grown to respect it all the same.

So today, he didn't try to put words to any of what he sensed. The song ran through him and around him, and he let it carry him where it would. A moment or an hour later, for time had no meaning in the song, he sensed Kaya's presence approaching, a bright star in a sea of light, and he drifted after her as she dove toward the heart of their Engine's song.

He could only get so close before the power threatened to consume him. The true danger of the song wasn't its strength, but its appeal. Some part of the human spirit longed to rejoin the song, but doing so meant the body's death. Kaya's presence served as his beacon, guiding him to his destination while keeping him safe.

This close to Underhill's Engine, its song was the only one he could hear, now familiar after a year of living in close proximity. He could have stayed and listened, but Kaya had other plans. She joined her spirit to his, and they dove into the Engine and surrounded themselves with the song. Distance meant as little as time within the song, but Radyn still had a sense of sudden movement, as though his spirit had been pulled far from his body.

Pulled into a deafening silence, one that squeezed him from all sides, tearing at his spirit as he clung desperately to Kaya. He was in the song, but the song had gone silent, and he couldn't find his way home. He tried to breathe, tried to calm the terror that sought to encase his spirit in ice and freeze it in place, but even Elora's training fled him.

If not for Kaya, that silent darkness would have been the end of him. While he froze and cowered, she dug deeper within herself, revealing an inner song, a light not even the rabid darkness could extinguish. He sensed something around his spirit snap, and he was once again beside Underhill's Engine, its song more enticing than ever, for if he gave his spirit to it, he'd never have to face that darkness again.

Kaya guided him through both the dark and the light, though, pulling his spirit gently beside hers, escorting him much as he'd escorted Jarrod earlier in the day. They put distance between their spirits and the song of the Engine, and then he was back in his body, gasping for air and clutching at his chest. Across from him, Kaya opened her eyes. The only distress she revealed was in the way she pressed her lips into a firm line.

"What just happened?" Miranda asked, a note of fear in her voice.

Radyn couldn't answer, certain his voice would crack and he'd lose the slim control he maintained over his body.

Kaya saved him the indignity. After a long, slow breath, she stood and brushed off her bottom. "Something terrible has happened to Maker's Mound, though I'm not sure what. Their Engine no longer sings."

Miranda dug her nails into her palms. "Their Engine has failed too, then?"

Kaya shook her head slowly. "No. Not failed. If it had merely failed, I would have sensed some sign of it. It's been destroyed or overtaken by another force. Something dark, but I couldn't tell you what it is. I've never felt anything like it, and it came close to tearing us both to shreds."

Miranda glanced down at Radyn, and he supposed his sudden panic at least had the effect of convincing Underhill's leader that Kaya spoke truthfully.

It was slim consolation, though. His heart pounded in his chest as though it were a prisoner trying to escape his ribcage. He remained connected to his shards, and the Engine sang beside him, but for the first time in his life, he had no desire to explore the song. He broke the connection with his shards, uncertain he'd ever use them again.

Miranda's gaze traveled back to Kaya, and her voice was hard. "What, exactly, are you saying?"

Kaya helped Radyn to his feet, and he could feel the tremble in her hands. "I'm saying that there's something else on this world we didn't know about, and it feels like it has already destroyed one of the soulkeeper projects."

Miranda dug her nails so tight into her palms Radyn feared she might draw her own blood.

Even though he stood in the middle of a warm Engine room, he couldn't stop the shivers from running up and back down his spine. He'd faced death dozens of times, and he'd been scared, but never so much he couldn't overcome the fear. What made this so different? The experience couldn't have lasted more than a few moments, and nothing had happened to him, not that he could notice.

He knew the answer, though.

He'd faced steep odds before, but he'd always known there was at least a chance of victory, and that had been enough to see him through. That darkness, though, was absolutely overwhelming. Winning a fight against it was as likely as picking up an entire city with one hand.

Miranda turned to leave, but before she exited, Kaya stopped her.

"Miranda, I don't know what that thing is, but whatever it is, it knows we're here now."

4

Jyn lay on the couch, hands behind his head, eyes closed, and breathed slowly and evenly. He wasn't asleep, but Nikki wondered if he was close. The Blade's chaotic schedule meant he worked all hours of the day and night, so it would be no surprise if he caught up on sleep whenever and wherever he could. Still, it seemed impossible that he could sleep so easily now. They weren't even in his apartment.

As soon as Magni had left them, Nikki had paced the length of the living room, but when it became clear Magni wouldn't be returning anytime soon, she used the opportunity to study the quarters of the Sword and his late wife.

Magni claimed it couldn't be, that he'd just seen her the day before, and had left them here while he searched all the places she could reasonably be. Jyn had let him go over Nikki's objections.

With no remains, they couldn't be certain, but Nikki knew. Magni's wife was gone, destroyed by the incredible power of the Engine. All that remained was understanding the truth surrounding her final moments, a mystery that would only become more difficult to solve the longer they waited for Magni to return.

She swallowed her frustration and forced her attention back to the room. Her heart cracked at the sight of every memento, every painting, and every sign of the life the Singer and Sword had built together. Her steps carried her to a small bookshelf. She tilted her head to read the foil-stamped titles.

"He's one of the best-read Swords in the clan," Jyn said. She glanced back. He remained flat on the couch with his eyes closed, but he spoke as if he was looking at her. "He's always borrowing books from me."

"Looking through these, I would have suspected it was mostly his wife who did the reading. Everything is about the Engines and the song. There's no history, no battlefield studies, no books of clan legends."

"He's a deeper man than you realize. He's obsessed with the song, even though he lacks the sensitivity necessary to become a Singer."

"Why?"

Jyn shrugged his shoulders. "I've never asked."

Nikki looked to the door. Though Jyn still hadn't opened his eyes, he sensed either her movement or her doubt. "He'll return."

The door finally opened an hour later, after Nikki had examined every corner of the apartment and Jyn had fallen fast asleep. Magni entered, a giant bowed over by a weight no amount of strength could help him carry. He shuffled over to the only vacant chair, leaving the door open behind him, and collapsed. The chair groaned and creaked but didn't break.

Jyn woke the moment the door opened, and he took a

knee before Magni and wrapped one of Magni's giant hands in both of his own. He leaned forward, and Nikki looked away, an intruder on a private moment between two men who had been friends for years. She didn't turn back until she heard the rustle of cloth as Jyn stood. The Blade nodded to Nikki, then took a seat on the couch close to Magni.

Nikki's tongue was dry and heavy in her mouth. She was no stranger to grieving widowers, but this grief had a presence, a weight that squeezed the air from her lungs. Both men had the strength to kill her easily, and both were consumed by barely controlled emotion.

She didn't fear for her life, but Firestone would feel the echoes of this murder for days, if not weeks, to come.

"Senior Sword, I'm terribly sorry for your loss. May I ask you some questions?"

It was never not awkward, beginning a questioning with a new widower, and the only way forward was to charge through.

Magni's eyes were fixed firmly on the floor between his feet, but he nodded.

"I didn't know your wife very well. Mostly just through reputation. Could you tell me about her?"

Magni nodded again, but his shoulders shook, and he didn't speak for a long while. "She was the best thing that ever happened to me, better even than my service to the clan. She was a private person who often seemed cold and aloof to those who didn't know her, but she was one of the kindest people I've ever known. Singing was her life, and both of us were obsessed with the song. Her curiosity was greater, though. It made her one of the best. She was going to be the best."

That matched closely enough with what Nikki knew of Rebecca. She'd never heard Magni's wife described as either cold or aloof, but that may have come from sometime deeper in her past. "Do you have any idea what Rebecca might have been doing in the Engine room last night?"

Magni's fists clenched. "She should have been in bed. She'd been a part of the morning chorus and wasn't scheduled again until this morning."

"Did she talk to you about anything unusual, or did you notice any different behaviors in the past week or so?"

"It seemed to me that she was more nervous about the Engine than she usually was. It's always something she's worried a lot about, but her concern seemed...more intense lately."

"Did she say why?"

"No. I asked her about it once, and she told me the Engine was fine, but she thought she'd been hearing discordant notes in the song."

Jyn gave the slightest shake of his head as Nikki looked at him. It was news to him.

"Did she talk to anyone else about it?"

"I'm not sure, but if she'd talked to anyone, it would have been Jelrik. He was the only one she went to when the song surprised her."

Firestone's Master Singer was already on Nikki's short list of people to speak to, but he climbed to the top.

"Is there anything you can think of that would help me figure out what happened to Rebecca last night?" she asked.

Magni thought for a while, then shook his head. Nikki thanked him for his time, then nodded to Jyn. The Blade stood. "We'll find out what happened. I promise it. Is there anything I can do for you?"

Magni was silent a long time, and when he answered, his voice was barely loud enough for Nikki to hear. "I'd like your permission to end my life, sir."

Jyn froze, halfway toward placing his hand on Magni's shoulder.

"She's waiting for me on the other side of the gate, Jyn. I want to be with her."

Jyn's hand dropped to his side. "I'm sorry, friend, but I need you, at least for a time. There's no one I trust more, and you know what still lies ahead."

Magni's head fell until it was almost between his legs. Tears dripped to the floor. He nodded. "After, though?"

"Of course."

"Thank you."

Jyn turned, eyes rimmed with red, and made for the door. "I'll expect you to report for duty tomorrow. Nikki will share anything she discovers."

He left before Magni could respond, leaving Nikki to stand awkwardly alone in the middle of Magni's living room. Not knowing what to say, she bowed deeply, held it a moment, then chased after Jyn. Before she could ask, he said, "We've seen growing evidence of a conspiracy against the clans, something that reaches far beyond the borders of any one city. It's proven frustratingly elusive to pin down, though. All we hear are rumors, and we can never prove anything."

"You think Rebecca's murder is related?"

"I have no idea, but I wouldn't find it surprising if it was."

Nikki debated about asking her next question, but it needed to be asked. "I didn't know Magni was a man of such faith. Did he ever associate with any of the Engine cults that spring up from time to time?"

"His belief is of a different quality. He's known the song for decades, and he's known enough warriors who have seen the gate to know something more exists beyond this world. The Engine cults thrive among those who seek something to believe in. Magni knows there is something more, and seeks only to understand it better."

Nikki didn't think the Blade was thinking only of Magni as he spoke. She had never thought Jyn the type, but he had always been a hard man to decipher.

"Are you worried he'll act without your approval?" she asked.

Jyn grunted. "I was already a Sword when Magni began his training to join the clan, but he was a giant even then. Do you know what the instructors made him do? They made him fight every student who wanted to become a Dagger. Half the kids took one look at him and decided they wanted nothing more to do with the clan. The other half he pummeled so the instructors could glimpse their character."

Nikki didn't know what that had to do with anything, but she waited for Jyn to get to his point.

"He's the only student the instructors were ever able to do that with. Whenever they tried to use a different student, they either ended up starting rivalries that divided the students, or the power of the position went to the student's head and they became more difficult to train. Do you know why Magni was the only one we could use?"

Nikki didn't have a clue, but she wasn't supposed to.

"It was because it was never about him. He knew the test served the clan, and he made sure, after each beating he handed out, to be the first to befriend the new arrival. Years he performed the task for us, and never once did a student come to hate him. Because he put the clan first."

Jyn slowed. "He'll do the same now, and I hope that he'll change his mind, but if he doesn't, I'll grant him what he wants. It's the least the clan can do for him."

GIVEN that she was already within the guarded neighborhood where the Singers lived, Nikki bid Jyn farewell and followed the hallways that led to Jelrik's quarters. A Dagger guarded the door, even though Nikki had already had to pass through a pair of guards when she'd entered the neighborhood.

Jelrik was worth the protection. As Firestone's Master Singer, no one had more responsibility when it came to the safety of the city. The clan might argue on the Blade's behalf, but even Jyn couldn't Sing with the Engine. Jyn kept them safe, but Jelrik kept them alive.

"Is the Master Singer in?" Nikki asked.

"He is, but he asked not to be disturbed for the rest of the afternoon. He spent the morning with the Engine."

"Will you tell him Nikki is here to see him? If he'd rather I come back later, I can, but I'd prefer to talk to him sooner."

The Dagger looked as though someone had ordered him to clean latrines, but he knocked softly on the door and let himself in. When he returned a few moments later, he held the door open and invited her in.

Nikki bowed and entered. The Dagger closed the door behind her. Jelrik lay on his couch, a ragged reflection of Jyn's rest in Magni's home an hour earlier. He didn't get up to greet her, but he said, "There's not much I can tell you."

Nikki helped herself to one of his stuffed chairs on the other side of the room. She glanced around his living room, which was filled mostly with books, but a few paintings hung on the walls, memories of a different time and a different man. Almost all featured a much younger Jelrik, confident, at ease, and smiling, a woman always on his arm.

He'd not been that man for as long as Nikki had known him. Elora, his wife, had died in a raid, in circumstances closely guarded by the clan to this day. If those paintings told a true story, he'd changed an incredible amount. Nikki knew him as a man who rarely smiled, barely spoke, and never raised his eyes to anyone. Jyn respected him tremendously, but Nikki had never been sure why. She assumed he was an excellent Singer, but that was the bare minimum required to become the Master Singer. There had to be something more, but she'd never known what it was.

"What can you tell me?" she asked.

"That short of losing me or Jyn, losing Rebecca was the worst murder that could have happened to Firestone."

She didn't speak often to Jelrik, but he wasn't prone to hyperbole. She covered her fear with a question. "I knew she was a skilled Singer. I didn't realize her loss meant that much to the city."

Jelrik cracked open one eye. His dark brown iris was surrounded by red veins, and he closed it after studying her for a few seconds. "Yeah."

Nikki pressed. "Why did she mean so much?"

"Because she was sensitive, even for a Singer. She heard everything in the song, and few do. We need that skill now, more than ever."

Nikki tired of his deliberate obtuseness. "Why?"

"Because our Engine is dying, that's why."

It was a deliberate non-answer, a half-truth. She was one of the handful of people in Firestone who wasn't a Singer and knew. But Jelrik would know that she knew, and Nikki had interviewed enough people over the years she could tell when her subject held back. Rebecca's loss hurt Firestone in a very specific way, but Jelrik clearly didn't plan on sharing it.

She switched angles. "You said Rebecca was murdered. Are you sure?"

Jelrik pressed his palms against his eyes. "Yes, but I'm the only Singer who will say so."

Nikki leaned forward. "What would the others say?"

"That she got herself killed."

"Explain."

"When she died, she was connected to the Engine. Probably alone, which was why she died." He paused, swallowed hard, and opened his eyes to glance briefly at one of the paintings on the wall before he closed his eyes again. "No one can connect to the Engine alone and survive."

He'd glanced at one of the paintings of him and his wife, and the pieces fell into place. Elora had died connecting to the Engine. But she'd just been a Sword, if Nikki remembered correctly. She noted her suspicion, collecting it with a dozen other guesses and theories, slowly building a story of what had happened when Firestone had been raided years ago.

"Other Singers sensed the connection she had made?" Nikki didn't need to know how Jelrik knew Rebecca had been connected, but she did need to know if the information could be confirmed.

Jelrik nodded.

"So why are you the only one who will say she was murdered?"

"Beyond the circumstances surrounding her death? It was because I knew her better than anyone except Magni. She wouldn't connect to the Engine alone, not without an unquestionably powerful need. So, murdered, though by who or what, I haven't the slightest."

He was lying about that, but if he was going to tell her he would have. He knew full well how Jyn used her to solve problems no one else could.

"Is there anything else that would help me?"

"No. Once I've napped, I'm going to speak with Jyn. I'll ask him to remove you from this investigation. This is beyond you."

Nikki stood. "You can try, but I will get to the bottom of this, even if you don't want to tell me everything you know."

Jelrik remained silent, which she took as her cue to leave. There was nothing more for her to learn here.

The Master Singer was hiding the truth, but she'd find it before long, no matter how he tried to stop her.

5

Many called him the Seer, though they revealed their own foolishness for doing so. They heard his proclamations, saw them come true, and believed he possessed some secret window into the future. They were almost as blind as the clans who falsely claimed the mantle of leadership. All he did was observe that which was hidden from everyone's eyes, the facts staring them all in the face, begging to be seen, and project current trends into the future. It wasn't prophecy, but it required a keen sense of observation most lacked. They buried their heads in tradition, in distractions, in arguing about that which didn't matter. Anything to avoid the obvious truth:

Humanity was a sickness, a stain upon this world that did not want them.

Many called him the Seer, and they were fools to do so, but he never attempted to correct them.

Humans were weak-willed and weak-spirited creatures who'd mistakenly raised themselves above the natural world. They destroyed everything good they touched and then cried desperately for some hope to cling to. Now many clung to him, believing that he would carry them through these times of trial.

And he would, though not in the way they believed.

He stood on the surface of Skykeep, beside the fence which served as the boundary of the city. There were no clouds today, and from his vantage point, his sight stretched for countless miles. Despite the decades behind him, the sight never failed to make him feel like a child again, filled with wonder and possibility.

The land below was beautiful. It always was. Whenever the burdens of his purpose threatened to overwhelm him, he came here, and the sight of the world strengthened and sustained him. Its majesty reminded him of why he fought so hard and why he sacrificed so much.

Slow footsteps behind him caused him to glance back, though he knew well who approached. The sight of him was almost as impressive as the land beyond Skykeep. He seemed as much mountain as human, as strong and unchanging as granite. The giant took position next to the Seer and drank in the sight.

They were two, but possessed of one purpose. Called, not by the song of the Engines, but by another melody, darker and more primal. A song few could hear.

For now. Soon, every human alive would hear and understand.

The Seer looked around, ensuring they were alone. He needn't have worried. Only the farmers came to the surface anymore, and they ran back into their holes as soon as their shifts were over, as though some part of them understood the sun didn't want to waste its light on their filth.

"You have news?" the Seer asked. Several messengers had arrived this morning, riding their dragons as though they owned the sky. The messengers served the clans, but carried news and letters from citizens, too. Buried within those letters was mail meant for the Seer, coded, so that any prying eyes wouldn't suspect the conspiracy taking root in the fertile soil of too many disaffected hearts. The letters went to the giant, who served as the barrier between the Seer and the mundane tasks of the world.

"Some. The attack on Underhill had mixed results. The banti attacked as they were directed to, but they were killed before they could do any meaningful harm."

"Radyn?"

The giant's eyes went wide, as though the event had been *seen* instead of merely predicted. Their agent among Miranda's soulkeepers was one of their best, but Radyn had a remarkable tendency to appear in the places where he caused the most problems. He'd possessed the gift for years now, so it stood to reason that if anyone was going to interfere with the attack, it would be him.

"Yes, sir. According to the stories we've heard, Radyn was surrounded by nine banti but still managed to fight his way free."

"Impressive. If true, he's gotten stronger since that nastiness at Starfall."

The news was unfortunate, but not a disaster. Radyn could kill as many banti as he wanted, but it didn't matter one bit in the grand scheme of things. Still, he couldn't be dismissed. Radyn was in exile, but the Seer didn't trust him to stay out of trouble. The former Sword was too well connected to his old clan. He'd have to be dealt with sooner rather than later, but for now, there were more important matters to attend to. "And the other attack?"

"Successful. Every soulkeeper within died."

The Seer allowed himself a smile. That was good news. Not only did it eliminate one of the most painful thorns in his side, but it also freed up servants for other tasks. He had eyes and ears everywhere, but strong, trustworthy hands were scarce. The clans' grip remained tight around the thoughts of most Manirah.

"I'm glad to hear it. How goes the training?"

"It goes. Finding spaces and times to train unobserved remains difficult, but we manage. The younger members require considerably more attention, but they make up for their lack of skill with enthusiasm. I wish you could see it, sir. You'd never suffer from doubt again if you saw them training."

"I don't suffer from doubt, but it's because you're by my side," the Seer said.

The giant bowed. "There is something else, though."

"What's that?"

"Our servants within Firestone missed their regular check-in. We haven't heard from them in some time now."

Another thorn in his side, then, and a difficult one to remove. "Do we have any idea what happened?"

"No, sir. We haven't received a dragon from Firestone in over a week."

The Seer leaned against the fence and stared out into the distance. Firestone was important, one foundation of his plan. Important enough to risk losing his reliable giant. "Can you create a reason to visit?"

"Easily."

"Please do so. Bring some of our younger members with you. Learn what has happened and use your best judgment about how to proceed. Don't risk yourself unnecessarily, though. If the situation has completely unraveled, return here so we may discuss it. But if you see an opportunity, take it. None of this succeeds unless Firestone falls."

The giant bowed deeply. "It shall be done. Do you want me to begin any action against Miranda or Radyn?"

The Seer weighed his options, imagined what would come from the success and failure of different actions.

They called him the Seer, and they were fools, but sometimes, he could almost convince himself. Especially during times like these, when he saw the narrow path through the chaos as clearly as if someone had erected signposts to guide his way.

Not *someone*, he corrected himself, but *something*. The other song, exerting its will in the world through him.

"Yes. I do."

He offered his plan to the giant, whose eyes widened as he listened. The giant bowed again. "Brilliant. I'll make sure it is carried out immediately."

The Seer would miss his friend as he traveled to Firestone. Together, there was nothing they couldn't accomplish.

The fall of Firestone and the end of Radyn were only the beginning.

6

Radyn stood on top of Underhill's mound and turned his face to the sun, welcoming the warmth on his eyelids and cheeks. He was delaying, and Aria knew it. She squeezed his hand and said, "You'll be fine."

He'd confessed to her after the encounter with what Kaya called the "shadow song," a name that he hated, but he couldn't think of one better. He hadn't thought of the darkness as a song, but that was how Kaya had experienced it. She described it as a song of silence, a song where the rests between notes had expanded to consume the noise, much as the darkness had wanted to consume the light.

Aria had listened sympathetically to his confession, but she couldn't understand his fear. Some days, standing in the light of the sun, he couldn't quite articulate it either. He'd fought murderers, dragons, and traitorous Singers, but that one brief experience with the shadow song rattled him in a way he couldn't shrug off like he did lesser fears.

Weeks had passed since then. Quiet weeks, filled with the mundane tasks of starting Underhill's fields and protecting the ruin when predators came too close. Aria and Kaya had been particularly busy with some project they wouldn't tell him about. Whatever it was, it was going well, because Aria returned to their apartment each night exhausted but smiling. There had been a handful of attacks, one of which was banti, but none that reminded Radyn of the day in the fields with Jarrod. Far from reassuring him, the lack of obvious threats led him to believe dark forces were gathering just out of sight.

He'd connected with his shards since that day, but never for longer than necessary. He didn't train with his maniblade, worried that the longer he spent in contact with the song, the easier it would be for the shadow to find him again.

Aria's patience with him had grown thin in the last week. Kaya hadn't stopped Singing to the Engine, and though she hadn't searched out the shadow song since that day, she hadn't avoided Underhill's song the way he had. Aria kept pushing him to return to his normal routine, and he kept putting it off.

Until today. This morning she'd woken him with a kiss and informed him, politely but in a tone that made it clear that no arguments would be considered, that he needed to fly today. He'd asked why, but she just smiled and told him that he would find out soon enough.

So he was here, delaying a few more precious moments before connecting with his shards and summoning Tanwen. He told himself that today would be good for him, and that was true enough. He was as disappointed in himself as Aria was becoming in him.

Aria leaned over and kissed him on the cheek. "Remember, we need to make sure the area is as clear as possible. I'll probably ask you to do another quick check tomorrow, just to make sure nothing has moved in overnight, but be thorough. It's important."

"I'd do a better job if I knew exactly what I was doing."

"Nonsense. You know exactly what you're supposed to be doing, you're just not sure why. But you'll like the reason once you find out."

Radyn arched an eyebrow. "You've been awfully mysterious lately."

Aria feigned innocence. "Have I?"

Radyn sighed. There'd be no getting information out of her, and they'd been together long enough that she knew how closely he observed everything and developed appropriate defenses. She was probably the only person alive who could keep a secret from him.

She turned his head toward hers and kissed him again. "Besides, you're stalling. Summon Tanwen and get going. Otherwise, you'll miss supper tonight."

Radyn could do nothing but agree, and he connected with the shards in his body. He flinched when he did, as though expecting some sort of spiritual punch to strike him through the song, but the connection went as smoothly as usual, and he searched for Tanwen's presence.

The dragon was easy to find, and Radyn asked if they might fly together for the day. Tanwen's pleasure flooded through Radyn's senses, and he felt a pang of guilt for avoiding Tanwen as long as he had. Riding meant a constant connection to the song, and so he hadn't flown with Tanwen since the encounter with the shadow song. It was by far the longest time they'd been apart since returning to the surface.

Tanwen appeared over the high hills to the west of Underhill, where the dragon had made itself a new home. He sped over the tops of the mountains, flying fast enough it looked like he was in a race. Once he cleared the last of the hills, he dropped low, no more than a few feet above the tall grasses of the prairie. Grass bent as Tanwen passed overhead, shoved aside by both air and the power of the song emanating from Tanwen's spirit.

Radyn couldn't help but grin at the sight. Dragons that served the clans weren't captives, but Tanwen's newfound freedom from the routines of Firestone's nest had served him well. He was leaner and faster than he'd been the year before, and when they were connected, Radyn sensed a deep contentment within the dragon.

Tanwen slowed and landed on top of the mound that marked Underhill. Radyn climbed up and shot Aria a questioning look. "Care to join us?"

She shook her head. "Too much to do today, but if everything tomorrow is successful, then yes."

"Love you," Radyn said.

"Love you, too. I'll see you tonight."

With that, they were off. Immediately, Radyn knew he'd been wrong in putting this off so long. He was connected to his shards and the song, but to Tanwen also, and he imagined it was something like having a bigger, stronger older brother to protect him. He relaxed into his connection with the shards and the song, and the Engine's energies flowed smoothly through him for the first time in weeks.

Tanwen banked in a gentle circle, and dragon and human alike turned their attention to the land below. Underhill was a large symmetrical mound that bubbled up from an otherwise flat stretch of prairie. Their first fields, struggling to survive both predators and inexperience, marked the western side of the mound. Farther to the west the land rose into hilly terrain, some of the hills steep and tall enough that Radyn thought of them more as mountains than hills.

They'd flown above this land countless times over the past year, and it was likely due to their efforts that Underhill was as successful as it was. Dangerous as the predators below were, few in this area could stand against the combined might and intelligence of a human and dragon paired together. If they were closer to the forbidden zones, it might be a different story, but Underhill was far enough north that they didn't attract the worst of the predators.

Their first few circles kept them close to Underhill, and neither Radyn nor Tanwen noticed anything alarming. Once Radyn was confident the prairie was safe, he asked Tanwen to fly in progressively wider circles. The dragon, disappointed in the lack of prey close to Underhill, was only too happy to agree.

Radyn noticed nothing to the north, east, and south of Underhill, but did spot a fresh kill several miles to the west, high in the hills. He asked Tanwen to land nearby, and the dragon obliged.

The dead animal had been a goat, a species that called these hills home. Its horns had barely broken free of its skull, and it looked surprised to be dead.

Radyn could hardly blame it. If he'd died in a similar manner, he'd be surprised, too. Its stomach was distended, with a gaping hole near the center, the flesh and bone turned outward as though something had killed the goat by breaking free. He used a knife to poke and prod around the fatal wound, but could make no sense of it. He recognized several organs, but some seemed to have gone missing.

Radyn stood and looked around, but saw no sign the organs had been carried off by either predator or carrion feeder. The goat didn't look like it had been here long. He looked at Tanwen. "Any ideas, old friend?"

Their connection was silent, and Radyn shook his head. "Me neither."

He climbed back on, the dragon's solid bulk under him reassuring. He took one last look at the goat, suppressed a small shudder, then urged Tanwen back into the air. They kept low, though, and flew as slowly as Tanwen could.

The hills here were thick with caves, from small depressions that only went a few paces into the hillside to monstrous, labyrinthine tunnels. He'd explored some of them before, but to complete a map of all the tunnels would take years, and it was time they couldn't currently spare. He focused his attention on the cave entrances, looking for any sign they were occupied or had been recently.

One cave looked as though it had attracted a bear, but he found little else of note. He and Tanwen kept flying west, but after a while it became clear that if there was any danger, it was both well concealed and far from Underhill. He asked Tanwen to fly higher so he could take one last look across the hills. Tanwen gained a couple of thousand feet, and for a moment, Radyn felt as though he were back on Firestone, standing on the observation platform and staring at the world below.

This was unexplored terrain for him. Their best hunting was typically to the south, and they never patrolled this far west. In time, though, he hoped to learn this land better. The rugged hills called to him, but for now he was needed at Underhill. Someday, when everyone was safe, he'd explore this land more thoroughly.

Just before he was about to turn home, a feature farther to the west caught his eye. At a glance it looked like a valley, but something about its shape was wrong.

Aria had asked him to be thorough, and he grinned as he urged Tanwen toward the strange valley. Tanwen's eagerness surged through their connection, and Radyn reminded himself that Tanwen had probably explored these hills every day since they'd moved to Underhill. "You know something?"

The dragon's only answer was to fly faster, and as they came closer, Radyn decided he was right to have investigated the area. What he'd first called a valley was closer to a caldera, although there were no volcanoes here. Perhaps it was a crater? He wasn't sure. Most meteors burned up before reaching the ground, and the depression didn't look like the one crater he'd seen before.

It was hard to tell, though. Whatever forces had shaped the depression in the hills had faded far into the past. Trees, shrubs, and grasses had moved in, and erosion had sanded the sharp edges of the rock away. A small, quiet lake reflected Tanwen's stomach as they flew overhead, but Radyn didn't see any streams either feeding the lake or draining it. The surface was as still as glass.

Radyn grunted to himself. Strange as the formation was, it hardly seemed important to Underhill's current problems. As he turned Tanwen back to Underhill, he spotted a new cave, maybe a quarter of a mile from the rim of the crater. A pile of branches had been stacked neatly inside the cave's entrance.

The exiled Sword and dragon descended once again. Tanwen landed a few hundred paces away from the cave and Radyn climbed down. He was already connected with his shards, but he advanced cautiously, the hilt of his maniblade already in hand. He neither heard nor sensed any sign of life, but he wasn't satisfied until he poked his head around the edge of the cave's entrance.

It wasn't as deep as it had appeared from the air. The back of the cave was easily visible, and a quick glance confirmed that the cave had been inhabited but was now empty. A fire had burned in the corner, and some of the embers were still warm, so Radyn guessed it had been last night's fire.

The floor of the cave was stone, leaving Radyn precious few clues to learn more from. The cave could have held anywhere from one to half a dozen travelers comfortably, but who would be out here? These hills were reasonably safe, as far as Radyn had seen, but it was still the surface, and even the "safe" areas could be incredibly dangerous for those who didn't know how to defend themselves.

He took one last look around, and as he exited the cave, he saw a small pile of bones behind a bush. The bones had been picked clean and bleached white by the elements. Whatever the bones had come from had been small, but there was nothing Radyn could identify. As he neared them, though, he heard a discordant note in the song, followed by a silence where there shouldn't have been one. Radyn backed off quickly, holding his hands before him as though to ward off an attacker.

His heart pounded even after he was well away. Those bones whispered fragments of the shadow song, and suddenly the twenty miles back to Underhill seemed a woefully short distance. He hurried back to Tanwen and climbed up in a rush. He'd search for the party that had spent last night in the cave, but he didn't hold out too much hope. The hills were filled with nooks and crannies, and it would be too easy to miss them.

Still, he had to try, and so he and Tanwen took to the air, searching the hills for trouble as they hurried back to Underhill.

7

Nikki bowed to Magni when she reached the door of the Blade's study. When she rose, she could see the question lurking behind his eyes, the one he was too proud to ask.

She saved him the pain. "I'm sorry, I haven't found anything yet, but I'm not giving up. There are a few avenues of investigation I haven't had time to pursue yet. I promise I'll do everything I can to figure out what happened."

Magni looked as though she'd punched him hard enough to break ribs, but he maintained his composure. Even if the world burned to ashes, she suspected she'd find him standing like a statue, guarding the Blade with the last of his strength. The vision made her think of Radyn, whom she hadn't thought about in weeks, and she wondered at that.

Magni lowered his head and his voice, his words for her alone. "I've been doing my own search. I've spoken to almost all the Singers, but no one knows anything. At home, I've been looking through all her papers, but there's nothing there, either."

He stopped and took a deep breath. "Losing her is hard enough, but we both swore our lives to the service of Firestone, and we both knew that someday, we might have to say goodbye before we grew old. We always thought it would be me, of course, but Singing isn't as safe as many think. It's not the losing her that torments me. It's not knowing why. I toss and turn all night, and sometimes I'm so angry at her for leaving without explaining herself."

Years of service as a Shield had conditioned her to grief in all its forms, but Magni's hit her like a mallet to the stomach. He carried the safety of Firestone on his shoulders and didn't so much as frown, but this, this tested his spirit like nothing had before.

"I can't promise that I'll solve this, but I promise I'll do everything I can for as long as I live," Nikki said.

Magni bowed, held the pose for a moment, and said, "Thank you."

When he straightened, his grief and weakness had been stuffed back within, deep where the clan's enemies would never find them. He knocked on the Blade's door on her behalf, and Jyn opened the door for her.

She entered and took a seat, waiting for Jyn to close the door and take his position on the other side of the desk. "I've been expecting you for several days now."

"If I'd had anything to report, I would have come earlier, but almost every question is a dead end. I've spoken to every Singer, interviewed every friend and acquaintance Rebecca ever had, and it's all come to nothing."

Jyn didn't miss her careful phrasing. "Almost every question?"

"Jelrik knows something, but he's not talking."

Jyn steepled his fingers. "And?"

"He won't speak to me unless you make him."

"Do you think he had something to do with Rebecca's murder?"

It was the same question she'd been asking herself since she'd left his apartments. "My instincts say 'no,' but he's the only one I've spoken to who has the slightest clue of what happened. Given that we think another Singer may be involved, it doesn't bode well for him."

Jyn leaned back in his chair and considered for a moment, but he reached his decision quickly. "I won't order Jelrik to speak to you. Make him talk yourself or find another way."

"You can't ask me to solve this and then not give me what I need!"

"I just did."

"Why?"

"Because Jelrik is one of the very few people in this city that I would absolutely trust with my life. If he didn't answer your questions, I can only imagine he had a good reason. If anything, now I'm wondering if it's wise for you to continue this line of inquiry."

Nikki stabbed her finger in the direction of Jyn's door. "That man is on the verge of breaking because of what happened to his wife, and I just promised him I'd do everything in my power to figure out why Rebecca died."

"Then your promise is safe. You promised everything within your power, not mine."

Nikki was on her feet in an instant, and if she'd been clan, she was sure it would have been with a maniblade in hand. "You can't treat him like this, Jyn. What would he do if I walked out there, right now, and told him that you were helping Jelrik keep secrets from me?"

"He'd bow, thank you, and continue guarding that door with his life," Jyn answered.

His confidence landed like a slap across her face, and for a moment, she stood there, jaw open, at a complete loss for words. When she found her voice again, it came out just slightly louder than a whisper. "I don't understand. Why won't you speak to Jelrik?"

"I told you, but you won't hear me. I trust him."

Her thoughts were slow to catch up, but she didn't miss the edge of hurt in his voice, so well disguised that none but those who knew him best would have noticed. What had she missed that he expected her to understand?

She slumped back into the chair, defeated. "I'm sorry, but I don't understand."

Jyn leaned forward. "When I tell you that I trust Jelrik, that means I trust Jelrik, fully and completely. It means I trust that when he decides to keep a secret from you, which ultimately is a secret from me, he has a very good reason for doing so. My trust is not conditional."

Nikki felt like a tree, ripped up from her roots and pulled into the air by a force she didn't understand. Jyn was no fool, but such blind faith in another was nothing but foolishness. He couldn't be both the insightful and decisive leader she'd known for years and hold to such childish simplicity in his dealings with others. And yet, he sat before her, seemingly both cunning and simple at the same time.

Jyn sensed her distress, because he continued, "It could be that Jelrik doesn't trust us, but I doubt it. More likely, what he has is knowledge he can't risk anyone having, not even you or I."

"But you're the Blade!"

"And too many people seem to think the title means I have some absolute control over Firestone. But all I truly have is the loyalty of most of the clan and the weight of tradition. I can't Sing to the Engine and keep us alive. I don't even have your ability to look closely and understand why and how somebody died. Firestone flies because all of us keep it in the air, not because I say so. I trust Jelrik, and I know it makes your life more difficult, but my decision is final."

"You're not going to remove me, though?"

Jyn shook his head. "I have little doubt Jelrik is doing everything in his power to find out what happened, too, but I don't think it hurts to have you approaching the problem from another angle. I owe Magni that much and more."

Nikki stood to leave. She couldn't claim to understand, but she could almost convince herself she would someday. Jyn had revealed something to her today, a truth, either about him or all of reality, but it would take her some time to reach her heart.

He stopped her before she left. "It isn't just that I trust Jelrik, you know."

"It isn't?"

"No. It's also that I trust you to figure out what happened, even when I make your life difficult."

Nikki grunted, gave him a half-smile, and shook her head as she left his study.

BACK AT HER APARTMENT, Nikki looked through all her notes again, hoping to find some detail she'd overlooked before. If the detail existed, though, it remained too well hidden for her to find. Lacking any brilliant insight and needing a change of pace, she stood from her desk, left the apartment, and made her way to Shield headquarters.

Her apartment was conveniently located, so she only

had to climb three ladders and travel down two halls to reach the square where the Shields were based.

Nikki paused in the square, both to see if she could smell any headquarters-delay-worthy scents in the air, and to get a sense of Firestone's mood. Unfortunately the nearby teahouses were closed for the day, and the mood was difficult to determine.

The square, as usual, was busy, with citizens trading for the goods they wanted and shopkeepers doing brisk business. Several public tables were occupied by craftspeople who were off shift, playing games with one another and enjoying the relative openness of the square. Firestone had twelve squares, but this one was the largest, an open cavern three levels tall and almost half as wide as the clan academy. The space was filled with tall buildings, constructed from the same alloy that shaped their halls and apartments, and each of those buildings held multiple shops.

Shield Headquarters squatted in the middle of the square, an unimaginative two-level tower that held the various administrators who ran the Shields. A handful of Shields, like Nikki, were stationed out of headquarters, but most were in smaller satellite offices scattered throughout Firestone's sprawling network of hallways and rooms.

Despite the typical busy-ness of the square, Nikki felt as though something in the air was off. The conversations at the tables weren't as loud as usual, and though neighbors smiled and greeted one another, many didn't linger any longer than manners required.

Shield Headquarters was also busy, though not overwhelmingly so. Nikki bowed to the rookie Shield running reception, then proceeded to the slightly quieter offices upstairs. She stopped by the commander's office and poked her head in.

Marian looked up when Nikki entered. On paper, Nikki reported to her, but in practice, their paths rarely crossed. Marian tried hard, and she made those who served under her feel appreciated, but she lacked the competence Nikki wanted in a commander. Unfortunately for Marian, Nikki spent enough time around Jyn that she recognized great leadership when she saw it.

"Nikki. I didn't expect you in today," Marian said.

"Didn't intend to stop by, but the work I'm following up on for the Blade isn't going well, and I figured a change of pace might do me good. Do you have anything that isn't too time consuming I could help with?"

The question from anyone else would have earned disciplinary action. Shields were supposed to follow the orders of their commander, no matter how hard or unpleasant the task might be, but Nikki had rarely had the patience for obedience, even before falling into Jyn's personal service.

"Funny you should ask. Jayke's been putting in extra time trying to break up a ring of petty thieves, and he hasn't had time to follow up on a missing-person report. Care to go through his notes and check off all the boxes? It's a kid, missing for two days now."

"Have we done anything?"

Marian gave her a look that said of course they hadn't. Firestone was a maze of hallways, rooms, nooks and crannies that weren't even entirely mapped out. If a child really wanted to hide and was halfway smart, no one would ever find them. Or they got curious, climbed over the fence, and were never seen again.

It wasn't exciting, and she doubted she would solve it,

but it was a change of pace, so she took the appropriate papers from Marian and read through them as she tracked down the parent.

She grunted to herself. The mother was clan, and the father had been a Shield who had died in the Nightkeep attack years ago. She went to the academy, where they produced a duty roster that informed Nikki the woman was on the surface with the dragons. Nikki considered waiting until she was off duty, but the Shields had wasted enough time already. She climbed the stairs to the surface.

The day was cloudy and gray, the air damp and cool against her skin. Most of the farmers had already finished their work for the day, leaving the surface of Firestone mostly empty. Nikki made as straight a line as possible to the walled-off section of the surface where the clan kept their dragons, realizing she hadn't been inside since Radyn. The guards at the gate reluctantly let her enter, and she was promptly greeted by Macken, a bear of a man who'd been in charge of the dragons' care longer than Nikki had been alive.

His eyes narrowed as he recognized her. The last time they'd met, she and Radyn had brought a truly unfortunate amount of chaos to his life, and she didn't think he'd ever quite forgiven her. Still, he found enough professionalism in his bones to ask, "What do you want?"

"I'm here to speak to one of your Daggers about a report they filed."

Macken's eyes narrowed to slits. "You'll be wanting to talk to Aella, then. She's at the landing area. You can't miss her. Taller than most."

Nikki bowed, somehow not surprised Macken knew of his Dagger's troubles. He cared for the dragons as if they were his children, and knowing him by reputation, she suspected he cared for those who served him just as well.

He showed her considerable honor when he let her walk to the landing area unaccompanied. The land inside these walls was some of the most precious and secure in all of Firestone, and most never saw anything inside the gate. Given their history, she was surprised he was so willing to let her wander.

She made straight for the landing area, a cleared rectangle of grass the dragons both left from and arrived at. As she neared, a delegation was landing, the clan rider dressed in Nightkeep's colors. Nikki stood aside as Firestone's Manirah carefully inspected the appropriate paperwork. When all was shown to be in order, a group of Daggers escorted the delegation to the gate.

Nikki shook her head as they passed. Most of the new arrivals looked like traditional members of trade delegations, filled with academic-looking men and women loaded down with papers. There was a giant among them, though, who looked strong enough to crush stone with his bare hands. She grinned to herself as the Daggers unconsciously gave him more space than the others.

Once they were past, Nikki approached the tall woman in the uniform of a Senior Dagger. "Aella?"

The woman turned, took in the sight of Nikki and her Shield uniform, and nearly crumbled to the ground. She caught herself just before she fell and forced herself straight. "Did you find him? Did you find Zak?"

Nikki hated lying, but sometimes, the truth served no purpose. "We haven't yet, but the Shields are continuing to work their way through Firestone. As I'm sure you know, there's a lot of space to check, and it usually takes several days."

The Shields would have drawings of the boy spread throughout their satellite offices, and Nikki was sure at least a few would be keeping a sharp eye out on their regular patrols, but there was no dedicated search.

"I came to ask you a few questions, to hopefully aid us in our search. To start with, can you tell me a little bit about your son? What was he like? How did he spend his time?"

The news her son hadn't yet been found almost brought Aella to her knees again, but she was no stranger to suffering, and after she cleared a stray tear from her eyes, she said, "I can't tell you he's a perfect child. He's a young boy and gets into trouble as young boys like to do, but I count myself lucky to be his mother. He's always meant well, and he's been working hard to pass his trials."

Nikki nodded and took notes. "Does he know when he's going to take them?"

"This summer. We're friends with an instructor who's been helping him acclimate to shards, so he should have a good chance of passing. I've heard he's quite sensitive to the song, so I'm hoping he'll become a Sword."

Strictly speaking, Aella had just confessed to violating clan law, but if Nikki brought it to Jyn, he'd have to deal with at least half his Manirah. The trials were open to all, and Manirah were prohibited from discussing the specifics of the trials, but many clan "helped" their hopeful students along. The child shouldn't have had any access to the precious shards, but Nikki let the matter go.

"Are there places he likes to spend his time when he isn't in school or training? Perhaps a favorite hideout?"

"If he has any, he hasn't told me, but as of late, I don't think he's done much more than school or training. He has his heart set on joining the clan."

Hopefully that dream wouldn't be cut short. "Does he

have any close friends I could speak to, people who might know more about him?"

"Of course." Aella gave her a list of names, as well as directions to where most of them lived.

"Is there anything else you can think of that might be important? Was there anything he was struggling with lately, or had anyone new come into his life? Was he dating anyone?"

Aella thought about the questions for what felt like a long time, but she shook her head. "I'm sorry, I realize this probably isn't any help at all, but no, I can't think of anything. For the last few months we've been in a deep routine, and if there was anything new in his life, I haven't heard about it."

Nikki closed her small notebook. "Don't worry, ma'am. This is helpful and gives me a lot of new places to start searching. We'll continue our sweep, and I'll go around and ask after him. Either I'll stop by in the next day or two, or I'll send another Shield with news. We'll find out what happened to him."

The effort of keeping her feet and bowing looked like it cost Aella the last of her remaining strength.

As Nikki turned and left, she had the sinking feeling in her stomach that she'd been making a lot of promises lately she wasn't sure she could keep.

8

Radyn found no trace of whoever had left the bones, but he wasn't entirely surprised. There wasn't even any guarantee they were moving toward Underhill. He and Tanwen found and killed a small pack of banti on their way back, but the flight was otherwise uneventful.

He was surprised by the commotion he found just inside Underhill's main entrance, and was even more surprised when he discovered Aria was the one in charge of the chaos. A line of men and women were carefully carrying what appeared to be long metal poles in teams of two and gently laying them next to the entrance. The poles were about six feet long, rounded at both ends, and capped with what looked like clear glass.

"What's all this?" he asked Aria.

"A surprise for you in the morning. Did you find anything?"

He briefly told her of the cave and the bones, as well as the caldera-shaped hole in the hills, and his tale distracted her almost until the last pole was carefully placed in the pile. The workers gathered together after, and Aria spoke to them. She chose several to help the next day, while the others were released to their normal tasks.

Whatever Aria was up to, Miranda must have deemed it important, because she'd recruited some of the most reliable farmers and repair crew in Underhill. With so much else to do, Aria's selections represented an impressive investment of Underhill's total work capacity.

Aria wouldn't give him any hints, though, and when he delivered his report to Miranda later, the soulkeeper was equally enigmatic. Radyn gave up, forced to be content to wait until morning to know what Aria planned.

Aria woke him early the next day, and for a moment he panicked, thinking that perhaps Underhill was under attack. She laughed at his distress, swept her hair behind her ear, and assured him she was only up to get an early start on the day. Radyn was reasonably sure she hadn't seen a sunrise in at least two months, so her project had her more excited than usual. They ate a quick breakfast together in Underhill's dining room; then Aria dragged him to the main entrance, where they found Kaya waiting.

Radyn looked between the two women. "What's this all about?"

Kaya was the only person in Underhill who slept later than Aria. She preferred the silence of late evenings, when most were asleep. She claimed she could hear the song more clearly when the halls were quiet.

Neither woman deemed it time for him to know, though. They asked him to pick up two of the poles and carry them out into the prairie. The poles weren't as heavy as they'd looked the day before, and he was able to hold one in each hand and follow the women into the earliest light of dawn.

The two women consulted a diagram they purposefully

kept out of his sight, pointing east toward the rising sun. Eventually they reached a decision, and Radyn followed them.

They walked perhaps three quarters of a mile, which was farther than Radyn had expected. His hands grew sweaty, and he was forced to connect with his shards to ensure he didn't drop the poles. When he did, he learned something new. The poles each had a small shard in them. Smaller even than the one that powered his maniblade, but still a considerable treasure from anyone's perspective.

The two women debated for a time, but eventually settled on a patch of soil that was completely unremarkable. "Would you carve out a posthole with your maniblade? The depth of a normal sword, please," Aria asked.

Radyn carefully placed the poles down, then grabbed his maniblade and lit the sword to its customary length. He stabbed it straight into the ground until it reached the hilt, then twisted until the hole was complete.

Aria took over, grabbing one of the poles and placing it into the hole. She filled the hole with nearby soil and packed it down tight with her foot. Half the pole remained aboveground, and for the life of him, Radyn couldn't guess its purpose. Aria was one of the smartest builders he knew, but even she couldn't fit much into a narrow pole. If it was some sort of trap or defense, he didn't understand its nature.

She asked him to pick up the second pole. Then she looked between Underhill and the prairie and started walking, verbally counting off her paces. When she reached two hundred and fifty, she pointed at the ground and asked for another hole. Radyn obliged, and the pole went in just as the first did. Aria examined the pole carefully, then said, "If you could stand about a dozen paces to the north, I'd appreciate it. Kaya and I need to run some tests, and if you're between the two poles, it won't work."

Radyn knew his questions would remain unanswered, so he simply nodded and backed away from the pole. Aria gave him a smile that he would have fought a dragon for, then hurried to a spot roughly halfway between the two poles. Once she was in position she waved to Kaya, who'd remained by the first pole.

For a moment, nothing happened. Kaya stood in place, as did Aria, who looked to Kaya as though she was waiting for some form of acknowledgment.

Cursing himself for his own foolishness, Radyn connected to his shards and listened for the song. He heard the new song layered on top of Underhill's engine, and recognized Kaya's techniques instantly.

He'd listened to a fair number of Singers over the years, and no matter their skill or experience, something about their singing had always struck Radyn as crude, as though they were trying to bully the Engines into obeying their commands with rude punches and pushes. Their techniques worked, and for what it was worth, they'd honed those crude techniques into an artform, like a Dagger who decided to master a club instead of a proper maniblade.

Kaya's technique had nothing in common with the other Singers, and Radyn suspected much of it had to do with the fact that she had been forced to teach herself so much. She hadn't known all that the Singers considered right and wrong, and so she'd had to feel it out on her own, relying on her own sensitivity to guide her. Fortunately, she was perhaps the most sensitive Singer Radyn had ever crossed paths with. Her songs were beautiful harmonies, laid gently on top of the song of the Engines. She didn't bully an engine so much as work in tandem with one, much the same way Radyn flew with Tanwen.

Unfortunately, being able to hear the song and know what it did were two separate abilities, and he didn't possess the latter. Kaya nodded, though, so whatever she'd done, it had worked.

Aria turned and gestured for Radyn, a smile wide on her face. "Once we have more time, we can measure the positions more precisely, and I imagine that in a few years we'll want to expand the circumference, but I think it'll do for a start."

"And what, exactly, have you started?"

"You haven't figured it out yet?" She shot him a mischievous glance, daring him to figure out the answer before she told him.

Radyn looked around. Circumference meant circle, and there were more than thirty poles waiting in the hallway to be placed. Something that required activation by the Singers. He frowned. "Some sort of perimeter?"

Aria's smile grew wider. "Took you long enough. The song reacts to all living things, and the poles are designed to amplify that reaction and feed it back to whatever Singer is connected to Underhill's Engine."

"You'll know if anything approaches."

It was brilliant, but he'd come to expect no less from Aria. They'd already built a pair of bells that served as warnings. All the Singer would have to do was alert someone to ring the bells, and everyone would rush in. The load on all Underhill's Manirah, and on him specifically, would be much less. He grabbed her face in his hands and pulled her lips toward his.

After the kiss, he said, "You're a genius."

"I know, but it's nice when others recognize it, too."

With the concept proven and the rough distances calculated, they returned to Underhill, where Aria's selected workers from the day before had gathered. She ran the crew as though she'd been doing it her whole life, and before long she had teams assigned to the poles. She and Radyn went out with the first wave, and she marked out the locations for each pole so that Radyn could dig with his maniblade.

There'd been a time when he would have considered digging holes a task far beneath a Manirah and a maniblade, but he no longer held to such foolishness. Survival meant far more than some outdated tradition.

The other farmers carried the poles, planted them, and ensured they were stable before returning to the main gate for another load. Radyn and Aria worked their way in a slow circle around Underhill, and with everyone working together, the task was done well before noon. After, it was Kaya's turn to contribute.

Radyn connected with his shards, but she was almost finished by the time he could still his mind and focus on the song. With all the poles connected, he was barely sensitive enough to feel the difference in Underhill's song. He doubted he would notice a predator breaking the barrier, but he could see how a Singer might.

The other farmers gathered and congratulated themselves on the work. Aria stood apart from them, and though her face revealed little to those that didn't know her, Radyn could see the satisfaction in her bearing, in the way she tilted her head slightly and turned the corner of her mouth into a smile.

"How long have you been working on this?" he asked.

"I had the idea not long after we arrived. It's not too far

off to say I've been working on this from our first day on the surface."

"Congratulations. I've never seen anything like it."

Aria's shoulders shrugged upwards a fraction of an inch. "I'd been working on something based on the same ideas back at Firestone, so I wasn't starting from nothing. I couldn't have done it without Kaya, though."

Kaya shook her head. "At best, I'll admit that it was a team effort. The song is a simple one, and it's the poles that do most of the work."

Radyn's eyes narrowed as his gaze traveled from pole to pole. "Speaking of, I can feel the shards in them. Where did they all come from?"

The two women glanced at one another, and though the expressions on their faces never changed, Radyn swore they exchanged the grins of co-conspirators whose schemes had been discovered.

"I've been growing them," said Kaya, as though growing shards was as simple as growing beans.

"You...grew it?

Kaya grinned from ear to ear.

Growing shards was impossible. Every Manirah in the world knew that shards were carefully carved out of Engines, and then only rarely. Most shards in Firestone could trace their origin to the city's earliest days. Radyn wasn't even sure Jyn could get more, short of attacking another clan or paying an exorbitant price. No one had carved a shard from Firestone's Engine in generations. They most certainly weren't grown and harvested like common wheat.

"How is that possible?" he asked.

"The Engines aren't stone, even if they appear that way," Kaya said, "They're more organic than stone."

Kaya's hands danced in the air, trying to express something her words weren't sufficient for. "We see their crystal lattice and we think of gems, but if you look closer they're more akin to plants with their thick cell walls. Only instead of plant matter containing life, it's a crystal structure containing energy."

Radyn stared at her and blinked. It would be a lie to say that he understood, but his trust in Kaya was complete, and he accepted her claim as truth. He was interested in the explanation, but the pragmatic repercussions of the claim were what his thoughts latched onto. "You can grow shards?"

The grin fell from her face, the thrill of surprising her friend replaced by the awareness of all her discovery meant. Battles had been fought over shards. Countless lives had been lost. All for a scarce resource that was no longer scarce. And if shards could be grown...

His eyes went wide. "What's the limit? Can you grow an Engine?"

Kaya's expression made it clear she'd been wondering much the same. "I don't know. What I've learned has helped me heal Underhill's Engine, and it's possible it might heal others, but I won't know without access to other Engines. And I don't know about creating a new Engine. What I'm doing is just extending the structure that is already there. I'm not sure I can build it from scratch."

Radyn looked to Aria, feeling a hope bloom in his chest he wasn't sure he'd ever felt before. At the very least, more shards meant fewer reasons for the cities to fight. At the most, he couldn't stop imagining possibilities. He saw his hope reflected in her face, and something more, too.

"That's not even the best piece of news today," Aria said.

Before he could ask what was better than a perimeter

fence and new shards, his senses screamed out a warning. He saw no threats, but Elora's training was written deep in his bones, muscles, and spirit, and he connected with both the shard in his maniblade and the shards in his body. The song and the power that came with it flooded his limbs and sharpened his senses.

Not for the first time, his training saved his life.

An attack struck him, one of a nature he'd never felt before, yet familiar. It wasn't physical, but spiritual, and it landed like a mountain on top of him. An invisible weight fell on his shoulders and squeezed his chest. Ribs threatened to crack and shatter as he fought to merely draw breath. If not for his connection to the shards, and several shards at that, the pressure would have crushed him in an instant. Even with the shards, he wasn't sure how much more he could endure.

There was no thought of striking back. He could survive and nothing more. The pressure on his chest increased, forcing the last of the air from his lungs. The edges of his vision went dark, and shadows loomed all around him. He was dimly aware of shouting, of voices calling out in support and despair, but they faded along with his sight.

And then, only malevolent silence, surrounding him and crushing him.

9

Nikki began her search for Zak in the corners of Firestone where Aella claimed he spent most of his free time. It didn't take long for her to find a group of young boys who claimed to be his friends. They were all too happy to answer her questions, and one particularly bold boy asked her whether or not she had a man in her life.

He shut right up when she told him that she reported directly to the Blade.

The story from the first group of boys was much the same as what she'd heard from Aella. Zak had been training hard to pass the clan tests, and from everything they'd seen and heard, he was doing well. Most fully expected him to become a Sword one day, although one boy suggested he had the sensitivity necessary to become a Singer. No, they hadn't seen him in a few days, but they hadn't thought anything of it. They suggested a training area that Aella had also mentioned, saying that he had spent most of his time there.

She thanked the boys for their answers, then took a ladder down a level and toward the training area they'd mentioned. She hadn't been certain Aella had spoken correctly when she'd first mentioned it, but the boys' confirmation overwhelmed her doubts. The training grounds were known to her, and she'd visited them herself on occasion. It tended to attract high ranking Shields and a handful of Daggers looking to improve their skill. It wasn't exactly a welcoming place for those who couldn't at least hold their own in a sparring match.

Maybe she and Zak had even trained at the same time, though she doubted it. She would have noticed if a boy had shown up.

She greeted some of her usual sparring partners, but disappointed them when she informed them she was there for work. They knew of Zak and had kind words to say about him, and they told her to speak to Clarise. She'd been working closely with Zak.

Nikki knew of Clarise. She was a mid-ranked Shield, young but well-regarded, as far as Nikki had heard. Their paths had never crossed, but that wasn't unusual. Nikki's relationship with Jyn precluded most work with other Shields. Clarise wasn't among those training, but it was prime shift, so Nikki made her way to the closest Shield office. There she found a duty roster and saw that Clarise was currently on duty up on level three. She thanked the Shield in the office, then began the climb up the stairs.

Other Shields complained about this aspect of their work, but Nikki had never minded. Sure, she might walk miles a day, but she was on the hunt for truth. The miles usually meant she was making progress.

She had to wander the third level for a while, but

eventually she came across Clarise on patrol. The woman recognized her, and Nikki fell into step beside her. Nikki told Clarise that Zak was missing, and asked what she might know.

Like everyone Nikki had crossed paths with, Clarise was happy to oblige. Firestone, like any city, had its share of lowlifes, criminals, and liars, but Nikki found far more often a shared sense of purpose among her fellow citizens. Though they rarely spoke of it, most were aware their situation was a precarious one. Being trapped in a flying city together did wonders to improve cooperation among neighbors and strangers alike.

"Zak's a good kid," Clarise started, and Nikki noted the other Shield refused to use the past tense. "He trains hard, and if he's got a weakness, it's that he hasn't yet run into a problem he can't outwork. That ethic is good, but his answer to everything is to throw more at the problem. If you pin him in a wrestling match, he'll practice new grappling techniques until he can't get off the mat. You beat him at chess, and he'll study a whole book of tactics."

"Seems like someone I'd like."

"I'm not sure you would. There's no intelligence or strategy behind anything he does, it's just always more. He doesn't adapt well."

Nikki conceded the point, but she didn't really care. She wasn't here to discuss whether or not she'd like the missing child. "Any ideas where he might have run off to?"

Clarise thought for a moment, then said, "He did mention he'd found someone new to train with. He was pretty cagey about it, which wasn't like him, though I did hear him say he was going down to the twentieth level one day after we trained together, and I thought that odd, as there was no reason for him to ever go down that low."

Clarise didn't know anything else, but the twentieth level was something to go on. There weren't any residential areas that low, and it wasn't too much lower that one started reaching the maze of storage areas and workrooms that formed the base of Firestone. Nikki grabbed a quick bite to eat, then descended to level twenty.

She decided Zak would be proud of her, because she had no real choice except to brute force the problem. She went around, knocking on doors and opening them, systematically working her way through the level. It wasn't pleasant, but it was much more doable than going from door to door on one of the upper levels. That would have taken her days.

Behind most of the doors she found the workrooms where the unsung heroes of Firestone labored day after day to ensure the city had all the materials and goods it needed to survive. Carpenters and metalworkers crafted everything from furniture to spoons, and then there were those who repaired lanterns, fixed hinges, and recycled old and battered goods. Most down here didn't even receive the recognition the farmers on the surface did, but their contributions were no less necessary.

Her search ended in a nondescript workroom, which she later learned had been empty for months, the previous carpenter who used it having passed through the gate.

The room was covered in blood, and it looked like all of it had come from Zak's body.

THE JELRIK that eventually met her in the hallway outside the workroom was a different Jelrik than she expected. Calling his appearance haggard would have been a compliment, and because he'd come without wearing his traditional robes, he looked like nothing more than a tired, worn-out old man, even though he couldn't have been much more than fifty.

His appearance raised all sorts of questions in her mind, but she'd asked him here for a different purpose, and was frankly surprised he'd shown up at all. Two Swords followed close behind him.

He noticed. "Yes, I know how terrible I look, and yes, I came. Your message told me I was the only one you trusted, so here I am."

He left much unsaid, adding even more questions to Nikki's pile. He knew she'd left their last meeting frustrated, and Jyn had informed her the Master Singer had officially requested her removal from Rebecca's investigation. She wasn't sure why he'd shown up without question or complaint, but hoped she might find out soon.

"I'd like you to help me investigate another murder scene. It's...very unpleasant, but my message was true. I think that if anyone can tell me what happened in this room, it's you."

He nodded and reached for the door, but his hand froze before it could push the door open. Nikki caught it trembling before he drew his hand back and pressed it tight against his side. Then he took a step back. "What happened in there?"

"A boy training to become a Manirah was killed. It looks like something exploded from his stomach, and someone used his blood to scrawl symbols on the walls."

Jelrik paled, but Nikki didn't think it was because of her description of the scene. There was something else happening, something the Master Singer feared. He stood in the middle of the hallway, as though someone had carved him out of granite and left him there, but Nikki waited patiently.

In time, some of the color returned to his face. He motioned to the two Swords. "I want one of you on either side of this door, looking away from it. No one else, under any circumstances, comes within five paces of this door. Am I clear? I don't even want you looking in."

His guards bowed their acknowledgment, and he turned his attention to Nikki, weighing her with his gaze. "It would be best if you forgot all of this and dropped both this investigation and Rebecca's immediately. I suspect you won't, because you're as stubborn as Jyn, but I assure you it would be best, certainly for you and possibly for Firestone. This is not your battlefield."

Such was the sincerity in his tone that Nikki actually considered his warning before dismissing it. "If there's a threat to Firestone, it is my battlefield."

Jelrik sighed and nodded, as though he'd expected nothing else. Then he gestured for her to lead the way into the room. "I do not think it is wise for me to touch anything."

The smell was what hit her first: not just the stench of the dead, which she had some familiarity with, but a rottenness beyond that, a wrongness that she inhaled with every breath. She fought the urge to plug her nose tight and let Jelrik observe the room without her commentary.

It was as horrible a sight as she had ever seen. The corpses she usually saw were rarely a pleasant sight, but she lacked the words for the anger that consumed her when she saw Zak's corpse. His face was twisted, a frozen reminder of the pain he'd suffered in his final moments.

She couldn't explain the wound in his stomach that had killed him. The best she could do was to say that it looked as though something had violently emerged from his stomach. Several of his bottom ribs had been cracked and blown outward.

And yet somehow even worse than all that were the symbols around the room, painted in Zak's blood. Not writing, but geometric lines and shapes, hinting at an order and a pattern just beyond the edge of her understanding. The sight of them made her stomach churn and made it feel as though the walls were closing in.

Jelrik had turned pale again, but not because of what had happened to Zak. His attention was focused on the symbols on the walls. He walked slowly around the room, hand outstretched, never quite touching the wall.

She didn't know what any of it meant, but she hated everything about it. The symbols hadn't been slashed across the walls, but carefully painted, the work of a killer taking their time.

Nikki knew, better than most, why most people turned to crime. Some were desperate, some were greedy, and some were driven by extreme emotions. There were a few more calculated criminals, but they tended to be self-interested thieves of various stripes.

This, though, had an entirely different feel. This was evil in the flesh, wandering somewhere among the halls of her city.

She suddenly wished Radyn were still here. Together, they'd be far more capable than she was alone.

After she'd given Jelrik enough time, she said, "You know something."

The statement was an invitation to share, but Jelrik licked his lips and looked like he might continue to keep his secrets. He broke his silence before she was forced to argue with him.

"I do, but not here. It's best we talk in front of Jyn. I now believe that Firestone is under attack and in imminent danger."

10

Trapped within the darkness, cut off from light and sound, memories long buried crawled to the surface like the dead reborn. A blurred memory of his father, fighting off Daggers from an invading city, and the sharp, crystal-clear realization that Father was not who Radyn had thought he was. Maniblade fought against maniblade, but it was no longer Father that wielded the weapon but Elora, blood running down her side, dueling the Swords from Nightkeep who hoped to bring Firestone to the surface. Then Elora no longer held her maniblade but clutched only at her side as she crawled toward the Engine, more than ready to sacrifice herself so the city could live. Finally, he and Aria on Tanwen's back, fleeing Firestone and the wrath of the clan.

Forced to confront all his memories at once, Radyn confronted a truth he knew but never acknowledged. Since he'd been young, all he'd done was lose. He'd lost the people he cared most about, surrendered the respect of his clan, and exiled himself from the only home he'd ever known.

Why bother fighting?

Caged by the darkness and surrounded by a bubble of silence, he found that he couldn't answer, at least not to his spirit's satisfaction. He tried to hold tight to what remained precious, but everything he grasped slipped like sand through his fingers, and the mere act of holding on brought so much pain.

It was so much easier to let go.

At first, he thought he was imagining the song, for what song could exist in this silence? It wasn't the song of the Engines, but was still familiar. His first instinct was to cover his ears, to bury his head under a pillow. Why couldn't the song just let him be? Why couldn't he have peace?

Almost despite himself, he turned his spirit toward the source of the song, drawn toward it like a moth to flame. It warmed his spirit and fanned its flames brighter, and he thought of Aria and Kaya and Underhill. He thought of the hills and mountains he hadn't explored and thought of Tanwen and their shared adventures in the air. The song grew louder yet and he reached for it. The song was Kaya's, and he would recognize it anywhere.

Her light banished the darkness, and he opened his eyes and found himself on his knees near the last pole in the perimeter. Kaya stood tall, but her eyes were closed, and her lips were pressed tightly together. Her song battled the silence to a standstill.

Radyn connected with his shards and stood, looking for the source of the attack. His stomach felt sore, but he ran his hand over it, and all seemed fine. He saw no threats but could feel all too clearly the silence lurking in the spaces between the beats of Kaya's song.

"Are you hurt?" Aria asked, and Radyn shook his head. He was about to say more when the silence intensified.

Aria groaned, and Radyn's heart stopped beating as her eyes rolled up in her head and she collapsed to the ground, both hands wrapped protectively around her stomach. He caught her as she fell and lowered her gently down, but he was at a loss for how to help. He looked to Kaya for assistance, but her teeth were gritted and veins bulged from her forehead, as though she was trying to lift a tree trunk on her own.

Radyn was no Singer, and this battle, for he was now certain it was an ambush, was beyond his abilities. But that didn't mean he couldn't help. He made sure Aria was as comfortable as she could be in the field, then ran to Kaya and put his hand on her shoulder. With his free hand he grasped the hilt of the maniblade and summoned its shard as well.

The air around them seemed suddenly lighter, and he thought he heard the soft song of Underhill's Engine in the distance. Kaya drew strength from the additional shards, and with that strength pulled more from Underhill's Engine. Together with the strength Radyn's shards provided, she beat back the silence with a vengeance that revealed her anger.

The silence soon fled, and perhaps Radyn was imagining things, but he swore it ran scared, as though at the very end Kaya had been the hunter and their mysterious assailants the prey. The heavy silence of the attack vanished, replaced by the mundane swish of grasses blowing in the breeze.

"How are you?" Radyn asked Kaya, who waved away his concern as though it was nothing. She stumbled to where Aria lay on the grass. Radyn's wife breathed steadily, her chest rising and falling, but she remained unconscious.

"I'm fine, but we need to get her to Pardin, and quickly."

Radyn heard the fear in her voice, and his heart threatened to stop again at the thought of Aria being hurt worse than he realized. With all the shards burning in his body, it was a simple matter to pick her up and carry her toward Underhill in his arms. They rushed through the main entrance, and Kaya led them toward Pardin's rooms, clearing the way for them as Radyn ran.

When they came close, Kaya ran ahead, pounded on Pardin's door, then threw it open before he could answer. "It's Aria!" she shouted, and Pardin came rushing to the door.

The healer guided Radyn to one of the padded tables he used to examine patients, then told Radyn to take a few steps back. "You can watch, but with all those shards burning I can't focus."

Radyn disconnected from his shards and was assaulted by a deep and sudden exhaustion. He slumped back against the wall and watched. As much as he wanted to run across the room and help, he was even less help on this battlefield. All he could do was watch Pardin and hope for the best.

The healer ran his hand over Aria's stomach, then left it there while he placed his other hand on her shoulder. He closed his eyes, and Radyn knew that if he was still connected to his shards, he would hear Pardin's own crude song, but he forced himself to stillness.

Pardin's examination only took a moment, and when he opened his eyes, he looked relieved. He breathed out loudly and took a step away from Aria. "The news is good. Whatever happened to her took most of her strength, but it's nothing that some rest and a big meal won't fix. Both she and the baby are perfectly healthy."

Radyn's eyes went wide, and his legs lost the last of their strength. He slid down the wall until he was sitting on the floor. He rested the back of his head against the wall and closed his eyes, shutting out the rest of the world.

"Radyn?" Kaya asked. "Are you alright?"

It took a moment, but eventually he smiled. "Never been better," he said.

ARIA WOKE SOMETIME AFTER MIDDAY. Radyn had pulled a chair next to the table and maintained a constant watch. Pardin had left them the room and closed the door behind him, reassuring Radyn that they could stay as long or as little as they liked. Kaya had left, too, and though she'd offered to bring Radyn food from the dining hall, he'd told her it was unnecessary.

Aria's eyes fluttered, then shot open. She saw Radyn and called his name.

He grasped her hand and held it tight. "Everything is going to be fine. This is one of Pardin's rooms, and he's already checked on you. You're healthy."

She gripped his hand tight, and he caught the searching look in her eyes, and he couldn't hide his knowledge any longer. "So is the baby, apparently."

Tears trickled down her cheeks, and she levered herself up so she could wrap her arms tightly around him. "Sorry you had to find out this way. I was just about to tell you."

He held her close. "I figured as much. It also explained why you've been working so hard on the perimeter project. Congratulations, by the way."

Her body shuddered as she half chuckled, half released the sudden fear that had almost consumed her. She wiped away some of her tears on his shoulder. "To both of us."

She pulled a little away from him so she could look him

in the face. They'd talked of having a child, but they hadn't been trying for one, and she was searching for any clue of how he felt. Thankfully, he'd had some time on his own to digest the news, and so he already knew his feelings.

He pulled her in close so he could whisper into her ear. "I'm excited to be a father," he said.

He didn't think he'd ever seen a wider smile on her face, and for a while they simply sat together, basking in their new shared purpose. Eventually, though, the moment passed, and both were reminded that they were in Pardin's rooms after the attack.

"What happened?" Aria asked.

Radyn told her what he knew, which was precious little. He was certain the attack had been from someone instead of something, but beyond that, there was very little he felt confident about. "If not for Kaya, I don't think I would have survived. Her song saved me, and you, too."

Aria shuddered at the memory. "After you told me what you'd sensed when you'd gone looking for Maker's Mound, I didn't understand what had frightened you. Now, though, I think that I do."

"You sensed the silence, too?" Aria was sensitive to the song, but she'd never been able to stand contact with the shards, which was why she'd never become a Manirah. Still, he was surprised and more than a little curious.

Aria nodded. "It isn't just the absence of sound. It's something darker, the absence of everything. I don't think I've ever been so frightened in my life. Even the fall of Whitehawk doesn't compare."

She wasn't prone to hyperbole, so Radyn understood how much that meant. She continued, "When it surrounded me, it made me want to give up, as though there was nothing worth fighting for anymore."

Radyn reached out and took her hand. "I had a similar experience. I saw all that I had lost and all that I was in danger of still losing, and it was more than I could bear. If not for Kaya's song, I might have given into it. It wasn't until I heard her that I thought of you, Kaya, and all the others, and I wanted to fight again."

"We can't give up," she said.

"We're not going to."

Aria looked up, and her eyes met his. She knew him well, and she knew what he meant. "You have a plan?"

Radyn grunted. "*Plan* might be a bit of a strong word, but I've been thinking. There's not much I can do alone, but I think that if Kaya, Tanwen, and I are together, we'll be able to fight against whoever did this. They caught us by surprise today, but they also failed. They attacked the three of us, and all of us are still here."

"They didn't attack anyone else?"

Radyn shook his head. "Only the three of us that were outside of Underhill. Not sure exactly what that means, but with Kaya and a dragon on my side, I'm feeling confident."

She squeezed his hand tight. "I know this is what you need to do, but you'd better be careful." She squeezed his hand one last time, then let go and gave him a mischievous expression. "After all, I'm sure I can always find myself another husband, but I think you should stick around to meet this child. It is yours, after all."

He grinned. "It is? That's a relief."

She punched him in the shoulder, but their forced humor couldn't last long. Her face fell, and he knew she was thinking of him out there, beyond the safety of Underhill's sturdy walls. "I mean it, though," she said.

He nodded, his own smile falling. "I know. And don't you worry, I know exactly what I'm fighting for now."

11

Nikki and Jelrik didn't meet with Jyn until that evening. The Master Singer had spent most of the afternoon copying the symbols on the wall onto sheets of paper, and Nikki had to call for other Shields to come and help her remove Zak's body. He was taken to the nearest morgue, where they would make him look as presentable as possible for his mother. Nikki had watched them take the body away with a stone in her throat. Once Jelrik was done, they sealed the room and locked it. For now, the walls would remain untouched, so that if there was ever reason to return, the evidence would be as they left it.

Nikki elected not to tell Aella of her findings that day. The morgue would need time with the body, and she wanted to wait until she'd spoken with Jyn and Jelrik before deciding what to tell Aella. Zak's mother would get the truth, but maybe not all of it.

When all was said and done, it was already the evening shift by the time Jelrik and Nikki made their way up to the academy together. The hallways of the academy were quiet at this time of night. Training was done for the day and dinner had been served. Some of the older students might be out, seeking fun beyond the clan's protective walls, but most students would be in their rooms studying.

As was usual, Magni stood outside Jyn's study, and his eyes narrowed when he saw Jelrik and Nikki walking down the hallway together. He remained professional, though. "The Blade is in a meeting with a group of Swords. Is it urgent?"

Nikki looked at Jelrik to answer. The Singer was the one who had claimed Firestone was under immediate danger, but he didn't act like enemies were at the gates.

"How much longer will it be?" Jelrik asked.

"Not long," Magni answered.

Jelrik bowed, then walked a few paces down the hallway and took a seat on a bench.

"Any news?" Magni asked, and the hope in his voice broke her heart all over again.

"None yet, but hopefully soon. I think there's been a development." She glanced meaningfully at Jelrik.

Magni nodded but was too disciplined to ask for more, even though the look on his face said that there was nothing he'd rather do than probe her for all the information she had.

Nikki paced the hall until the Swords left. Magni poked his head in the study, and a moment later, she and Jelrik were sitting before the Blade. Jyn looked between the two of them, clearly trying to figure out what had transpired without his knowledge. He quickly gave up. "What is it?" he asked.

Nikki glanced at Jelrik, who gestured for her to start. She told Jyn of Zak and how she'd tracked his body down. Then she gave a brief description of the room. "I asked Master Jelrik for aid, and what he saw concerned him, so now we're here. From what I can gather, Zak's murder might have some bearing on Rebecca's."

All eyes turned to Jelrik, who stared at a point above Jyn's head as though it possessed all the answers in the world. Finally, he gave one slow nod. "I'm sorry, old friend, for not having spoken with you earlier. Even now, I'm not convinced it's wise, but I believe it is necessary."

If Jyn was disappointed by Jelrik's confession, he didn't show it. He waited patiently for Jelrik to continue. After a time, the Master Singer did. "For a few years now, I've become aware of—something—conspiring against the Engines. I haven't said much to anyone because what evidence I have is scant, more conjecture and feeling than anything solid I can point to. I'm afraid that even the amount I know now amounts to less than a thimble's worth."

"Another clan?" asked Jyn.

Jelrik shrugged. "It's possible, but I doubt it. Perhaps it is best if I start at the beginning, when Elora died." His voice caught then, and he needed a moment before he could continue.

Nikki couldn't help but lean forward. Elora's death was one of the greatest mysteries she'd ever come across, sealed up behind a wall of secrets so tight not even she'd been able to peer through the cracks. She noticed the corner of Jyn's mouth turn up in a smile. She'd been begging him to tell her what had happened for years, so he knew just how much any clue Jelrik might reveal would mean to her.

"The Singers knew that something within the Engine had changed after Elora's sacrifice. Most obviously, the Engine was healthier than it had been in generations, but there was a difference in its song, too, a quality none of us were quite able to wrap our heads around. To investigate further, a group of the most sensitive Singers were given the task of completing the most detailed investigation of our Engine to date. Rebecca and I were both part of that team. The team discovered one thing, and Rebecca and I discovered another."

Nikki fought the urge to barrage Jelrik with questions about what had happened to his wife and barely succeeded.

Jelrik continued. "The team discovered that there was a new song within our Engine, one so close and so true to the Engine's song we never would have discovered it unless we were looking. We're still not sure what that means, but it's what is keeping our Engine healthier than those of any of the other cities. That doesn't matter as much as what Rebecca and I discovered: a third song, more subtle and more dangerous than any we'd heard before."

Jyn frowned. "From a person, or from an Engine?"

Jelrik shook his head. "I don't think it's coming from either. Rebecca and I were the only two to hear it, and we were lucky to catch it. The song isn't like any we've heard before. It's silent, and Rebecca and I believed it represented a force equal to but opposed to the Engines."

Nikki gripped the armrests of her chair tighter. Interesting as Jelrik's story was, and she certainly had questions, it didn't explain what had happened to Zak or Rebecca. But Jelrik was talking, and she'd long ago realized the best way to conduct an interview was to let the subject talk as much as they could. They often revealed more than they realized.

The Master Singer seemed to expect some of their questions. "I'm afraid there's not much I can explain. Only Rebecca and I have been able to sense this other song, and even then, only intermittently. We know that when this dark song comes into contact with the Engines it causes problems. It may even be why the Engines are failing, but we're not sure."

Jelrik paused. "We also believe it has human allies. When we hear it most clearly, we can sometimes sense other presences, much the same as how we can sense other Singers when we're singing to the Engine."

Jyn kept his reactions controlled, but Nikki had known him long enough to see the way the news struck him. Strong as Jyn was, Jelrik had just piled a city's worth of problems on his shoulders. "What kind of threat are we talking about?"

Jelrik started to shrug, then saw Jyn as Nikki did, and stopped. "I don't know, but I fear the worst. The song of the Engine is what gives our Manirah the ability to do all that they do. I have to assume this dark song gives its followers unusual abilities as well."

"Like cause one of our Singers to vanish, as though she'd been burned by the Engine?" Jyn asked.

"Possibly," Jelrik admitted.

"Or make it look like a child died because something crawled from it?" Nikki asked.

"Also possible."

"Why didn't you tell me?" Jyn asked.

Jelrik glanced at Nikki, then back at Jyn, and Jyn nodded. Whatever it was, he didn't care if Nikki knew it.

"Rebecca believed, and I agree, that the dark song has a corruptive influence on our spirits. The stronger one is, the greater the risk of corruption. Both of us experienced anger, frustration, and a deep cynicism after listening to the dark song, so much so that we only explored it together. We carefully examined ourselves after and talked over how we were feeling. I feared that if I let you know too soon, if I let you know before I had answers, you would go searching for it yourself, and given the foolish number of shards you're playing around with these days, I feared we'd lose you to it."

Jyn leaned back in his chair and crossed his massive arms, and Nikki watched him closely. He didn't deny any of Jelrik's accusations. What exactly had Jyn been doing in his free time?

"You're still worried about me, aren't you?" Jyn finally asked.

"Shouldn't I be? Ever since Rebecca's death I've been trying to study the dark song on my own, and I'm to the point where I hate everything about Firestone. Elora is dead because of you and Radyn, and there are times when I consider just singing to the Engine and dropping Firestone from the sky. None of the other Singers could stop me, and I know better than any why I feel this way. Nor do I keep shards anywhere close to me when I'm not singing. What would you do if our positions were reversed?"

Jyn had gone silent and still, and even Nikki, who wasn't that sensitive to shards, felt the power radiating off him. Jelrik almost looked as if he wanted Jyn to end his suffering, but Nikki personally hoped for a good long life. Except here she was, trapped in a cage with an angry dragon.

The moment passed and Jyn stood, turning his back to Jelrik and Nikki. "You said that you believe Firestone is in imminent danger. Why?"

"Zak's body. Nikki tells me he was sensitive to shards, possibly enough to someday become a Singer. As soon as I approached the room where he died, I felt the dark song more strongly than I have before. It has allies in this city, and they're either preparing for something or have already started. We don't have much time."

"*I* don't have much time," Jyn said.

Jelrik frowned.

Jyn turned around, his decision made. "I'm sorry, too, old friend, but I can't lose you."

Realization dawned on Jelrik's face, and for a moment, he looked horrified, but then he passed into resignation. "I'm still your best bet for finding out what has happened. For finding who did this."

"Perhaps, but don't underestimate Nikki. She's never failed me."

"She can't hear the song," Jelrik protested.

"No, but she's almost as observant as Elora. The two of them would have gotten along well. She'll solve the problem using her own methods."

Jelrik looked as though he might argue, but then he surrendered, and he looked like an old man ready for his deathbed.

Jyn wasn't done, though. "You'll stop singing, too. You can keep the title, but I don't want you near either the Engine or a shard. Not until you've recovered your health, and maybe not until Nikki has dealt with the allies of this dark song."

The declaration was like a slap to Jelrik's face. "You don't trust me?" he asked.

Jyn came around the desk and took a knee before the Master Singer. "Jelrik, I would trust you with my life. But you just told me that you've been corrupted by this song and that you've entertained thoughts of dropping Firestone to the ground. You leave me no choice."

Jelrik tried one last argument. "You know I'd never drop Firestone, Jyn, and my life isn't more precious than everyone who lives here. Let me help."

Jyn shook his head. "I'm sorry, friend. My answer is final. Get some rest. You look terrible."

The two leaders of Firestone stared at one another, but

Jelrik was no match for Jyn's commanding presence. He sagged and nodded. "Very well."

"Is there anything else we need to know?" Jyn asked.

"Now you know as much as I do. If I should learn more, I'll let you know, but if I'm not allowed to sing, I'm afraid I'll be no help at all."

"Don't sell yourself so short. There's no one else I want as the Master of Firestone's song. Get some rest, and I'll stop by to check on you as soon as I'm able."

Jyn's tone made it clear the meeting was over, and both Nikki and Jelrik stood to leave.

"Nikki, a moment, please," Jyn commanded.

She bowed to Jelrik as he left, then took her seat. Once the door closed behind Jelrik, Jyn said, "Thoughts?"

"Making progress will be hard without Jelrik's help."

"Agreed, but after his confession, I can't risk having him singing. Firestone needs to stay in the air. I've been receiving messages from other cities, and the problems with the Engines are getting worse. None of us know how much time we have left, but it feels as though it's getting close. Our Engine is now in the best condition of all cities, and Nightkeep has even approached me about moving some of their citizens here."

"You told them no, I hope." She couldn't imagine ever allowing Nightkeep's citizens within Firestone, not after all they'd done in the past.

"Under normal circumstances, I would have denied them and grinned as their cities went down in flames. Recent events have made me take a longer view, though. I haven't answered their request, but it's not so simple."

"They've tried to take Firestone down, maybe more than once."

Jyn's sharp look reminded her that he was well aware.

He'd ascended to his position after his predecessor had fallen during one of Nightkeep's attacks. The look only lasted a moment, though, and then he sighed. "Remember this, Nikki. The cities that are afloat are almost all that remains of humanity. We've fought in the past and we might fight again in the future, but I have to think about the children, and their children. If Firestone is simply the last city to fall, that doesn't make us the victors. It only makes us the losers that lasted the longest. We'll need the help of the other cities if we want our descendants to have a future."

She offered a smile as an apology. "This is why you're the Blade and not me."

Jyn grunted. "Can you do it? Can you find whatever allies this dark song has?"

"I can only promise that I'll do all I can. There's been little to go on."

"Dig as hard as you can. I want reports twice a day, just before prime shift and right after. Is that clear?"

"Yes, sir." She hesitated.

"What?"

"If what Jelrik said is true, there's a chance I'm going up against forces I'm not equipped to challenge. Is there any chance of support?"

Jyn consulted a duty roster. "I can spare a pair of junior Swords. They can figure out what shifts they want, but that way you'll always have one Sword with you."

She bowed deeply in thanks. "There is one other thing."

"What's that?"

"Jelrik is still among my suspects. He knew more than he told us, and he's one of the few Singers who had access to the Engine room. I'm inclined to believe him, but he's still one of the most likely people to be involved with Rebecca's murder. I'll want to investigate him."

Jyn's cold eyes settled on her. She admired his loyalty to those he considered friends, but she needed more than trust. He gave the smallest hint of a nod. "He's not behind it, but I won't stand in your way. You have my permission to investigate him however you see fit."

She thought he meant it as a dismissal, but as she rose to leave, he held up a hand. He twisted around and pulled something out of a cabinet. It was a thin leather thong, but a lone shard was cleverly embedded in the middle. He tossed it to her, and she held it in her hand. A closer examination confirmed that it was, indeed, a shard.

"A new type of training band, sir?"

"Something like that. I want you to tie it high up on your leg once you get home, where it won't be seen or found during a search."

"Sir?"

"Don't ask. It's a shard, and I feel like you might need it as you continue this investigation. It's designed to be hidden, though, and I expect you to keep it safe."

"Yes, sir. Now, if you'd be so kind as to give me the names of those Swords, I'm going to get back to work. I'll report to you before prime shift tomorrow."

He scribbled an order on a piece of paper, signed it, then passed it over to her.

"Good luck."

Nikki nodded. Even with the Swords and the generous gift of a shard, she felt as though she was going to need it.

12

Radyn, Kaya, and Aria waited on top of Underhill for Tanwen to appear. Radyn had summoned him already and expected to see him flying over the hills any moment now. His attention, though, was firmly fixed on his wife. It had been since he'd learned of her pregnancy the day before. He'd always found her beautiful, but never more than now. He couldn't quite put words to what he sensed, but everything about her seemed brighter, as though some part of her spirit was lighting her from within.

Kaya coughed loudly into her hand. "Are you two going to need some privacy?"

Radyn caught his first glimpse of Tanwen and shook his head. "Unfortunately, no."

He would have rather torn a shard out of his body than leave Aria, but allowing the enemies that had attacked to escape was more dangerous. Tanwen landed and Kaya climbed on first, then waited for Radyn. He took Aria's hand. "I'll be back as soon as I can."

"I know. You be careful out there." She tilted her head up for a kiss, then shoved him away.

It was good that she did. He might not have been able to summon the courage otherwise. He climbed up Tanwen's side and took his position behind Kaya. The young Singer glanced back. "You with me?"

He understood. He watched Aria until she was safely within Underhill's main gates, then nodded. "I am now."

"Good." Kaya connected with Tanwen, and they took to the sky. It had been months since Radyn had been a passenger on a flight, but he and Kaya had agreed it was more important that she have access to the song. If they were attacked while Radyn was flying, Kaya would be unable to defend them. Given she was the only one capable of defense, it made the decision a simple one.

As they had on the flight two days ago, they started with a slow circle of the area. Radyn searched with his eyes as Kaya searched with her song. He wasn't surprised when she noticed something first. She pointed to the hillside facing Underhill. "There was something there."

She asked Tanwen to fly in that direction and he banked his wings and turned. As they approached, Kaya nodded. "There's definitely something there."

Radyn saw nothing but a barren hillside. The top of the hill was steep and exposed enough to be mostly stone, but the lower one descended, the thicker the grasses, bushes, and trees grew. A handful of places provided some cover, but it was scarce. The side of the hill was too steep for Tanwen to land on, so Kaya asked him to drop them closer to the top of the hill.

Kaya disconnected after she climbed off. Tanwen took to the air again, and Radyn shot Kaya a questioning look.

"I asked him to keep an eye on us from above. It's harder to sense anything when he's nearby."

Radyn checked to ensure his maniblade was securely attached to his hip, and Kaya did the same. She wasn't as proficient with her blade as he was with his, but she was able to protect herself if needed. He'd made sure of that over the past year. Once certain they were ready, Kaya led the way down the hill.

Most of the descent was easy, but Radyn was tempted once or twice to connect with his shards. They picked their way down the rocky slope until Kaya stopped behind a clump of bushes and squatted. She pressed her hand to the ground, but Radyn didn't follow her lead.

He had a clear view of Underhill from here, and they were close enough he would have been able to make out individuals, had there been any outside. The grass and vegetation behind the bush were bent and broken, which was all the evidence he needed. He looked around and found the tracks leading away. They were faint, but visible enough.

"They were here," Kaya confirmed.

Radyn pointed up the hill. "And they went that way."

He took the lead back up the hill, following the tracks. He lost them once but found them again higher up the slope. The trail led to the top of the hill and over, and they descended down the other side, where they ended at the entrance to a cave.

"I know where this one comes out," Radyn said.

He called Tanwen down and had the dragon carry them over the next hill. They dismounted on the other side, near another entrance where they picked up the trail again. It appeared to head west, deeper into the hills. He was tempted to hop on Tanwen, but he wasn't sure he could follow the faint trail from the air. They continued following the tracks on foot, which led them down into a valley carved by a slow-moving stream. Their assailants had followed the stream for about a mile, then crossed. The mud on the opposite side revealed the first set of clear prints Radyn had found since they'd started tracking. He squatted next to the mud, casting his gaze around the area.

He counted three sets of distinct prints, and perhaps a fourth. They'd lingered near the stream after crossing, possibly filling waterskins before carrying on. "Notice anything unusual?" he asked Kaya.

She'd been letting him study the tracks while she watched the surrounding hills, but his question drew her gaze down. She studied them for a moment, and then her eyes narrowed. "They're not wearing boots."

"Good work. Couldn't say what it means, though, except I've never known anyone not to wear boots."

The prints were nearly perfectly foot-shaped, although the part around the toes was rounded. If Radyn didn't know better, he would have said they were chasing a group that only wore socks on their feet.

He stood and followed the tracks away from the stream. Thankfully, the ground around the stream was muddy for maybe twenty feet, so he was able to learn more. There had been four, but one was not like the others. He considered asking Kaya as another little test but decided against it. "I think one is wounded, or at least not feeling well."

"Why?"

Radyn pointed to one pair of tracks, the one that had been the last to leave the stream. "Look. One is dragging their right foot, almost as though they're shuffling forward."

He looked at Kaya for an explanation, but she only

shrugged. "It's possible I hurt one of them when we fought, but I couldn't tell you."

"It's good news, though. Means we might catch up to them more quickly than I'd thought."

They filled their own waterskins at the stream, then hurried after the tracks. Thanks to thicker grass and more brush the trail was easier to follow, and they made good time. By noon they were climbing another hillside, one far enough away from Underhill that Radyn hadn't explored it.

The tracks led them to another cave, and Radyn and Kaya paused to consider their options.

"I don't know where that cave lets out, or if it lets out at all," Radyn admitted. "We could ask Tanwen for a ride, but there's no telling where it leads. I think we have to go in."

Kaya hardly seemed enthused by the prospect. She closed her eyes, and Radyn sensed her connection with the song. "There's darkness within," she said.

Radyn arched an eyebrow. "It's a cave. It would be more unusual if it was bright."

She opened her eyes to glare at him, and he smiled. "What do you think? This is why we came, but if you're not sure, we can consider a different approach."

Kaya looked at the cave again and Radyn was reminded of just how young she was. Because of her strength and the way she carried herself, he tended to think of her as older than she was. In a better world she'd just be leaving childhood behind and starting to think about her own future. In this world, though, she'd shouldered the burdens of adulthood years before. He didn't like the idea of taking her into danger, but the alternative was to leave the rest of Underhill under the threat of this shadow song.

After a moment, she nodded. "You're right, this is why we came."

He would never fault her for her courage. "Then let's go. I'll lead the way. Tap me on the shoulder if we're approaching something dangerous."

He took his maniblade in hand and lit it, relying on the pale blue glow of the blade to light their way through the cave. The initial entrance was wide, with more than enough space for five or six warriors to take shelter for the night. It quickly narrowed near the back of the cave, though, becoming little more than a crack barely wide enough for him to slip through.

He shuffled sideways through the crack, stone scratching against his shoulder blades as he worked his way to the other side. Thankfully, the crack didn't last long, and he soon found himself in a wider tunnel running perpendicular to the crack. He waited for Kaya to come through, then asked, "Which way?"

She pointed left without hesitation. Radyn nodded and led the way.

He'd explored just a few of the caves and tunnels closest to Underhill, and they never ceased to amaze him. Before he'd come to the surface, he'd always imagined caves as not being that much different than the maze of hallways he'd grown up in. Though his city had flown through the sky, he'd always felt as though he'd grown up underground.

Natural caves had little in common with the hallways of Firestone and Underhill, though. Stalactites dripped water from the ceiling, reminding Radyn that though an incredible amount of stone was above him, it was more porous than he thought. Puddles in a hallway would have been a sign of problems in Firestone, and a repair crew would have found the source of the leak in no time at all. This ground rose and fell, and the tunnel grew narrow in spots and opened in others. It lacked any of the uniformity of the hallways the Makers had created.

Without landmarks, Radyn had little idea of how far they'd traveled. Twice the tunnel had split into multiple branches, and both times Kaya had chosen one without more than a moment's consideration. At each intersection Radyn carved an arrow into the stone with his maniblade, so if they had to retreat the way they'd come they wouldn't get lost.

They'd been walking for a good while when Kaya put her hand on his shoulder. He stopped and she leaned close so she could whisper into his ear. "There's something close. The strength seems to swell and fade, but it's not far away."

Radyn nodded slowly. He let the maniblade die, but the darkness of the cave was absolute, reminding him of the dreadful day he'd been stuck in the Engine room with Elora when the Engine flickered and went dark for a moment. He gave his eyes time to adjust, but there was no light to work with, and he had no choice but to light his maniblade again. They wouldn't surprise whoever waited for them, but they had probably already sensed Kaya. Even so, he advanced quietly, placing his steps carefully and keeping both eyes and ears open for an ambush.

He needn't have bothered. Two turns later they spotted a light in the darkness, and as they continued down the tunnel it brightened into the flame of a torch, which lay beside a young man who was seated with his back to the wall, eyes closed.

Radyn stopped a dozen paces away and glanced at Kaya, who nodded. This was the source of the shadow song, one of the group that had attacked him, Aria, and their unborn child. He tightened his grip on the hilt of his maniblade and forced himself to look, the way Elora had taught him.

The young man stirred and reached for a sword lying on the other side of him. Not a maniblade, but an actual sword, forged from metal. Radyn had never seen one, but the edge looked plenty sharp.

Little about the man's appearance made sense. He wore something that resembled a vest, although it was several layers of leather thick. His pants were also leather, and instead of boots on his feet he wore some sort of leather covering that explained the strange prints Radyn had found. The young man's skin was tanned darker than a farmer's, and he glared at Radyn with eyes that were impossibly dark.

Curiosity overwhelmed revenge. "Who are you?" he asked.

The young man responded, but in no language Radyn had ever heard.

He glanced back at Kaya, but she was every bit as confused as he was.

"What?" he asked.

The man said something again, and the sounds were the same, but Radyn still didn't recognize them. Who didn't speak their language? It was shared across all the cities, a subtle reminder that though they were separated by steel, sky, and clan, they were all still human, fighting to survive on a world that no longer wanted them.

"Radyn, watch out."

He appreciated the warning, but there was little need for it. The man got to his feet slowly, pulling his sword up with him but leaving the torch to burn against the stone. He moved as though he'd been injured, and Radyn noticed he put most of his weight on his left leg. He shifted his feet until he reached an unfamiliar stance. As before, most of his weight was on his left foot, which he moved behind him, and he held the sword out, tip pointed at Radyn's heart.

Radyn took a defensive stance. From what little he'd seen of the man, he had no chance in a duel, and his stance seemed weak. Radyn would be able to knock any stab off its line with a twisting of his wrists, leaving the man completely at his mercy.

But he'd never make the mistake of underestimating an opponent again. He connected with all his shards and focused his full attention on the dark-eyed man. He was debating whether to defend or attack when his opponent took his decision away from him.

Radyn sensed it first with his shards, a spiritual pressure similar to what he'd felt the day before outside Underhill. The air in the tunnel grew heavy and oppressive, as though a storm approached just over the horizon. The weight didn't bear down on him like before, but he tensed all the same.

Kaya called out another warning, but there was no need. He sensed the man's power growing and saw how it gave him strength. His stance became more balanced, and he trusted his injured leg more than before. The muscles in his arm bulged, filled with a dark song Radyn didn't understand.

The man leaped forward, faster than Radyn would have thought possible a moment ago. His sword tip jumped toward Radyn's chest, eager to slide underneath his ribs and pierce his heart. If Radyn hadn't been connected to his shards, he might have lacked the speed to save himself.

Radyn blocked, slapping away the thrust with the flat side of his maniblade. Steel met song, and for a moment, Radyn feared he hadn't struck hard enough. The steel pushed forward, and Radyn had to flex his wrists to shove the steel to the side. The sword drifted wide, and Radyn stepped into the gap, disconnecting their weapons and cutting his blade down. The weapon went through his opponent's skull without slowing and buried itself in his chest.

Radyn let the maniblade die. The body collapsed, the steel sword clanging and echoing in the tunnel. He lit the maniblade a moment later, but the black-eyed man was dead and still.

"Sorry you had to see that," he said.

Kaya's lips were pursed in a thin line, and she forced her gaze away from the body, though they kept drifting back toward it. Radyn stepped between her and the corpse. "Why don't you take the torch and go a little way farther into the tunnel? I'm going to look over the body."

She nodded slowly, but she didn't turn until he put a gentle hand on her shoulder and guided her away. Once she was around the bend, torch in hand, he returned to the corpse. He'd landed facedown, so Radyn patted down the backside of the body, finding a beautiful knife made out of bone and steel. He took the knife and sheath and slipped it into a pocket. Then he flipped the body over and searched it, too. The young man had been left here by his friends without food or water, and Radyn wondered if it was due to cruelty or tradition, or if they planned on returning soon. Regardless of the answer, the only item of interest he found was a stone tied tightly to the young man's wrist. Radyn ran his thumb over it and sensed—something. A shard?

It didn't feel quite right, but similar, perhaps. Once they were out of danger, he'd have Kaya examine it more closely. He used his new knife to cut the leather thong that held the stone in place. Knife and stone went back into his pocket and he stood. Then he rejoined Kaya.

"What do we do now?" she asked, her voice trembling just a little.

"We keep going," Radyn said. "At the very least, our enemies are up ahead, but perhaps there are answers, too."

13

Nikki bobbed her head as Stephen tried to land a jab against her chin. His punches came quickly, but most missed. One grazed her ear, but if that was the worst she suffered today, she'd be pleased. Stephen took a step back to plan his next attack, but Nikki didn't offer him the chance. She followed him as he retreated, mixing jabs and hooks in an attempt to land a clean blow.

One of her punches sneaked through his defense and caught him in the side. He winced from the blow, but without assistance from a shard, she couldn't hit him hard enough to bring him down.

Stephen recovered quickly, returning her punches with a little extra interest. Again, she avoided most, but one solid body shot from his left fist left her stumbling back and gasping for air. She forced herself to stand straight. The corners of Stephen's lips were turned up in a self-satisfied grin.

"You've gotten better," Nikki admitted.

"So have you, and recently. I couldn't go nearly this hard when we last sparred, and that wasn't that long ago."

"What was it? Six months?" Nikki asked.

"Closer to a year, if my memory serves. But the point stands. Where have you been practicing?"

Nikki swore under her breath. Had it really been a year since she'd been to this training area last? She remembered why she'd come. It had been after the investigation she'd worked with Radyn, which had taught her how much stronger she was going to need to be if she planned on defending Firestone from the dangers it faced. Too late, she realized she hadn't answered Stephen's question. "All over, honestly. I mostly train with the top Shields, though."

"You should train here more often. You're good enough now, and I don't have any doubt you'd be able to defeat some of the younger and less experienced Daggers. Do some of them some real good to get beaten by a Shield, I think."

"Ego problems?"

Stephen nodded. "No more than usual for new Daggers, but the youngest graduates of the academy haven't experienced any real battles yet, so they're more confident than they should be."

"I suppose I'd rather have that problem than having our young Daggers be really experienced in battle."

Stephen's grin widened. "That's a good way of looking at it. I'll have to remind myself of that the next time I want to slap the mouth off of one of them."

Nikki laughed out loud. Stephen was a Senior Dagger and would never advance higher. He couldn't handle enough shards to become a Sword, but he'd spent the better part of two decades in service to the clan, and Nikki knew he was invaluable. It was the Senior Daggers, far more numerous than the Swords, who truly ran the clan's day-to-day operations.

Stephen was an excellent example. He was one of three Senior Daggers who ran this training ground, which was open to all but tended to attract a more skilled group of students, usually Junior Daggers looking to advance their techniques to a Senior Dagger level. When he wasn't here, he acted as the connection between the clan and the neighborhood Shield office. And if all that wasn't enough, in what free time remained, he kept regular patrol hours in the neighborhood, a familiar face to all who lived here. Oh, and he was the loving husband to one of the cooks for the dining hall and father to two beautiful young girls. So if there was anyone in the neighborhood who would have noticed something amiss, it was someone like Stephen.

"Another round?" Stephen asked.

Nikki undid the wraps around her hands. "Not today. I can only get beat up so much before it starts to affect my work."

Stephen's grin faded. "So why are you really here?"

"I did want another chance to spar with you, but I also wanted to ask if you'd noticed anyone unusual hanging around the training ground lately. Or if you've seen anything that made you suspicious."

Stephen started unwrapping his own hands. "That's a bit vague. Care to fill in some details?"

"I think there's someone aboard Firestone recruiting talented young men and women. I can't say much else at the moment, but one of my guesses is that they're keeping an eye on training grounds for any promising up and coming warriors. My best guess is they're targeting kids who want to get into the academy, but it's possible they're recruiting from the academy, or even trying to recruit Junior Daggers. Any of that ring some bells for you?"

Stephen searched his memory for a moment, then shook

his head. "Sorry, but no. It's been nothing but regulars around here as of late, excepting yourself. Haven't had any lurkers, and I haven't heard anyone talking about anything like that, either. What are they recruiting for?"

"I'm not exactly sure, but it didn't end well for the last kid."

"Sorry I can't be more help, but I can promise you that if I do hear anything, I'll come personally to your place to let you know right away."

She bowed toward Stephen. "I really appreciate it. And please, spread the word. I've been stopping by the different training areas, but the more people on the lookout, the better."

"Of course. I'll do all I can. And you should stop by again soon. If you have the time, I can probably teach you a few tricks that will help you even against old Senior Daggers like me."

"I'll take you up on that."

Nikki left the training ground, and her stomach reminded her that she'd skipped breakfast that morning. She meandered through the halls, her mind racing while she made her way to the dining hall.

They were serving lunch when she arrived, and she turned in her ration card in exchange for a meal. Not wanting to be disturbed, she found an unoccupied table in the corner of the dining hall. She barely tasted the food as she considered what she knew.

Unfortunately, it was precious little. For all the digging she'd done since finding Zak's body, she'd found nothing. No one who worked on the level where Zak had been found had seen anyone or anything suspicious. That wasn't entirely surprising. Most workrooms kept their doors closed, for their neighbor's sake, throughout the day, and it would be easy to come and go without being observed.

She'd also combed the training grounds. If someone had recruited Zak, it stood to reason they might try to recruit another student, but everyone told the same story as Stephen. She'd stared at the drawings of the symbols in the room until her eyes ached, but she couldn't make anything of them. Zak's friends and family were likewise unhelpful. Aella had been as broken as it was possible for a parent to be when she heard the news, but hadn't been able to give Nikki any more information than she already had. Zak's friends didn't know much, either. The only useful piece of information she got from them was that he'd been recruited recently, probably within a week of when he died.

There weren't many leads left for her to track down, and she was rapidly running out of ideas.

Despair waited at the edge of her thoughts, eager to be allowed in, but every time she sensed its presence, she remembered the look on Zak's face and the state of the room where she'd found him.

Giving up wasn't an option.

She just wasn't sure how to continue.

She was looking through her notes in her apartment that evening when there was a knock on her door. She looked up and frowned, then went back to her notes.

The knock repeated, and Nikki pushed her chair back. "Who is it?"

A male voice answered, but too quietly for the words to penetrate through the door. Nikki grabbed a dagger resting on the table. The shard Jyn had asked her to wear was tied around her upper thigh, so if her visitor meant her harm, they were in for an unpleasant surprise. She planted her right foot a few inches behind the door, then opened it a crack.

She needed a moment to recognize the man on the other side. He wore a hood over his face, casting most of it in shadow, but the lines she caught were familiar. "Jelrik?"

"May I come in?" he asked.

One didn't typically refuse any request from the Master Singer, but she hesitated a moment before moving her foot and opening the door. "Of course."

She led him into her living area, suddenly self-conscious of her bare walls and lack of furniture. She pointed to the one chair she'd been sitting on at the table. "You're welcome to sit, if you like. Can I get you some water?"

Jelrik tossed off his hood, gave her a wry smile, and shook his head. "No, but thank you, and I can stand. I don't plan on being here long."

He looked better than he had the last time she'd seen him. He wasn't quite as gaunt, and there was a spark of life in his eyes that hadn't been present in Jyn's study. If such a change was the result of the dark song alone, it was more powerful than she'd originally given it credit for.

"How can I help you?" she asked.

"Actually, the question I came here to ask is if I could help you," Jelrik said.

"The Blade gave you strict orders," Nikki reminded him.

"And how has the investigation gone without me?"

Her look was answer enough.

"I don't question your ability, but we're dealing with a conspiracy of clever and determined individuals. I suspect they've been active for many years, and we have nothing but the slightest whispers about them. Without a Singer, I don't know how you'll track them down."

"I haven't exhausted all my leads yet," she said.

"Be honest with yourself. How likely are any of your remaining leads going to be? Let me help."

"How?"

"I know that you have a shard. Let me use it, and I'll see if I can track down the dark song in Firestone."

Her eyes narrowed. Had he somehow become addicted? She dismissed the thought after a moment. He looked healthy, his eyes were clear, and there was no sign of physical need.

But even if it wasn't an addiction, she wasn't any more confident about allowing him near her shard. Jyn's caution hadn't been without reason. With a shard he could connect to the song, and given his ability, there was little limit to what he could do. He could be exactly what she needed to proceed in the investigation, but he might also take the opportunity to drop Firestone from the sky.

She couldn't take the risk. "I'm sorry, Jelrik, but I can't."

He reached out to her but stopped as she pulled her hand away. "Nikki, please. I need to help."

"Why?"

"Because I'm the only one who can, and because I fear that if I don't, whoever killed Rebecca will kill again."

"What if I think you killed Rebecca?"

She didn't, not really, though his name was on the short list of suspects who could open the door to the Engine room.

Her accusation robbed him of his strength. He shook his head, eyes wide, and took a step back. "You don't mean that."

She advanced, studying every facial muscle, every twitch

of his eyes. "Why wouldn't I? You've already confessed to being under the influence of this dark song, and as far as I know, you're the only one left in Firestone who can hear it. You can also open the Engine room. Maybe Rebecca was getting too close to the truth."

Her words were heavy boulders placed on his shoulders, and he shrank from her until he was close to cowering in a corner. He kept shaking his head, trembling from toe to crown. He was either very guilty or completely innocent, but Nikki couldn't tell which.

She let him stew in the accusations. In time, his trembling stopped, and he found his strength. He stood up straight, and his eyes were bright again. "That was cruel, even for you. I didn't kill Rebecca, but if you refuse my help, you might as well be killing everyone in Firestone. I'm sure our enemies are on the move, and you can't afford to waste any more time."

The transformation before her eyes was remarkable. This was the Jelrik she was most familiar with, a man she'd happily put her trust in. But if she trusted him, which Singer would help her? The man who stood before her now, or the one who cowered under her accusations, the man susceptible to the corrupting influence of the dark song?

In the end, it all came down to trust.

It might lead to disaster, but if she continued as she had, disaster was nearly certain. Jelrik was right about one thing, at least. She wasn't making any meaningful progress.

"Why should I trust you?" she asked.

He thought about the question for a moment before answering. "Because of Elora, my wife. She gave her life so that Firestone would survive. I'll accept no less from myself."

It was as good a promise as she could have asked for, and it pushed her over the edge and into a decision. She walked over to a dresser, pulled open the top shelf, and pulled out a leather band with a single small shard embedded in it. The band was a slightly nicer version of what the students at the academy wore. She tossed it to him.

He caught it and tied it around his wrist, then covered the band up with his sleeve.

"Let's get started, then," Nikki said.

As they turned to leave her apartment, all she could hope for was that she hadn't made the wrong decision.

14

Kaya remained quiet as she followed Radyn deeper into the tunnels. She was no stranger to violence, but from the way her gaze jumped away from him, he guessed she was working her way through a complicated mess of reactions. He didn't fault her, but her refusal to answer any question with more than a gesture left him at a loss for how to help.

The tunnels branched twice more, and both times Kaya directed them with a tilt of her head. Radyn marked the path with his maniblade and continued the pursuit. He was troubled by his own questions. Why had the warrior been left behind, and why was everything about him so odd?

They'd covered at least another mile when the tunnel started to rise in fits and starts. For a time, a stream smaller than the width of Radyn's wrist trickled down the side of the tunnel, disappearing into a crack he hadn't even noticed as he had passed it below. They came to another branch, and for the first time Kaya hesitated. She eventually pointed right, and when Radyn gave her a questioning look, she nodded.

He followed her directions. The tunnel grew wider and more uniform, and they ended their journey under the hills ascending a long line of flat stones that had clearly been placed as stairs. No mortar or frame held the stones in place, and a few shifted as Radyn stepped on them, but he never felt as though he was in danger of losing his balance. Light seeped into the tunnel from above, and it wasn't long before there was enough light for Radyn to let his maniblade rest. He breathed a slow sigh of relief. It had been ages since he'd been connected with the shards for so long, and though the connection strengthened him, the aftermath left him exhausted.

The stairs ended near the back of another cave, and Radyn slowly stepped into the light, grateful his eyes had already adjusted during the climb. The sun had passed its zenith for the day, and he was forced to shield his eyes as he looked out west from the cave. He didn't recognize exactly where he was, but that wasn't surprising. He let his eyes roam across the terrain. A valley stretched out below them, and the hills here were more rugged than the ones closer to Underhill. Most revealed their dark stone near their summits, but below were covered with grasses, bushes, and trees, all green and vibrant in the heart of spring.

Distant movement caught his eye, and he focused his gaze west-northwest. A trio of dark figures, barely more than dots, climbed a trail on a distant hill. The trail carved a zigzag line up the hill, but the figures made steady progress. Radyn watched for a moment to ensure they weren't one of the wild animals that called these hills home. Once he was sure, he nudged Kaya and pointed in that direction. "Can you tell if that's them?"

She stared alongside him for a bit, then nodded. "That's them."

Radyn rubbed at his chin. He hadn't truly believed that they would leave their partner behind. He supposed it was a question he could ask them later, although if they didn't share a language, he might never get an answer.

The hill was miles distant, but Radyn called Tanwen, who had been resting near the summit of a nearby hill. Before long they were on the dragon again, flying across the valleys. The dots on the hillside had disappeared, but Radyn knew their approximate location and suspected he would find a cave there. Given the complexity of the tunnel system they'd just been in, it seemed their assailants knew this land far better than anyone in Underhill, which was another question he was eager to find the answer to.

Radyn pointed out their destination to Kaya, who spoke with the dragon and brought them closer. They circled the hill once on the chance the tunnel let out on the other side, but they found no other exit. Tanwen landed, and Radyn thanked the dragon for the help. The dragon returned to the air, and Radyn turned to Kaya. "I'm sorry I had to bring you into this."

She huffed and set her shoulders. "Let's go."

Radyn followed after, connecting to his shards and preparing to enter this new cave. This cave dropped almost straight down, and Radyn was surprised to find a ladder of wood and nails. It looked new, and when he tested his weight on it, he found it as sturdy as a rock. He added the ladder to his list of mysteries for the day and climbed down. The three they were following didn't have that much of a lead, and he fought the desire to run headlong through the tunnel.

Fortunately, the tunnel itself helped him fight the temptation. Instead of a wide tunnel, they had to traverse a long and narrow crack. Radyn turned sideways and started shuffling through, his heart starting to race as the stone pressed against both chest and back. He sucked in his stomach and thought skinny thoughts. More than once, he feared he'd wedged himself into the crack for good, but each time he pushed himself just a bit harder and squeezed through. Kaya was smaller and had an easier time, but she looked just as relieved to be done when the crack ended, and they found themselves in another tunnel.

Radyn tapped his feet against the stone and looked around. Light entered the tunnel through the crack, but what little he saw made no sense. "Are they close?" he whispered.

Kaya shook her head and pointed to her right. "They're down that way, but farther than I would have expected."

Radyn nodded and connected with his maniblade, adding its pale blue glow to the light from the crack.

Kaya swore.

"Yeah," Radyn agreed.

They found themselves in a tunnel, but not a tunnel like any they'd spent the rest of the day in. This, finally, reminded Radyn of the hallways of Firestone, except here the tunnels were made from stone instead of metal. The floor and walls were smooth and even, and when he went over to one to run his hand along it, he shook his head. The wall was stone but was as smooth as one of Firestone's metal hallways.

"This has to be the work of the Makers, right?" Kaya asked.

"I think so." Radyn glanced at the crack they'd entered in, a crack he suspected hadn't been here when the tunnel was first made. He looked around, and though it all struck him as unreal, there was little to see beyond smooth walls. Long as the tunnel was, there were no doors. He pointed the same direction Kaya had a moment ago. "They're down that way?"

She nodded, and once again, Radyn led the way. Thanks to the smooth stone, they made quick progress, and Radyn hurried them along. The faster he killed Underhill's attackers, the faster he could return to Aria.

They hadn't gone that far, though, when Radyn felt the weight of the shadow song pressing against his senses. He connected with his shards and took a defensive stance, but he could see nothing in the darkness ahead of him.

Kaya grunted and took a knee.

"Kaya!"

She shook her head, as though to clear a buzzing sound from her ears. "I'm fine. It's not an attack. But someone just summoned a fair amount of power."

She sensed the power better than he did. "What should we do?"

Her gaze hardened as she stared down the tunnel. "Catch them."

Radyn didn't need to be told twice. He ran down the tunnel, restraining his speed so that Kaya could keep up. The tunnel curved as it descended, but it wasn't long before Kaya slowed. Radyn slowed down with her, thinking that she had run out of strength, but she wore a frown of confusion on her face.

"What's wrong?"

"I don't sense them anymore," she said.

Radyn couldn't think of anything to do except keep running, and his steps echoed in the empty stone halls of the Makers. The tunnel ended suddenly in a cavernous space, and Radyn and Kaya skidded to a halt.

Radyn held his maniblade high, trying to make some sense of what his eyes were telling him. Something about the area made him think of Firestone's nest, where they staged all the dragons to both leave and arrive, though he couldn't place his finger on why he thought that.

The cavern, like the tunnels they'd arrived through, was carved out of stone, the walls as smooth as glass. The floor of the cavern was cut by two wide incisions, about three feet deep and eight across. A steel beam was secured to the bottom of the incision, and as Radyn studied it, he realized he could hear the faint notes of an Engine's song coming from the steel.

Each of the incisions led to a separate tunnel that appeared to be a perfect circle. Radyn walked to the entrance of one, and the light of his maniblade was swallowed by the darkness. The steel beam ran the entire length of the incision, and the whole construction felt like it carried on for some ways.

"Any idea what this is?" he asked.

When Kaya didn't answer, he turned around and saw her concentrating. She'd moved to the second incision and was staring at the steel beam. He hopped across the first incision and joined her. "What is it?"

"There's something here."

He sensed her singing to the steel, testing different notes and harmonies until she found the music that resonated. Radyn sensed when it matched, the steel at the bottom of the incision coming alive as Kaya sang.

He couldn't think of another Singer that could so easily accomplish what she just had. Being forced to learn so much on her own had left her with gifts other singers could only dream of. She wasn't glued to the traditions that so bound other Singers.

His appreciation didn't last long as sudden motion drew his eye to the tunnel the incision led to. He first thought he was staring at a dragon bearing down on him, but it was no beast. It was—well, he didn't have the slightest clue what it was, but it ran along the steel beam at the bottom of the incision.

"It's a track," Kaya said.

Radyn shot her a questioning look.

The shape stopped in front of them, and it was a long metal capsule with chairs. It was entirely enclosed, but as it came to a stop, its doors opened, and Radyn took a step back, taking a defensive posture.

Kaya laughed. "You don't need to worry. Aria taught me something about tracks, although the ones she works with are nothing like this. I think this carries people from one place to another."

Radyn looked down the dark tunnel.

"Underground?"

"It seems that way, but there's no way to tell. It is powered by the song, which makes me think that somewhere, it's connected to an Engine."

"And that's why you aren't able to sense the attackers anymore? They've gone too far away?"

Kaya shrugged. "It's my best guess."

Radyn swore, but an intrusive thought brought a surprising smile to his face. "Aria would love this, if she was here."

"Absolutely," Kaya agreed.

"What do you think?" Radyn asked. He wished he could be more decisive, but this was far beyond his understanding.

"I believe I can control the motion of the..." Her voice trailed off, and she gestured to the thing that ran on the track, "But there's no telling what we find on the other side."

Radyn sighed. They had to know, and it wasn't as if there

were any strong Manirah back at Underhill he could turn to for more help. "I think we should travel on it."

He was surprised Kaya agreed so easily. She extended her arm. "After you."

Radyn stepped through the door, halfway expecting it to be a trap, but nothing happened. He took a seat and Kaya followed after him. She resumed her song, and the door closed, and they sped off into the darkness.

15

Now that they were on the hunt, Jelrik seemed a different man. He led Nikki through the hallways with his head high and his steps sure. She'd rarely seen him outside of his official duties, where he'd always maintained a certain aloofness. She'd not thought much of it, assuming such an attitude came naturally when one was the most revered Singer in a city, but now she wondered if she hadn't been witnessing an act all along.

Jelrik led her so confidently it took her some time to realize she hadn't stopped to ask if he had a plan. She was grateful for his assistance, but wasn't sure what difference he could make. She hurried so that she was walking beside him. "What are you thinking?" she asked.

Jelrik turned down a quiet hallway, stopped, and asked the young Swords following them if they could have a moment. The Swords bowed and took position ten paces away. Jelrik leaned close. "When you asked me to come see Zak's body, I felt the dark song before I reached the door. It wasn't a great distance, but it was about twenty paces."

Nikki followed the thought. "So if we can get you close, you should be able to sense them,"

This was exactly the sort of break she needed, but there was only one obvious problem. "Even so, you're talking an enormous search. Firestone is no small city."

Jelrik looked like he had already thought of that. "You're forgetting an important detail, the detail that will help us find the monsters who did this."

It was a test, and she hated that he thought it necessary. She shoved the frustration aside. He'd noticed the dark song at the scene of Zak's murder. What was she missing?

Her eyes narrowed as she understood. "Zak had been dead for a time, and you still sensed it. The presence lingers."

Jelrik's look made it clear he wasn't surprised she'd figured it out, but he was satisfied that she had. "Exactly. We don't need to find where they are. We can find where they've been and track them that way."

"Firestone is still a big city, and that's a lot of ground to cover for two people. Or one, really, as you're the one who will have to do the sensing." Her thoughts raced ahead of her objection, though, planning how they might approach the search.

Jelrik had already done the same, likely before he'd even come to her door. "True, but we can make some guesses, can't we? They'll likely prefer the lower levels that are quieter, someplace where their work won't be noticed accidentally by a passing Manirah."

The Master Singer's thoughts paralleled her own. Because Firestone was shaped almost like an enormous top, the bottom levels would be much quicker to search. "And if we find them?" she asked.

Jelrik shrugged. "I suppose it will depend on exactly

what we find, but I am fortunate to be guarded by two Swords and accompanied by one of Firestone's finest Shields. I'm sure we'll think of something."

Nikki also had a Sword assigned to her, but she'd given him the night off after returning to her apartment. She supposed she could summon him, but they already had two Senior Swords thanks to Jelrik. They were set. It was the most optimistic Nikki had felt in days, and she nodded her agreement. Jelrik motioned to the guards, and the four of them worked their way through the hallways and down into the bowels of Firestone.

As a Shield, Nikki spent more time within the lowest levels of Firestone than most. There were of course the crafters and recyclers who worked below, and almost everyone had served shifts as laborers carrying supplies up from the cavernous storage rooms near the very bottom of Firestone, but those reasons all affirmed life and purpose. When Nikki took stairs or ladders below the twentieth level, it was almost always because of trouble.

It wasn't that the upper levels were idyllic. Stuffing so many people into so little space was always going to be a recipe for conflict, and there was plenty of it. People got too drunk and acted like fools. Children would try stealing what wasn't theirs. Couples would fight.

Keeping the peace up top wasn't always easy, but the crimes on the higher levels were rarely premeditated. They were most often the result of strong emotions and poor judgment, a moment's error that often led to days or weeks of regret. Thankfully, between the efforts of the clan and the Shields, most conflicts were resolved quickly, if not always peacefully.

Dealing with the problems up top had been how Nikki had started as a Shield, but it wasn't long before her skills were identified, and she was given more difficult problems to solve. Problems that all too often led her to the lower levels. Because of the sheer number of people, combined with the frequent clan and Shield patrols, anybody planning a crime naturally fell to the bottom of the city. Few spaces in Firestone were empty, and even fewer were empty for long, but if anyone wanted privacy, the lower levels were the place for them.

She'd tracked down smuggling rings, pursued a kidnapper, and at one point, even found a family huddled down here, afraid the clan was out to kill them. In her view, humanity was a mixed bag of roses and dung, but these walls on the lower level saw a lot more dung than flowers.

She and Jelrik started, as the Shields usually did on their searches, at the very bottom levels, working their way quickly through the enormous storerooms filled with foodstuffs, recycled metal, old wood, and more. Supplies were the lifeblood of the city, and nothing was thrown out that could be saved, repurposed, and used again.

The rooms were empty at this time of night, and most were locked to prevent theft, but given that someone had broken into the Engine room, it seemed likely that the storage rooms would pose little problem. As a Senior Shield, Nikki also had a master key to the doors in Firestone, allowing her access to any door. Jelrik moved quickly, confident in his ability to sense the dark song without problem. They ascended several levels in little time, and Nikki began to fear they'd either moved too quickly or that one of their assumptions had been wrong.

Her doubts vanished when Jelrik stopped outside a workroom door. "There's something in here," he said.

"Active?"

"I don't think so, but it's hard for me to tell."

Nikki considered the door for a moment. She tested it gently and found it was locked. Her master key would grant her entrance, but would it be more effective to have the Swords storm the room?

She chose to trust Jelrik's senses. She slid the master key into the lock, grimacing as the sound of the tumblers shifting into place echoed down the quiet hallway. The key turned easily, and she held the door so that the deadbolt wouldn't snap open.

Nikki cracked open the door, so slowly the motion was almost imperceptible. As soon as the crack opened, though, the sickly-sweet odors of death and decaying flesh snuck through the door. She nearly gagged on the smell as she pushed the door open wide.

She didn't turn on the light, because what she saw from the light of the hallway was gut-wrenching enough. The workroom was, in many ways, a mirror of the one she'd discovered Zak in. Instead of only one body, though, there were many, and the walls had been covered with a correspondingly large amount of blood.

SHIELDS ONLY MAINTAINED one neighborhood office in the lower levels, but they responded promptly to Nikki's requests. Before long, the area had been cordoned off, and she and Jelrik were given scented scarves to wrap around their mouths and noses. It wouldn't be enough to eliminate the smell, but hopefully it would allow them to focus while they studied the room.

Nikki entered first and turned on the light. The sight that greeted her was every bit as grotesque as she'd first imagined. There were five bodies in the room, and they lay in a circle with their heads all pointed toward the center. Their eyes were closed, and their arms lay stiffly at their sides. Nikki intended to examine them closer, but she ran her eyes over the symbols on the wall first. There were many of the same symbols she'd just been studying earlier that night in her apartment, the same symbols found on the walls around Zak's body. They made no more sense here than they'd made around Zak.

Jelrik entered the room after her and looked around. He studied the bodies for only a moment, but it was clear that most of his attention was for the walls and their symbols. He noticed the same detail that had been bothering her.

"This isn't their blood?" he asked.

"Doesn't look that way," she agreed. They were dead, but their bodies hadn't been drained of blood.

"Then...what happened here?"

Nikki crouched down and examined the bodies more closely before answering. She lifted the smallest one, a young woman who couldn't have been much more than twenty, on her side. There were no wounds on their skin, either front or back. No fresh scars, either, as far as Nikki could tell. "I couldn't say. Zak was killed, and then his blood was used to paint the symbols. This? I'm not sure. Either the blood was here when they came in and lay down, or someone came and painted it after they died."

Jelrik's eyes narrowed. "You said 'died' instead of 'murdered."

Nikki made a sound in the back of her throat, the verbal equivalent of a shrug. "No obvious signs of violence, and it sure looks like they came and lay down of their own free will. They might have been poisoned, or perhaps it was even a group suicide, but I can't tell. Once the healers examine the bodies we'll know more. Unless you're noticing something that says different?"

Jelrik shook his head. "No, I have no evidence. It simply feels like murder, and that's all."

Nikki nodded and stood up, understanding what Jelrik meant. Death by unnatural causes, certainly, though not necessarily murder.

She noticed the Master Singer looking again at the symbols painted upon the walls, that frustrating pattern of geometry that seemed just beyond her understanding.

"What are you seeing?" she asked.

"I'm not sure, and any guesses I might venture would tend towards the esoteric."

Nikki gestured at the room, encompassing both the symbols and the nearly arranged bodies. "At this point, I'm open to anything."

Jelrik rubbed absentmindedly at the side of his neck, then spoke softly, so his voice wouldn't carry much farther than Nikki's ears. "Ever since Jyn has been made aware of the condition of the Engines across the cities, he's been encouraging Singers to share their insights with one another. These symbols remind me, in a way, of the work done by one of Nightkeep's Senior Singers."

Nikki's heart skipped a beat at that. "You think Nightkeep, or one of their Singers, is behind this, too?"

Jelrik shook his head, taken aback as though he'd never considered the implication. "No, not at all." He struggled for a moment to explain, then said, "One question that has endlessly captured our imaginations is the question of what, exactly, the song is. We know it is connected to the Engines and the dragons, and somehow connected to all of life itself, but that doesn't answer the question. With the Engines failing, answering it had gone from an intellectually stimulating pastime to a matter of vital urgency.

"Most of us listen to the song more closely to find the answer, but one Singer in Nightkeep has turned to math and geometry and tried to map out the Song using various models. Few of us believe he'll find the truth, but at this point, we're encouraging all unique approaches. His work, though, often results in similar patterning, except here we see more emphasis on three pointed shapes and straight lines, where his model results in more circular patterns and curves."

Nikki stared blankly at Jelrik. "What does any of that mean?"

A sad smile turned up the corner of his lips. "Maybe nothing at all. Probably nothing at all, honestly, but I can't help but wonder if maybe these symbols map out the dark song Rebecca and I heard, the same way we've been trying to map out the song of the engines."

"Does any of that help us catch the person or people responsible for this?"

Jelrik thought for a moment, then shook his head. "If it does, I don't know how."

Nikki would have liked some sort of straight line to her antagonist then, but life was rarely so simple. "Is there anything else you need here?"

Jelrik looked around. "No."

"Then I'm going to send you home for the night. Get some rest, and I'll find you sometime in the morning once I know more."

His expression was one of distaste, but there was nothing here for him to do. He'd helped her uncover a slew of new leads she'd have to track down, and that would have to be good enough for him for the day. He bowed and turned to leave.

She cleared her throat and held out her hand.

Jelrik grimaced but took the band off his wrist and handed it to her.

"Thanks for your help tonight, sir. I promise I'll be by in the morning."

Jelrik nodded and left, his thoughts someplace distant.

He was out of her mind the moment he was out of sight. She ordered a number of younger Shields in and gave them their tasks. Two were responsible for copying all the symbols on the walls, in case they proved to be useful later. Another three were to discover the identities of the dead and find out everything about them, to be reported by noon the next day.

Once she was satisfied that all her leads would be pursued, she left the scene with the intent of returning home. She'd just left the cordon when a young Dagger found her. "Ma'am, the Blade wants to see you."

Nikki yawned. "Can it wait until the morning?"

The young Dagger shook his head, his face paling at the thought of failure. "No, ma'am. Whatever it is he wants, he's angry about it. Even Magni is keeping his distance."

Nikki swore, but turned to follow the Dagger into the den of an angry dragon.

16

In the darkness of the tunnel, it was impossible to tell how fast the machine carried them from place to place. Radyn had sensed the quick acceleration, but now the machine moved at a constant speed, and he could have walked around the seating area without a problem. He left his maniblade lit, though there was little to see.

Like all the work of the Makers, this machine left him both in awe and unsettled. For all he knew, they were speeding through the tunnel faster than a dragon could fly, but where he sat there was no sound and no sense of motion. It should have been impossible, but he'd grown up in a city in the sky, so impossible wasn't entirely unfamiliar.

Not for the first time, and certainly not for the last, Radyn wondered about the Makers. How could they have been capable of so much and yet not been able to survive on the surface? It was a question that had bothered him since he was a child, and none of the answers provided by adults had ever satisfied him.

Behind him, Kaya ran her hands along the walls of the machine, her eyes wide with wonder. He smiled to see it.

Her expression changed. "We're coming to a stop," she said.

Sure enough, a moment later he felt the machine start to slow. It was a gentle force pushing him forward, and even if he'd been standing, it wouldn't have been a problem. The tunnel turned gradually, and Radyn saw light beyond. He killed his maniblade and watched the light grow steadily larger.

"Are they ahead?" he asked.

She nodded, and her face fell. "And I don't think they're alone."

Radyn cursed. "Is there any way to turn this around?"

She pressed her hand to the wall. "Once it comes to a stop, yes, I think I can send it back the other way."

"Not earlier?"

She shook her head.

That left them little choice, then. "Let's see what the danger looks like when we get there. If it looks clear, I'll step off and explore a little while you stay here. But if we're surrounded by enemies, send us back right away."

He hadn't expected to find others, but why not? Their assailants were clearly familiar with the tunnels and hills outside Underhill. The light ahead wasn't from the sun. It was too bright and too white, reminding him of the lamps in Underhill and Firestone.

Had he accidentally stumbled upon their enemy's home?

The machine slowed gradually and then suddenly, sliding and stopping beside another platform similar in design to the one they'd just left from. The only difference was that this platform was brightly lit. Radyn held his maniblade at the ready, but the machine's doors opened on an empty platform.

He stepped out and looked around. Low, regular sounds came from a tunnel about fifty paces distant, but he saw and heard nothing that gave him pause. He retreated back to the machine. "I think we should investigate. Thoughts?"

Kaya sent her senses questing, then said, "I agree."

She stepped off the machine, which remained in place with its doors open, waiting for the next passengers. Radyn shook his head at the sight, then hurried over to the tunnel the sounds were coming from. He peeked around the corner.

The tunnel possessed all the markers of a Maker construction. The stone walls had been carved to an almost mirror-like perfection, and instead of lanterns powered by the song of the Engine, there were strips of light embedded in the stone ceiling. The tunnel sloped downward and was empty.

Radyn glanced back at Kaya, who nodded. She didn't sense that anyone was too close. He popped around the corner and walked quickly but quietly down the tunnel, Kaya no more than a step behind.

The tunnel ended at a junction that traveled either left or right, and Radyn looked to Kaya for guidance. She sent out her senses once again, and a moment later answered. "They are to the left, as well as something else. An Engine, perhaps?"

"You're not sure?"

She shook her head. "It feels a little like an Engine, but if it is, it's even weaker than Underhill's was when we first arrived."

If retreating would have improved their odds of success, Radyn would have turned around in a moment, but there were no meaningful reinforcements waiting back in Underhill. If he'd still been a member of the clan he would have turned to them, but down here he had only Kaya to help, so they crept out into the hallway and followed her guidance.

They ran into more and more hallways, with doors carved into the stone at regular intervals. Radyn couldn't say for sure without more investigation, but it had the feel of a city, and if the distance they'd traveled was any indication, it was larger than any of the cities flying today.

He felt as though he was buried under an avalanche of questions. He'd explored all the underground cities the soulkeepers' Singers knew of, and this wasn't one. Why was it so close to Underhill? Even if the machine had been moving faster than a flying dragon, the trip hadn't taken long, so they couldn't be that far away. And why was it so large? The Makers had never built without a reason, but what possible reason justified this place?

He didn't even know how to begin to answer those questions. If he could make this city safe, his first plan was to bring Aria here. Maybe her mind would prove equal to the task.

Kaya grabbed onto his arm. "They're close."

"Approaching?"

"Not that I can tell."

Kaya guided him around another corner, and this time he came to a stop of his own accord. The tunnel they'd been following ended in the largest enclosed space Radyn had ever seen, and it wasn't even close. His vision swam and his knees threatened to buckle as he took in the awesome sight.

Ahead of him, the floor sloped away, falling gradually at first and then more quickly, a pyramid turned upside down and bored deep into the stone. Something glowed faintly at the bottom, and Radyn didn't think it was an Engine, but believed it was what Kaya had sensed. Though they were far from it, he was close enough to sense it now, too, a faint humming sound where he expected the song of an Engine to be.

Giant machines, of a scale he found difficult to comprehend, broke the smooth line of the floor. They stood as statues now, but gleamed as though they'd just been cleaned the day before. Radyn stared, but he couldn't comprehend their purpose.

Kaya tugged at his arm and pointed to a set of stairs just ahead. Radyn nodded and climbed them. They went up several levels and emerged onto a small balcony overlooking the space.

Radyn rode Tanwen across the sky without problem, but the height of the balcony gave him a sense of vertigo so strong he sat down. Somehow the space seemed even larger from higher up. His eyes drifted to the ceiling, which also sloped down, but not as sharply as the floor.

He was so distracted by the size of the space he almost didn't notice the movement far below. Halfway between the balcony and the center of the cavern, a group was gathered near the base of one of the machines. They were in the middle of a heated conversation, based on their sharp gestures. Radyn crouched so as to be less obvious. He counted eight dark figures, but they were too far away for him to make out details.

"The three we've been chasing are among them," Kaya whispered.

Radyn's heart sank. He couldn't guess how strong they were, either individually or as a collective, but if they were all warriors, he didn't think he stood much of a chance. If they were as strong as the wounded man he'd faced in the earlier tunnel, he had no chance at all.

He was considering his options when there was

movement directly below them. Another pair of men exited the hallway Kaya and Radyn had just wandered down, shouting for the attention of the others. Again, the language was like nothing Radyn had heard before, but the tone of their voices and the way they gestured back at the hallway gave Radyn a pretty good guess of what they were concerned about.

"I think they discovered the machine we took here," he said softly.

"Looks that way."

With any chance of surprise gone, only one realistic path remained. "I think we need to find another way out of here," he said.

They crawled away from the edge of the balcony and didn't stand until they were out of sight. They took the hallway behind them, choosing directions more or less at random.

"Are we trying to make it back to the machine?" Kaya asked.

"I'm hoping to find another exit. If they've discovered the machine, it's likely they'll have the area guarded. I'd like to avoid a fight if it's possible."

It didn't take them long to find another stairwell, and Radyn took the steps two at a time, climbing as far as the stairs would carry him. They climbed twelve levels before reaching the top, and Radyn was grateful when the door silently opened. It revealed a long hallway on the other side, made no longer of stone walls but the Makers' metal he was so familiar with. He looked up and down the hallway, first for enemies, then simply to understand.

If there'd been any doubt about the origin of the structure, the hallway would have banished it completely. Radyn and Kaya could have been in Firestone, or Underhill, or any of the other cities. The doors here were evenly spaced, and Radyn guessed that if he were to open a door at random, the design of the apartments would be the same as his own apartments in Underhill.

"Can you sense anyone near?"

Kaya shook her head. "What I can feel is faint and below us."

Whatever this place was to their enemies, it didn't seem to be filled with them, and Radyn thanked the song of the Engines for looking out for him. Coming here had been more foolish than he'd thought. They chose another direction at random, but all the stairwells went down. They seemed to be on the top level of whatever this was, but there wasn't easy access to the surface, which didn't make sense. Both Underhill and the floating cities had numerous paths to the surface, so why didn't this?

He was just about to suggest they turn around and find the traveling machines again when a door caught his eye. It had markings on it that Radyn didn't recognize, but it wasn't spaced the same distance as he would have expected if it was just another apartment. He tested the door, and it opened easily, revealing a small tunnel that rose straight up. A ladder was bolted to one side.

"What do you think?" he asked Kaya.

She shrugged. "Want me to explore so that you can stand guard down here?"

"Can you sense any danger up there?"

She shook her head.

He didn't like the idea of sending her alone, but it was the best of their bad options. He nodded, and she started climbing the ladder while he took position in the hallway. His hand went to his maniblade, and his fingers tapped against the hilt. Every few moments, he leaned over and looked up, though shadow had swallowed Kaya whole. He would sometimes catch a hint of motion, and he reassured himself that she was as competent a person as he could ask for in a partner.

After an uncomfortably long time he heard her call down, "This is it."

He leaned over again and looked up the tunnel in time to see her open a hatch. Bright light from above silhouetted her, and he watched as she climbed to the surface. Then she poked her head over the hole and waved at him. He stepped into the tunnel and closed the door behind him. He gripped the ladder and began the long climb to the surface.

Kaya was sitting cross-legged on the grass when he finally reached the surface and hauled himself to safety. He closed the hatch behind them and looked around.

He swore to himself.

They were near the rim of the crater Radyn and Tanwen had just discovered a few days ago, and if his sense of direction was correct, the center of the crater was located directly above the enormous cavern they'd observed from the balcony.

Pieces shifted in his mind, and he swore again. Kaya looked up, a question in her gaze.

"I know what this place is," he said, "and it should be impossible."

17

The Dagger led Nikki through the hallways of the academy, unnaturally quiet during these early morning hours. The rest of Firestone could never afford to completely sleep through the night. There was too much maintenance, too much work that needed to be done. Many slept overnight, but Nikki had always taken comfort, back in the evenings when she'd been responsible for overnight patrol, that she was never entirely alone. She could always count on coming across someone walking to or from their work.

The academy wasn't like the rest of Firestone, though. Here was the heart of the clan, the strongest warriors in the city and those ready to sacrifice their lives should the city ever come under attack. Here, almost everyone rested through the night so that come morning, they could resume their grueling training.

The light was on, though, in the Blade's study, seeping underneath the closed door like blood. Nikki started when she realized that it wasn't Magni standing guard, but another Sword she didn't recognize. Apparently even the giant needed sleep sometimes. The Sword recognized her and stood aside, and there was something in his bearing that made Nikki feel as though she was walking toward her execution.

It wasn't the first time she'd gotten Jyn angry at her, but it didn't mean she looked forward to their meeting.

She knocked on the door and Jyn told her to enter. She did, closing the door behind her and standing with her hands clasped behind her back.

Even though it was past the middle of the night and Jyn had no doubt endured a long day, he looked as immaculate as ever. He stared at her the way a teacher might stare at a misbehaving child. After a moment, he gestured to a sheet of paper on his desk. Nikki could have read it upside down, if she'd been so inclined, but she already had a pretty good idea of what it said.

"I received a report from my Swords not long ago, detailing the unusual events of their guard duty. They say you and Jelrik went on a long walk through the lower levels of Firestone until you happened to stumble upon the scene of a brutal murder. They say Jelrik was the one who knew where to look."

Nikki allowed herself one quick glance at Jyn. Put that way, it implied something very different, a possibility she'd already dismissed. Had Jyn come to believe that Jelrik knew more about the murders than he'd let on?

Her hesitation only lasted until the next sentence, when Jyn's tone made the subject of his displeasure perfectly clear. "Tell me how, exactly, Jelrik knew what door you would find the murder behind?"

Nikki's feet ached from walking most of the day, her mind was tired from constantly working on the problem of the murder, and there was an emptiness in the pit of her stomach from observing the ritual nature of the crimes. Simply put, she was in no mood for a rhetorical question. "They say he has an excellent sense of smell, sir."

She knew it was the wrong thing to say the moment she said it, but she was too tired to care about the consequences.

Jyn stood, and it seemed as though the air itself bent around him. Nikki was reminded of something Jelrik had implied when she'd last been in this office, when he'd spoken about Jyn playing with more shards than any human should have. Jyn's strength with shards was well-known, and had been known long before he'd become the Blade. Standing before him now, she wondered just how far past anyone else he'd progressed. Even the strongest Swords could rarely handle more than three or four.

Whatever the number, perhaps it wasn't wise to anger him.

He breathed deeply, the tension in his shoulders visibly relaxing as he calmed himself. "I'm not in the mood, Nikki. Not today."

"Then don't ask questions you already know the answer to, sir."

"You loaned him one of your shards."

"I did."

Jyn stared at her again, and she imagined that he was weighing the different punishments he might assign.

"Why?"

"As I suspect you already know, he came to me tonight and convinced me that his help was necessary. I've been investigating every lead, and whoever is doing this isn't leaving much of a trace, sir."

"Stop with the 'sirs.' Feels disrespectful, coming from you."

"Sorry. The truth is, I wasn't making much progress and

was running out of ideas. He came and offered to help, and he convinced me that he had the best interests of Firestone at heart. I believed the risk was worth it."

Jyn rubbed at his eyes. "That wasn't your decision to make. It was mine, and you were in the room when I made it."

Nikki made no further effort to defend herself. She hated it when people made excuses or tried to spin stories to protect themselves. She'd made the choice, knowing full well it might bring her back here. If she had the choice to do it again, she would. It was her responsibility, and she'd accept it.

"We're talking about the fate of all of Firestone here. If you'd been wrong, there's nothing you could have done."

Nikki considered speaking, then decided against it. She'd known all that, too, and had made her decision. She kept her lips sealed.

Jyn sat back down, and in that motion, Nikki caught just the slightest glimpse of the burdens he carried. Strong as he was, he was still only a man, and there was a limit to how much he could take. She wondered, and worried, if they were approaching that limit.

When he spoke again, his voice was soft. "I need to know who I can trust, Nikki. Firestone is beset by enemies on all sides, and the worst of them sit around pretending they're friends. There are precious few people that I know I can rely on, and you've been one of them for years. Are you still?"

She caught the hint of doubt in his voice with the question, and it stabbed more deeply than any knife. She swallowed hard and stepped around the desk, taking a knee before Jyn. There were few people in her life that she respected, and that respect was all the more precious for it. She bowed her head. "I am."

Jyn was silent for a moment, then grunted. "Get off your knees. It doesn't become you."

She obeyed.

"Will you be giving him the shard again?" he asked.

"Possibly. The new victims might yield more clues, which I hope to know by this morning, but if they lead to more dead ends, I might need him. He can feel traces of the dark song, which is how we found the bodies."

Jyn considered for a moment, then nodded. "My official order to him still stands, but I'll look the other way. I trust you, and I hope for the sake of Firestone you know what you're doing. Now get out of here and get some rest."

Nikki bowed and obeyed, hoping, as Jyn did, that she knew what she was doing.

~

NIKKI KNOCKED on Jelrik's door the next night, and the Singer answered promptly. Despite last night's excitement, he appeared well rested and more than a little surprised to see her.

"Care for a drink?" she asked.

His eyes narrowed. "I don't drink. It interferes with my ability to listen to the song."

She gave him a look that told him that of course she already knew that, and his eyes slowly widened in understanding.

"May I come in?" she asked, trying again.

"Of course." He stepped aside, let her in, and shut the door behind her.

"I figured you'd have your hide tanned by Jyn by now," he said.

Nikki held out her first shard toward him. "He tried, but we have more important matters to discuss."

Jelrik looked at the shard as though it were a trap. He didn't reach for it. "Such as?"

"Such as the fact that we found links between the bodies we discovered, and I think you and I should investigate a few of them. There might be other places where you can catch a whisper of that dark song, and if so, we can narrow down our search even further."

Jelrik looked between her face and her hand, as if he was weighing the truth of her statements. Then he sighed and took the shard from her. He strapped it around his wrist, then covered it with the sleeve of his tunic.

Nikki grinned and led him back into the hallway. As they started walking, the two Swords standing guard followed them. Nikki felt better having them near. She was getting closer to the monster that had killed so many, and a part of her feared what they would eventually find.

"What did you find?" Jelrik asked.

"Last night I had a group of Junior Shields start collecting information on the victims we found. Names, locations, favorite taverns, occupations, families, friends, everything they could. It's not terribly surprising, but the victims knew each other. Not only that, but they'd been spending a lot of time with each other as of late. We're heading to the tavern where they liked to meet."

Jelrik frowned. "But they won't be there, obviously."

"No, but there might be others, or the owner might be able to identify other people of interest. It's also why I'm bringing you along. Maybe you'll hear that dark song and have an insight. We won't know until we get there."

Jelrik nodded.

"We also discovered another link, and this one connects

to Zak, too. All the victims had at one time applied to become a Manirah. All failed their trials, but all had believed they could connect to shards easily."

"Someone is either hunting or recruiting people who have a connection to the song," Jelrik concluded.

Nikki agreed. "But as far as we know, they aren't going after Manirah, nor Shields. I suppose it's smart. It ensures they keep a low profile. Can't help but wonder if there's something else, some other quality we haven't noticed yet."

"I guess we'll find out."

They made the rest of the trip in silence. The tavern they needed to visit wasn't the seediest in Firestone, but it would definitely make the top three, if the city's Shields had to vote on a list. Nikki was well familiar with it. It was in one of the market squares on level thirteen, and Nikki knew the quickest route. She paused outside a two-story building that looked more like a metal cube than a respectable business establishment. Drake, the owner, had been the only one who'd seen potential in the nearly windowless place, and arranged the licenses for the tavern almost on sight.

Nikki paused before they entered. "Sense anything?"

Jelrik stopped beside her and stood silently for a moment. Then he nodded. "Just a whisper, but something happened there."

She turned to the Swords, who kept a respectful distance. "We're going in there, but I'd like one of you to lead the way. There might be trouble."

The Swords guarding Jelrik weren't rookies straight from the academy. They were some of the toughest Swords the clan had, with plenty of experience. They also weren't above questioning orders. "Are you sure that's wise?"

Nikki let Jelrik answer, as he was the one who could

most clearly sense what was ahead. "I think we'll be fine. Just be careful, please, there's no telling what we'll find."

The Swords didn't look pleased, but they chose to obey, and the commander of the guard stepped in first. He took a look around, then said, "Nothing seems out of the ordinary."

What Nikki heard was his unspoken question, wondering why Firestone's Master Singer would want to visit such a place. He'd have to keep wondering, at least for a while.

Nikki and Jelrik stepped in together, and Nikki took a look around. It had been months since she'd been here, but most of the tables were filled with the same familiar faces as the last time, as though she'd just stepped out for a moment. A few raised their mugs in her direction, a silent acknowledgment of times past.

The lower level was dark, the lights turned down so low she had to squint to see into the farthest recesses of the tavern. Drake was behind the bar, as he always was, but he hadn't yet looked up and noticed her. Her eyes settled, on their own accord, on a pair of faces she didn't recognize. One man was a giant, nearly as tall as Magni, and he was scrutinizing her and Jelrik as though they had a code written across their foreheads. The other man was slim, though nearly as tall in his seat as the giant.

Everything happened at once, faster than Nikki would have believed possible. Jelrik tapped her on the shoulder, and she felt his face close to her ear. He was looking at the table too, and he said, "The dark song is—"

He never had a chance to finish. The giant man rose from the table he'd been sitting at, and though there was nothing aggressive about the move, every hair on the back of Nikki's neck suddenly stood on end. The thin man joined the giant, and they stepped together toward the exit where Nikki and Jelrik were standing.

She had to give credit to the Swords. Even though she didn't have time to warn them, the commander had his maniblade in hand and lit before the two men took their second step. Nikki reached for her steel dagger, but by the time her hand made contact with the weapon, it was already over.

She didn't see the giant move. One moment he was standing a dozen paces away; the next he was among them, and Jelrik was folded over his fist like a piece of cloth. Nikki heard the Master Singer's breath as it rushed out of his lungs, eager for a more welcoming home.

The Sword behind Jelrik raised his lit maniblade and cut down, but the giant wasn't there anymore. He was behind the Sword and there was a second smile cut across the Sword's throat and he was falling, his eyes blank.

Movement in the corner of Nikki's vision tore her gaze back inside the tavern, where the thin man held something long and dark in his hand, a darkness that seemed to absorb the surrounding light. He swung at the commander, fast but nothing like the giant, and a maniblade blazed through the darkness, leaving a bright streak in Nikki's vision.

The line of darkness vanished, and something hit the ground. Nikki looked down and saw that it was a hand, which she was sure hadn't been there before.

The Sword commander cut again, but it wasn't a cut. The hilt of his maniblade struck the thin man in the forehead and he crumpled like a worn piece of paper.

Nikki turned back to the door, but the giant was gone and Jelrik was on the floor, surrounded by blood. The guard behind Jelrik was dead, his eyes gazing at the gate that would someday welcome them all.

Nikki frowned. The giant had only punched Jelrik, hadn't he?

She squatted, ignoring the chaos spreading like fire around her. Jelrik was gasping for breath, but when she pulled gently on his arms, she saw the stain spreading from the hole in his side.

She was no healer, but she knew enough. She ripped off the top of her uniform and stuffed it in the hole and called for help. With her free hand she gripped one of his, staying with the Master Singer as he bled out all across the floor of a seedy tavern.

18

For three days, Radyn had wondered how their enemies would respond. He'd taken to thinking of them as an enemy clan, based not in a city but in a Makers' ruin. They possessed Singers, of a sort, those who had launched the first attack on Underhill, though now he wondered, with the eyes of a man whose view of the world has been violently shifted, if the attack he and Aria had survived was the first. Perhaps the first had been the banti, connected to this enemy clan by a thread he couldn't quite see.

All he knew was that the banti had been the first sign something was wrong around Underhill, and he didn't hold much stock in coincidence.

Now the enemy clan knew their home, or their camp, at least, had been discovered. Knew, most likely, that one of theirs was dead. Would they attack in response, and if so, how?

The weight of uncertainty weighed heavy upon him, made worse by his lack of ability to act decisively. Miranda had listened to him and Kaya upon their return, but there was little they could do. They didn't have the Manirah to launch an assault upon the ruin, and they couldn't pause their planting or alter the routines of the settlement in any meaningful way. They spread a warning through the community and made sure the farmers were well protected every time they left the safety of Underhill, but that was all.

On the fourth day, Radyn discerned the shape of the enemy's plan, more terrible than he'd imagined. It started with a knock on his and Aria's door, too early for it to be anything but trouble. He rolled out of bed, bleary-eyed, and opened the door. Kaya waited on the other side.

"There are creatures wandering out around the new perimeter," she said quietly.

He gestured for her to come in as he started preparing to go out. Aria rose from bed and leaned against the doorway to the living room, listening in. "What do you know?" he asked.

"Not much, except it doesn't feel natural. I can't tell what they are, but they're circling around the perimeter, coming in and out of range. But when they get close to any of the poles, I swear I can hear some of the shadow song."

"Do others know?"

Kaya nodded. "I've already spread the word. Everyone is staying in behind locked doors."

"Good." Radyn finished his preparations by clipping his maniblade to his belt. "If the worst should come to pass, I want you to take Aria and get out of here on Tanwen."

"We're not going to leave without you," Aria said.

"Only if the worst comes to pass. You and our child need to live, no matter what happens here."

She looked like she wanted to argue, but they both knew there was no time for it. They shared a quick embrace; then he strode out into the hallway with Kaya. When they came to the intersection that would lead her to Underhill's Engine, she said, "I'll protect you as well as I can, but be careful."

"You, too. There's no telling what their Singers are capable of."

They separated and Radyn hurried to the main gate, where two of the bigger warriors stood guard. One was a former Shield, and the other a Junior Dagger, so at least they had one maniblade between them. It wouldn't be enough if Underhill came under a concerted assault, but it was something. They opened the gate for him, and he hurried through, squinting his eyes in the predawn darkness.

He called for Tanwen. There was little point risking himself if there were groups of beasts wandering around when he had a hungry dragon who was always eager for another meal. Tanwen answered, though it would be a bit before he arrived.

Radyn fought the temptation to wander around. Again, there was no point in exposing himself to risk when he had a dragon to protect him. He couldn't make out any of the invading creatures from where he stood, but he could sense the danger. The prairie was too quiet, and the morning air felt thick, even though it wasn't humid. The rising sun was starting to illuminate the sky, and soon he'd see them.

Tanwen arrived before the light.

"It's good to see you, old friend. We have some unwanted visitors."

He connected with the dragon and climbed on, and Tanwen launched them into the air, though they kept low to the ground.

Tanwen's gaze was sharper than Radyn's, and he found a pack of the invaders before long. His neck stretched out and snapped up—something—and crunched it in his massive jaws. Satisfaction flowed through their connection, and Radyn wished he could have known what Tanwen had just used as a snack.

By the time the sun rose high enough for Radyn to see, Tanwen had cleared most of the area. He'd snapped up at least two banti that Radyn had noticed, which likely meant several of the others had been banti as well. Radyn had also heard the pained howl of at least one wolf as it died in Tanwen's powerful claws.

They made another circle around the perimeter, but neither he nor Tanwen sensed any danger, and so they landed near the main gate. He'd barely hopped off when his stomach felt as though it was being torn up from the inside, as though a pack of rats had gotten lodged within and were trying to scrape their way free. He wrapped his hands tight around his gut to hold his organs in. Thankfully, the feeling only lasted a moment, soon replaced by the comforting and familiar sounds of the song of the Engines. Radyn stood up straight and glanced toward the hills. The enemy clan couldn't be that foolish, could they?

He caught a hint of movement, and he had his answer. Only two this time, unless his sight betrayed him. Maybe even the same two who had tried to hurt Aria several days ago. He was on Tanwen's back and flying toward the hill before he even registered a conscious thought. This time, they weren't going to escape. It was the only thought in his mind as he raced toward them.

Another round of pain wracked his core, but Kaya's control over the Engine and its song was greater than whatever force the other clan relied on, and it passed quickly. He said a silent thanks to Kaya and urged Tanwen to hurry. The dragon seemed eager, too, and thrust itself faster through the air.

The two saw him coming but didn't run. A small voice in the back of his mind warned him of traps, but they had hurt Aria and almost hurt his unborn child. Tanwen swept over them, attempting to catch the warriors in either jaw or claw, but they were quick and evaded tooth and talon. Tanwen spread his wings and bled off his speed, landing with a powerful flex of his legs.

Radyn was off Tanwen's back before the dragon had found his balance on the slope of the hill. He asked Tanwen to help in the fight, then broke the connection to focus on the two enemies before him. They wore the same strange clothing as the man he'd fought in the tunnel, and when they spoke to one another, it was in the language he didn't understand.

Unlike the man he'd killed in the tunnel, these two didn't carry steel weapons. They opened their hands, and two thin blades of darkness appeared. They grasped the blades and advanced, spreading to his left and right as they approached, two hunters nearing their kill. He stared at the blades and wondered at their nature. The shadow song version of the maniblade? If so, their control was considerable. Few Senior Swords could shape and maintain a blade of such a length without the help of the maniblade's hilt.

Radyn leaped toward the opponent highest up the hill. He liked the slight advantage higher ground conferred, and he intended to take it. His enemies reacted with inhuman speed. The one higher up the hill took a guard position while the one below hurried to join the fight.

Radyn and his target passed, then passed again, maniblade meeting darkness and making no progress against it. The second enemy closed quickly and left Radyn few options. He connected to all the shards within his body and attacked again. This time, he had the advantage of speed, slight as it was. He broke through the warrior's guard, cutting through his upper arm. The dark blade in his hands vanished and Radyn cut again, his blade passing halfway through the young man's neck before he had to turn his attention to the second warrior.

His next opponent had every bit as much speed and strength as the first, but he'd just watched his friend die. He swung with too much power. Radyn avoided the cut and slipped within his guard, snapping his wrists and slicing deep through neck and shoulder. The second enemy kept his blade alive and even as he fell and died, he cut at Radyn again, but Radyn stepped back and avoided the dying effort.

He let his maniblade sleep and returned it to his belt. He was about to bend down to investigate the two attackers for clues when he caught the sight of distant motion. Kaya's song suddenly echoed loudly in his spirit, and he turned toward Underhill. He focused just in time to see several dark shapes pour through the main gate. He cursed and called for Tanwen.

It was certainly possible these two might have killed him, had they been a little stronger. But they'd always been the decoy, and he'd fallen for it without a second thought. He was a fool and more, but his recriminations could wait. Tanwen landed, and Radyn connected to him as he climbed on. The dragon leaped off the side of the hill and spread its wings, gaining speed as it allowed itself to fall. Within moments they were whipping over the long prairie grasses, but each moment was one in which the invaders could walk freely through his home. A few of Underhill's Manirah might slow them, but if the skill he'd already seen was any indication, their resistance wouldn't last for long.

Was this what had happened at Makers' Mound? He'd met several of the Manirah there, and they'd been skilled and respected before they made the journey to the surface.

Maybe he'd get answers if this assault sent him to the other side of the gate. Not his most pleasant thought, but depending on how many invaders had broken through the front doors, he might not have much of a choice about it.

Tanwen landed him at the front gates, which had been carved open with what appeared to be maniblades. He suspected the work of the dark blades and stepped into the settlement carefully. The two men who'd been guarding the front gate were dead, sliced open with casual indifference. Neither looked like they'd put up a meaningful fight. Of the attackers, there was no trace. They'd gone deeper into the settlement.

Radyn ran down the familiar hallways, wishing he had Kaya close to tell him where to go. Enemies could hide in the labyrinthine passages for days or even weeks, and he'd never find them on his own. He kept moving in the general direction of the Engine room, certain that was their ultimate destination.

He paused when his path intersected that of a crowded residential hallway. Bodies lay still on the floor, eyes wide. Several had been killed by cuts to their back as they ran away. He glanced down the hallway, then back down the passage that led to the Engine room. In case of trouble, that was where Aria would have gone.

A cry of pain down the hallway sealed his decision. He ran through the neighborhood, avoiding both the corpses and the pools of blood that spread around them.

He found the invaders in a family's home. Aaron, the

husband and father, stood with his arms outstretched before a pair of the same invaders Radyn had already killed once today. The one closest to Radyn casually turned, as though expecting nothing but a nuisance, while the one furthest away cut through Aaron as though he were a piece of paper. His wife and daughter screamed and backed deeper into a corner of their living room.

Radyn didn't even reach for his maniblade. He swung a punch, and when the warrior blocked it, he formed a blade with the song of the Engine. It extended from his blocked hand into the warrior's skull, and he crumpled without a sound.

His partner's death finally made the other man realize the trouble he was in, and he turned in time to greet the tip of Radyn's maniblade with his face. Like his partner, he collapsed, and Radyn shoved his maniblade through the skull, simply to ensure his death. He looked at Aaron's wife and daughter, whose names slipped through his memories at the moment. Aaron had been a carpenter, and a skilled one, who had wanted to come to the surface because he wanted something better for his family than the clans could offer.

Radyn wished he could stay and offer comfort, but there was no time. Aaron's wife met his gaze, and through her shock, seemed to understand. She gave him the barest hint of a nod, and that was more than the permission he needed. He turned his back on the carnage and stepped back into the hallway. He paused and listened for a moment, but he couldn't hear any other sounds of violence nearby. Perhaps it had only been the two working their way through the residential area.

Regardless, his objective was clear. He ran back down the hallway and turned to follow the passage that would lead him to the Engine room. A pair of bodies, friends of Aria's, told him he was on the right track.

Kaya's scream through the song nearly brought him to his knees. In that moment, he sensed some fraction of the power she was fighting and hurried faster. Kaya's unique skill with the song kept her alive, but if that power he sensed was any indication of her opponent, even she might not last long. He gave no thought to stealth, his feet pounding against the metal of the floor as he raced toward the battle.

He found it just outside the Engine room. Several familiar faces had already fallen, but not from the cuts he'd come to expect from the dark blades. Their stomachs were distended, their organs strewn across the floor. One poor soul was still alive, though the light faded quickly from his eyes. Three men, two of whom wore the strange clothing that had so recently become common in Radyn's life, attacked the Engine room door, which was, for the moment, resisting their efforts. They attacked it with the dark blades, but the blades didn't penetrate, much to the surprise and dismay of the warriors.

Radyn paused and studied the third man, who was short and pale and had long blond hair that stretched well below his shoulders. He wore the clothing one would expect to find in a city, though it was well past the date it should have been recycled. Dirt was caked into the fabric, and it was ripped open in half a dozen places that Radyn could see.

The third man either saw him or sensed him, for he barked a command and pointed back toward Radyn. One of the two warriors with the blade gave up his assault on the door and turned to face the new arrival. He looked like a man who was well familiar with all the different ways he could use the sword in his hand.

Once his footing was clear, he launched himself at

Radyn. Radyn blocked the first cut and then the second, surrendering ground while he studied this new opponent. The man cut again, and Radyn's maniblade was there, but the opponent's wasn't. It disappeared and Radyn found himself out of position. The man came in with fists, driving one straight into his chin that had Radyn seeing stars. He hadn't been hit that hard since the days he was training with Magni. Radyn staggered back, then saw the shape of his opponent's hand change.

He squinted and focused, realizing that the man's hand hadn't changed, but that he had formed a spiked band of darkness that rested across his fist. Radyn had never seen a technique like it. He retreated quickly, not stopping until the world stopped spinning around him. Once he was steady, he stopped and took a defensive stance.

The other man seemed content to wait, and Radyn swore under his breath. He wasn't sure exactly what Kaya was doing to the door to protect it, but she wouldn't last much longer. If there was going to be a way through, he was the one who had to find it.

Radyn approached slowly, leading with the tip of his maniblade. He sensed the strike a moment before he saw it, the hairs on the back of his arm standing on end as the warrior embraced the shadow song. Radyn leaped forward, closing the rest of the distance as the man prepared to strike. A dark sword appeared in his hand, but Radyn was a moment quicker, and the man fell to his maniblade.

That was the moment the door to the Engine room finally fell to the assault. The last warrior stepped inside, but Radyn wasn't far behind. The short man in city clothes died as Radyn sprinted past, and he sensed he was the shadow singer who'd been battling with Kaya.

The last warrior turned as his final accomplice fell, but

there was no force in the world that would have saved his life from Radyn's maniblade. He was too slow and too weak, and Radyn cut him down before he could take another step into the Engine room.

As the man fell, Radyn looked first to Kaya, for she would know if it was over. She nodded, and it felt as though a group of friends had come and pulled an enormous stone off his chest. He breathed freely and let go of the shards, afraid he might well get lost in the song this close to the Engine.

His second look was for Aria, and she was there, on the other side of the Engine room, a dagger in her hand and a determined look on her face. Radyn bowed to her, then half-sat, half-collapsed onto the floor. His heart pounded in his chest, harder than if he'd just fought off an entire clan.

Aria was safe.

He didn't know about Underhill. The Engine still sang, and Kaya still lived, which meant they were in no immediate danger, but the number of bodies behind him was high. Maybe too high for the small settlement to recover from.

But that was a question for the future. For now, all he wanted to do was rest, confident in the knowledge that Aria was safe and he hadn't failed her too.

19

The Seer stood on the edge of the city and looked out across the landscape, searching the horizon for an answer he couldn't find in his thoughts. His song, his primal, beautiful song, wailed like a wounded animal whenever he listened to it. Its servants were dying, their shadows burned to ash by the light of the cursed Engines and their cultists.

He knew that much. He just didn't know why, or what had happened, and so far no word had reached him. Perhaps today. Dragons from several nearby cities were expected with messages, and perhaps one would trickle to him through their web of allies.

Somehow, his allies had been wounded, struck down by warriors who didn't realize their days were numbered, their fate sealed. Such strength shouldn't exist in the world, but he knew well enough who had been responsible. Radyn and Kaya, an unfortunate pairing if there ever was one.

What might he have accomplished if she'd joined him, as had once been planned? How quickly might his dreams have become reality? She was a generational talent, shaped for this moment by forces she still didn't comprehend. If not for Radyn, she'd be his.

He shook his head and cleared his thoughts. What was past was past, and not even the power of his song could change that. There was only now and the future, and the longer he delayed, the longer it would be until his dreams unfolded. So what did he do now? That was the question which troubled him, the question which demanded an immediate answer.

Alone, he was almost nothing. His strength with the song was considerable, but not much more advanced than those of his allies on the surface. He was an organizer, the one who weaved the web and then made sure every strand did as it should. Unlike Radyn, who survived through some combination of luck and sheer strength, he survived because his mind was superior.

Today he feared he would have to begin rebuilding the web again. Which he would do a hundred times, if necessary, but the delay was unacceptable. He was not getting any younger, and even his power had limits.

Still, all was not lost. His friend was still on Firestone, and his friend was a man of action. He would find a way.

He was thinking of his friend when the footsteps approached from behind, hesitant and uneven. Bad news, then, but he'd already known that. Here was a chance to remind them that he was their Seer. It was more important than ever, when plans didn't go as expected. He held out his empty hand. "How bad is it?"

"You already know?" the surprised girl asked.

"Of course I already know. But I need the details."

She pressed the paper into his hand, then backed away, waiting for his orders.

He looked at the notes, for several had come through

Nightkeep at once. The first notes were from the surface. Underhill's Engine had survived, but they didn't know how successful the attack had been. If they'd succeeded in at least killing their Singer, Underhill wouldn't last long. Even if they hadn't, an entire team had made it into the settlement, and though they hadn't come out, it was assumed they had caused havoc while they were within.

The Seer could add to that. Kaya still survived, for Underhill's Engine and its cursed song were as loud as ever.

The latter message was from Firestone, though not from his friend. The city still flew and his friend had gone into hiding, though from what, exactly, the message didn't say. There'd been trouble, though, involving the Shields and one of Firestone's Singers.

He crumpled the paper and let his mind wander over these new problems. There was still a way, he just had to find it. He had to see it.

He followed different plans to their logical conclusions, then weighed where each would take him. As much as it pained him, Underhill could wait. Firestone needed to fall for anything else to happen. Once it was nothing more than a burning hunk of metal and stone, then he could turn his attention to scouring the surface of the world of humanity's blight.

He gestured to the young woman, and he was made uncomfortable by the eager look in her eyes. Like all the rest, she couldn't even see him, though he stood right before her. She saw something greater than him and wouldn't unsee it. Such was the power of her belief.

"What can I do, sir?" she asked, in the tone of voice that made it clear she would be willing to do absolutely anything he wanted.

"Get in touch with the team that's been training here.

Send them to Firestone and have them rendezvous with whoever is left there."

"That's all, sir?"

"For now, thank you."

She bowed deeply to him, holding the position for far longer than he was comfortable with, then turned and walked away. He noticed the sway of her hips and couldn't help but think it was intentional.

He snorted. How little they understood. He proclaimed salvation, but it was as though they only heard the words they wanted to hear.

No matter. He trusted in his friend, and more than that, he trusted in his song. Even wounded, it was more than strong enough to defeat the weakening Engines.

The Seer looked one last time at the horizon, but it didn't relax him the way it used to. When the beauty of the world failed to stir his spirit, it meant it was time to take a break, to find his center once again so he could continue to push forward.

Soon.

As soon as Firestone was nothing more than a scar along the landscape, he would rest, then finish the work of his life.

20

Nikki winced in sympathy as Magni's giant fist drove the air from Brendan's overworked lungs. The man bent over as far as his bonds would allow, the rope creaking against the chair as he coughed out blood and tears ran down the side of his face.

She stood in the corner of the room, pretending that her awareness was somewhere outside her body, that she didn't feel anything.

She had to stay dispassionate. If she told herself that often enough, she might even come to believe it.

Magni didn't ask any questions. He just paced around the room like he was the one that was caged in here, then stepped over to the chair and punched straight down on Brendan's thigh.

She swore she felt the impact of flesh on flesh in her bones and in her lungs. Brendan screamed, the sound ripping apart the back of his throat. Magni only retreated a step, then began pacing again, working himself up for the next blow.

Nikki knew enough anatomy to know that the femur was

the thickest bone in the body, and thus one that wasn't likely to break like a twig, but Magni was more powerful than a force of nature. His fists landed like mallets, blurring with a speed she could barely comprehend.

In the past, when she'd met him, he'd always come across as silent and reserved. He walked so quietly it was as though he was afraid he'd break something simply by walking beside it. She'd known, in the back of her mind, there was more to him than his demeanor suggested. One didn't become Jyn's personal guard, or even a Senior Sword, for that matter, without the ability to fight and kill. Peaceful as the clans seemed most days, their true purpose always lurked just beneath their skin.

Still, knowing Magni's abilities and seeing them firsthand were two very different experiences. Brendan had been part of a conspiracy to bring down the city, and Magni's beloved wife was dead, but somehow, Brendan was the one she felt sorry for.

Except no. She felt sorry for both men. Magni hovered on the edge of control, and if Brendan's knowledge had been any less vital, he would have been beaten to a pulp an hour ago.

Magni finished his loop and drove his fist down into Brendan's other thigh, and once again he screamed. He screamed until he whimpered, and Magni gave Nikki a small, tight nod. She swallowed the bile collecting in her throat and took a step toward Brendan. The young man looked up as though she had the power to deliver him from Magni.

No one had that power, but he didn't know that. Jyn had already gifted the criminal to Magni, and that was that. His name would be wiped from the city registry, and it would be as though he never existed.

The power of the clans, in all its brutal glory.

She kept the thoughts out of her mind, kept herself focused on him. She needed to know the truth, and this was their first chance at it. "Will you tell me what happened now?"

He'd resisted before, bravely, even when Magni had first stepped into the room.

Even now, he shook his head, and Magni stepped forward. Nikki held up a hand, and thankfully, Magni obeyed.

"He won't stop. Not until you've told me what I want to know."

Brendan tried breathing deep through his nose, tried to center himself and regain his courage. Nikki's stomach twisted, but she didn't have the time to wear him down slowly. Brendan was a follower at heart, someone who wanted to be told what to do. But he viewed himself as a man of honor, and he'd hold onto that honor long enough to frustrate them, if given a chance.

Nikki shrugged before his breathing could return to normal. "I'm sorry, then."

She stood up. His eyes went wide as Magni approached, silent as a ghost.

Brendan shook his head. "Stop! I'll tell you."

"Start at the beginning," Nikki commanded.

He did, and when Nikki had heard everything twice, she stood and glanced at Magni, who held himself stiffly against a corner of the room, his massive arms crossed.

In a wiser world, they would keep him alive in case they needed any further information. Nikki thought Brendan had shared everything he knew, but she didn't know what she didn't know. Her thoughts of pleading for consideration vanished when she looked into Magni's face, its passivity more terrifying than any snarl. She gave the smallest nod of her head, then went to the door.

"Wait—" Brendan said, realizing something was wrong.

She thought Magni would wait until she was out of the room, but he moved faster than she thought possible, and there was a flare of a maniblade, and then Brendan's head fell from his shoulders, looking about as surprised as Nikki felt. She hadn't expected such a quick end.

Magni met her gaze. "We have a report to give to the Blade."

He led the way out of the room, and Nikki followed.

Nikki and Magni found Jyn not in his study, but in his private living quarters. It was the first time Nikki had visited, and she had to admit that she had started to believe that Jyn simply lived in his study. She was curious about what she would find on the other side of the door, but when Jyn opened it and let her in, she was quickly disappointed. The apartment was spacious, as befitted the leader of the clans, but it looked so barren, she could have been easily convinced Jyn had just moved in that morning. What personality he possessed had all gone into his study.

They remained standing, as there were no places to sit. Jyn asked, "What did you learn?"

Magni looked at Nikki, but Nikki answered the Blade's question with one of her own. "What about Jelrik? Will he live?"

Jyn nodded slowly. "He will, though it will be some time before he's regained even a fraction of his former strength. The healers told me he came as close to passing through the gate as one can without actually crossing. If you hadn't thought to put pressure on the wound, he might no longer be with us."

The rest of his accusation went unstated, but it lingered in the air all the same. Jelrik never would have been there if not for him leading her into danger. If Jelrik had followed Jyn's instructions, he'd be at home, healthier than he had been in weeks. But if he hadn't come, she wouldn't have learned all that she had. Firestone couldn't risk its Master Singer. But given that he was alive and would recover, she had to consider the sacrifice as being worthy.

Jyn crossed his arms. "Now, what have you learned?"

Magni folded his arms and leaned against a wall, allowing Nikki to take the lead. She was happy to.

"The group that we are up against calls themselves the Disciples of the Seer. The young man that we captured was vague on a lot of the details. Not because he was new, but because they strictly control the flow of information. Whoever the Seer is that is in charge, he's a careful man."

"What do they want?" Jyn asked.

"From the sound of it, they want to bring humanity toward a second reckoning. They believe that we have lost our way, and that the Engines' failures reflect the spiritual failure of humankind. They want to bring down the cities and build a new society with the survivors."

Jyn shook his head, as though he heard her words but couldn't bring his mind to understand them. "That's madness. If they bring down the cities, there won't be any survivors. At least, not for long."

Nikki shrugged. She didn't disagree, but she wasn't a member of the cult. "I cannot speak to their plans. But I can tell you that the young man we captured believed in these plans with his entire heart. He was willing to die for those plans. And if not for Magni's persuasion, he never would have spoken. We're dealing with a group of people who believe. Not only that, but they might have access to a power that allows them to accomplish their aims."

Jyn nodded. "I heard from the surviving guard of the powers he thought he witnessed. And Jelrik's wound makes no sense based on what was witnessed, so my mind is open. What did you learn?"

"This Seer calls it the shadow song, and claims it is a force even greater than the song of the Engines. Those who can hear the song are capable of impressive feats similar to those of a Manirah. They can temporarily increase their strength and speed, and like Manirah, can manipulate this shadow song into physical shapes. From what I understand, though, these are new techniques that are only now starting to spread through the group. They are improving. But there are few who can use it on command."

"The giant in the tavern seemed to have an impressive degree of control over it," Jyn observed.

"He did. Brendan said that he had only recently met with the large man who never gave his name. He arrived here from another city, and claims the right hand of the Seer. From what we were able to witness, there is no doubt he is a dangerous opponent. I would rate his skill as being equal to that of a Senior Sword, if not higher."

She studied Jyn for a reaction to this news, but it didn't seem to come as a surprise to him. If anything, he seemed disappointed to have his fears confirmed.

"The guard said something similar. But I had hoped your evaluation might be different," he said as a way of explanation. "What else?"

She glanced at Magni, but his blank look was all the invitation she needed to continue her tale. "We think we know what happened to Rebecca," she said.

She looked at Magni once again, but he continued to stand as still as a statue, letting her tell the story of his wife's death. She swallowed hard and continued. "From what we were able to gather, it was part of the first attempt to bring down Firestone."

She had already had Jyn's full attention, but now he hung onto her every word. "There was an attempt to bring down Firestone?"

"There was, yes. The bodies that Jelrik and I found when we were searching together were the result of that attempt. Brendan, being newer to the group and incapable of manipulating the shadow song, was a witness who'd helped prepare the scene and watched what happened. It was a ritual of blood and will. The disciples that had gathered tried to use their mastery of the shadow song to bring Firestone down. Although we do not know for sure, we suspect the attack was aimed at the Engine. Brendan reported that the attack had been going well, but then they encountered an obstacle. Not being connected to the others, he didn't know the nature of the trouble, but he claimed there was a colossal contest of wills. From what little he could gather, there was a Singer fighting them, although they believed it should have been impossible. We believe that Rebecca somehow sensed the attack and did her best to defend the Engine. In the course of so doing, she may have connected directly to the Engine and sacrificed her own life to defend the city."

"So there was no one else in the room with her?"

Nikki shook her head. "I don't think so. I think it was her and her alone."

The room was silent for a long time, and then Jyn walked slowly over to where Magni stood. Nikki looked, and she couldn't be sure whether Magni stood on his own or if he only stood thanks to the support of the wall. Jyn took a knee before his friend and bowed his head. No words passed between the two men, and yet Nikki was certain that in those moments of silence, those two said all that needed to be said. Jyn held the pose for another long moment and then asked, "What can I do?"

Magni's answer came less than a heartbeat later. "When the time comes, let me be the one to kill him."

Jyn stood and nodded. "Of course."

The Blade turned his attention back to Nikki, as though remembering for the first time that she was still there. "Can you find him?"

She wished she had a better answer. "With enough time and people, maybe. You know as well as I do how hard it is to find somebody in this city who wants to remain hidden, and Brendan made it clear the giant still had friends in Firestone. Without Jelrik, I'm not sure if we can find him before he strikes again."

A new silence descended over the group, one heavy with despair.

Nikki wasn't sure what made her say it: a casual slip of the tongue she would have guarded more closely at any other time. But it was a true thought, and it slipped easily from her lips. "If Radyn were here, I might be able to find him."

When Jyn looked at her as though she had uttered some form of mysterious incantation, his face possessed none of the anger that she had expected to see. "What makes you think that?"

A hint of color rushed to her cheeks as she consciously realized what she had said. But the words were out. There was no taking them back. "If there was anyone left alive who might help me, it would be him. He's sensitive enough to the song that he might be able to track these disciples. And if he's still alive, he might be fast enough to fight them."

Jyn looked at Magni, and once again, a look passed between them that said more than she could guess at. Magni remained as still as a stone, but Jyn seemed to find whatever he was looking for in his friend's countenance. He turned to Nikki with the barest hint of a smile on his face. "Well, if you think he's the only one who can save us, why don't you go get him?"

21

The next few days passed by Radyn in a flurry of activity. Bodies had to be collected throughout the settlement and buried in a long ditch south of the fields. The main gate needed to be patched and repaired, to the degree that they knew how. There was work to be done in the fields, and doors to be guarded. Radyn wasn't sure if his enemies would attack again, but he planned on being ready for them if they were.

He was far from the only one pushing himself to his limits. Every soulkeeper that had survived threw themselves into the suddenly overwhelming list of tasks that mere survival demanded. It was as if they had collectively decided to ignore the grief that hung in the air and push forward, doing all that they could to outrun the sense of loss that haunted their steps. Some escaped the grief for a time, but none for long. Radyn saw the evidence time and time again. A farmer would slow his hoe and bring it to a stop, and he would stand there as though he were a carved tree, staring off into a future Radyn couldn't imagine, or perhaps, as was more likely, staring off into the past before the times when so much had been taken from them.

Radyn had been among the fortunate few. He had not lost his family nor any of his closest friends, but the cumulative losses of the attack weighed like a heavy stone around his neck. He had been the fool. He had been the one so eager to seek revenge for Aria that he had abandoned Underhill. No matter how many times Miranda, Kaya, and Aria told him that it wasn't his fault, he couldn't bring himself to believe it. He might not have been the one who wielded the blades that cut his neighbors down, but he was the one who had left them to die.

Two days after the attack, Miranda held a ceremony for those that had fallen, when all those who had survived and were able to move emerged from Underhill into the light of day and paid their respects to the mass grave. Miranda spoke about the need to carry on, the need to keep fighting in their memory. But the words rang empty and hollow.

The next day, Miranda sent a runner and summoned Radyn into her study. He finished planting the section of field he was working, then wandered into Underhill. The hallways were unnaturally quiet for this time of day. This neighborhood in particular should have been bustling with people wandering through the hallways on any number of tasks. Now it was as if the hallways had become a second shrine to the fallen, a hallowed space too sacred for the day-to-day necessities of life.

When he found Miranda in her study, he thought that she looked the way his spirit felt. Her eyes were sunken into her cheekbones and her flesh seemed to hang from her cheeks, the animating spirit that had pulled them all forward flickering and sputtering like a candle at the end of its wick. She had a pile of papers scattered before her filled with numbers, figures, and notes to herself.

"I don't know how we're going to survive," she said simply.

Her confession was another weight added to his already considerable burdens, but it was one he was already prepared to carry. Aria had wondered much the same, her math no doubt less precise and considered than Miranda's, but the conclusion inevitable. There were far fewer mouths to feed, true, but also far fewer to do the work. It wasn't just the farming that needed to be done, but the maintenance around the ruins, the repair of the things the Makers had created so many generations ago, as well as dozens of other tasks Radyn could only begin to guess at.

"How bad is it?" he asked.

She looked down at her figures and considered. "I don't see how we survive another winter."

Radyn leaned back against the wall. "What do we need to do?"

She shook her head. "I don't know. Without an influx of both people and supplies, there's just too much to do. We were already balancing on the edge before the attack, and it pushed us right over."

Radyn closed his eyes. This wasn't an enemy he could fight with his sword, not something he could attack and kill. There was no hidden secret that he could find if he simply looked hard enough or observed what no one else had noticed. This was simple physical impossibility, and he had never faced it before.

For a moment, he let the despair wash over him and consume him. There was a sense in which he was sure that everything would be fine. He had Aria and he had Tanwen, and together there was nothing they couldn't overcome. But that was only true for the three of them, and it meant nothing to survive without a greater purpose.

He allowed the despair into every pore of his skin and deep into his bones, and then, with a long breath, he exhaled it all out. He forced a smile onto his face. Maybe if they smiled for long enough, they could even make it true. "We'll find a way. I don't know what it is now, but we'll find a way."

Miranda seemed to take some strength from his lie, and she nodded. "We'll find a way," she repeated, as though whispering the words to herself to make her believe.

Radyn left her to return to the fields. She'd wanted something more from him, but all he could offer was his support and his strength. It wasn't enough, but it was all he could give.

RADYN WAS STANDING watch on top of Underhill's mound when he saw the familiar shape of a dragon flying toward him. He tensed at the sight but relaxed a moment later. He didn't know how Miranda arranged it, but he also knew that dragons frequently appeared, carrying both necessary supplies from the cities as well as messages. He watched as it grew closer, then frowned as he saw its standard flying openly.

Radyn swore under his breath, for it was a dragon from Firestone. He almost ran back into Underhill to warn the others, then reminded himself that he was being foolish. Kaya would be certain to sense the dragon as soon as it came close, and she would send the appropriate warning through the community. It was the same problem that faced them with every unexpected visitor. He was the only one capable of dealing with the largest problems.

He summoned Tanwen from his home in the hills and walked down the mound to show the dragon where to land. Did Jyn really plan on hunting him all the way here? It seemed impossible, but Radyn had to admit that he didn't understand the thirteenth Blade of Firestone as well as he wished he did. He stood and waited, wishing that Tanwen would arrive more quickly. He squinted as the dragon came closer, not believing the faces of the two who rode on the dragon's back. The tension in his shoulders eased, if only a little. If Jyn had come to hunt him, those weren't the two he would have sent.

His belief was reinforced when the dragon didn't try to take him in his massive jaws. It landed a few dozen paces in front of him, kicking up dust and flattening the grass as it landed. A moment later, Nikki and Macken climbed off the dragon.

He shook his head, still not able to believe what he saw. "What are you two doing here?"

In answer, Macken strode up to him. In a moment too late, Radyn realized the danger he was in. Macken's hand came back and slapped Radyn hard across the face. Before Radyn could react, he felt the old Sword's giant arms wrap around him and pick him up in an embrace.

Radyn was confused, but he managed to get a breath and say, "I've missed you too, I think."

Macken looked around. "Where is he? Have you been taking good care of him?"

Radyn needed a moment, but then he laughed. "He's on his way as we speak. I summoned him when I realized I didn't know who you were. I think he'll be excited to see you."

It made sense, of course, that Macken would care more about his dragons than Radyn's well-being. As if on command, Tanwen's silhouette appeared on the horizon, and Macken practically rushed to greet him. Dragon and trainer were reunited, and Nikki and Radyn watched with matching smiles on their faces. Radyn was almost a little embarrassed on Macken's behalf. Nikki leaned toward him, "The whole way over, he talked about almost nothing but that dragon."

Radyn grinned widely. "Tanwen always was one of Macken's favorites. I'm surprised he didn't hit me harder than he did."

"He was probably afraid he would break you."

Radyn chuckled and shook his head. "You still haven't answered the question of why you're here—or how you found me, for that matter."

Nikki looked to the sky, and Radyn got the sense that she was looking for Firestone, as though to somehow check that it was still in the skies above. She saw nothing, though, and turned back to face him. "The usual. There's trouble, and I need your help."

He waited silently for her to answer the other question.

"Jyn knew where you were. I don't know how, exactly. All he said was something about not letting one of his greatest Swords go missing without his permission, but that was it. He had Macken help me, because he claimed that Macken knew the surface better than almost anyone, and he was one of the few Swords that wouldn't kill you on sight."

"Generous of him."

Macken finished the reunion with Tanwen and rejoined them. "Well, are you going to show us this new home of yours, or are you going to make us beg?"

Radyn was surprised that their visit meant so much to

him. He had come to believe that Firestone was nothing more than a chapter of his past. But seeing them here made him homesick in a way he hadn't been almost since the day he had left. "Come on in, I'll show you around."

The arrival of the unexpected visitors raised some commotion throughout Underhill, but less than it normally would have. Nikki was quick to pick up on the sullen atmosphere of the place. "What happened here?"

"There's a lot more to say, but we were just attacked by a group of people with strange powers. Kaya—you remember her, I'm sure—calls it the shadow song, but they just broke in and hurt us bad. We lost a lot of good friends."

He didn't miss the look that the other two shared. "What?"

Nikki licked her lips. "We've been dealing with a similar threat. They attacked our Engine, and Rebecca died defending it. Since then, another one of their disciples stabbed Jelrik and almost killed him. We think they're going to attack the Engine again soon."

"And that's why you're here."

Nikki nodded. "The shadow song can be sensed. At least, Jelrik was able to. I was hoping you might be able to do the same and defend yourself once you find the disciple. He's one of the strongest warriors I've ever seen."

Radyn considered for a moment. He still didn't believe in coincidences, and it was nearly impossible to believe that the attacks against Firestone and Underhill weren't connected. And if they were going to talk about it, it was best if they were all together. He suggested a meeting with everyone, and Nikki and Macken agreed without complaint.

If not for the reason of their visit, he would have watched their reactions with amusement, knowing that they had mirrored his not all that long ago. Like them, he had grown up thinking that Firestone and the cities like it were all that remained of the Makers and their work. But to be here, in a place that was so similar and yet so different, it wrenched a person's worldview wide open and made them realize that there was far more to the world than they had previously thought. Someday, when the threats were behind them and all they needed to worry about was the food that would be on their table that winter, then maybe they could compare their notes.

As it was, they followed him into the Engine room, where he grabbed Kaya and then dragged the whole crew towards Miranda's study. She looked up when they entered, surprised to see such a group, but maybe not quite as surprised as Radyn thought she should be.

"What's all this? And who are they?" she asked. Radyn handled introductions while explaining briefly how their arrival had come to pass. Nikki took up the explanation after Radyn was finished, and before long, everyone knew everything that had happened both in the sky and upon the surface.

Miranda's attention was focused entirely on Radyn. "What are you thinking?"

He'd been considering the problem since Nikki had first spoken of it, and the meeting had taken long enough that he'd come up with his answer. "I would like to help Firestone, but I don't dare leave here, not after the attack."

It was Macken, of all people, who came up with a solution. "If all you're worried about is keeping this place protected, then I'm sure we can get the Blade to leave people here while you're gone."

Radyn shot Macken an incredibly skeptical look. "Somehow that doesn't seem like a thing that Jyn would do, not after all the trouble he's gone to to keep this place and the ruins like it a secret."

"Don't be so sure. He sent me down here with a Shield with next to no notice. Something tells me he's taking these threats more seriously than most. If all you want is some muscle for a few days, I'm sure he can provide it."

"Not just muscle," Radyn said as he was looking at Kaya. "Although I appreciate Nikki's estimate of my abilities, I cannot sense the shadow song. She can, so we'll need Singers to replace her, too."

Macken shrugged as though it was no big deal. "I think you should ask. You might be surprised."

Radyn supposed the answer was simple enough, then. "Fine. If Jyn is willing to part with at least a team of Swords and two Singers, I'll come up. If not, then I'm sorry, but I have to stay here."

Macken actually laughed. "Rating yourself kind of highly there, aren't you?"

Radyn shrugged. "It is what it is. He can take it or leave it, but those are my terms."

No one was more surprised than Radyn when, two days later, two dragons arrived carrying the Swords and the Singers.

When Radyn saw them, he could do nothing but shake his head, laugh, and go to prepare his things to return to the first home he had ever known. It was time to save Firestone, and hopefully, he wouldn't destroy any more lives in the process.

22

Nikki glanced at Radyn as they approached Firestone on the back of Tanwen. She sought some clue, written across his face, of how he felt about his return. No matter how long she searched, though, she saw nothing that revealed his innermost thoughts. His face was as expressionless as a wall.

Kaya, at least, was easier to read, her face an open mix of excitement and nerves, closely matching Nikki's own feelings. The Shield was no stranger to big bets and risky gambles, but this one left her squirming uncomfortably upon Tanwen's back. Trading Radyn and Kaya for a squad of Swords and two Singers was a foolish trade by any estimation, but Jyn had hardly blinked when Nikki first brought him the proposal.

She'd never fully understood the Blade of Firestone. In many ways, he was the greatest unsolved mystery in her life, and that mystery was one of the reasons that she remained glued to his commands. At a glance, he was an impressive man, and well loved by most, including the clan. She'd never seen him fight, but she'd heard enough awed conversations to understand his skill was far beyond that of even a Senior Sword.

But everyone knew that. She was more interested in what they didn't talk about. Facts such as his knowledge of Radyn's location, or his willingness to station Swords and Singers in Underhill, thereby as much as guaranteeing word about the settlements would spread from the Swords despite their oaths to secrecy. At times, she swore she caught glimpses of some larger plan, but she couldn't guess at more than its vaguest shape, and certainly couldn't guess its ultimate goal.

All she could say for certain was that her trust in Jyn was absolute. Whatever plan he advanced, she was glad to be a part of.

Her thoughts ended as Tanwen spread his wings to land. He landed softly, as though he were a leaf dropping easily from a tree instead of a dragon capable of eating half a horse in a single bite.

The nest was as quiet as she'd ever seen it, and Nikki didn't doubt for a moment that all activity was being held until Radyn could be hidden inside the city. Jyn had issued a formal pardon, but that did little to keep Radyn safe from the clan's baser instincts. They couldn't keep Radyn a secret, but Jyn was doing all he could to keep his arrival quiet.

Nikki noted Radyn's moment of hesitation when he disconnected from Tanwen. It was unlikely, but possible, that the clan might conspire to keep Tanwen from Radyn's grasp, and the dragon was his only way back to Aria and Underhill. Radyn said something quietly to Tanwen, and then dragon and rider parted.

A messenger was waiting for Nikki. The note was from

Jyn, telling them not to begin the hunt until he'd spoken with them. He'd kept a guest room open for Kaya and Radyn, and ordered the group to wait for him there.

When Kaya heard the orders, she shook her head. "I'd like to talk to Jelrik, if I could."

"Why?" Nikki asked.

"He'll know exactly what this disciple feels like, and if he describes it well enough, it may make it easier for me to find him."

"I would like to see him, too," Radyn said, then added, "if he'll have me."

When Kaya saw Nikki's hesitation, she said, "We'll save time once we get started, and it's not strictly against the Blade's orders."

"It's not obeying them, either."

But Nikki relented. Jelrik was still being watched by the healers, and so Nikki led them there. The Sword who'd been with them in the tavern was standing guard outside his door, letting her past after a brief questioning. She knocked on Jelrik's door and entered alone.

Physically, Jelrik looked better than he had the last time she'd seen him. The color had returned to his face, and his sharp glance revealed the active mind trapped in the recovering body. "You're looking better than the last time I saw you," Nikki said.

A hint of a bitter grin flashed across Jelrik's face. "The last time you saw me was immediately after I'd had a hole in my stomach healed. Saying that I look better isn't saying much."

"Better than you looking worse."

He acknowledged the point with a brief dip of his head. "What's the occasion?"

"I brought visitors. I wasn't sure if you wanted to see them, though."

He frowned. "You've piqued my curiosity."

"One is a Singer from the surface who seems to possess a remarkable gift, and the other is her friend, Radyn."

She couldn't put a name to the emotions that twisted his face. He sat up straighter for a moment, then leaned back. He stared at the ceiling for a long while, then shook his head. "I'll see the Singer, but not Radyn. Not now."

Nikki knew that Radyn had been involved, somehow, in the death of Elora, Jelrik's wife, but she didn't know the details of that involvement. Whatever had happened had left scars that still ached. She didn't ask any questions, though, just bowed toward Jelrik and left to pass on the response.

Radyn's reaction was muted, but Nikki thought he looked hurt by Jelrik's refusal to see him. He didn't complain, though, and Nikki brought Kaya in.

The two had never met, but as soon as Kaya entered the room, the Singers stared at each other as though it were a contest between them. Jelrik paled at the sight of her, and it seemed to Nikki that Kaya was more in control of this meeting than the Master Singer.

Kaya bowed as though she wasn't. "Thank you for seeing me."

"What do you want?" Jelrik asked, his voice suddenly hoarse.

"To compare our experiences. You've fought against the shadow song, too."

He shook his head again. "Not fought. Just tracked."

Kaya stepped closer, and Nikki swore Jelrik flinched away.

"You should fight it," she said.

There was a weight behind her words, and Nikki sensed that she was saying far more than what she said, but her true meaning was lost on the Shield.

Jelrik, though, looked as though her words had struck him like a hammer. "You know what it promises, though."

She knelt beside his bed like a mother soothing her child back to sleep after a nightmare. "You know better. The path it would lead you down ends only in oblivion."

"You don't know that." Jelrik's voice was barely above a whisper now.

"I do, and so do you. If you follow this path, you surrender Elora."

He'd already been shrinking away from Kaya, but now Jelrik wilted like a dead flower. Tears sprang to his eyes and ran down his cheeks, and his voice was stolen from him. Nikki didn't understand it, but Kaya's gentle nature kept Nikki from interfering.

"How did it happen?" Kaya asked.

"I was listening for it. To it. That was all. I listened and listened, and I left myself open so I could listen. And then, when he struck me, it was inside of me. But I can fight it."

"Not if it's still with you. But we can fight it together, if you'll help."

Jelrik shook, half-spasm and half-sob. "I'm not strong enough to get rid of it."

"I don't think it has anything to do with strength. It compromises your spirit, instead."

"You can help?" Jelrik asked. He even had the look of a child, believing his mother when she claimed she could dispel his nightmares.

"I can. Will you sing with me?" Kaya asked.

Jelrik nodded, and the two began their silent song. Nikki felt it through her shard, soft but carrying an unfathomable depth of strength. The room grew warmer, as though someone had lit a fire where Jelrik and Kaya sang together. Nikki tried not to listen, feeling like a stranger invading a neighbor's privacy, but her proximity was such she couldn't ignore it.

She couldn't understand the song, as she wasn't a Singer and not sensitive enough, but she could understand how the song made her feel. Hopeful at first, and then resolute as she sensed the danger approaching. It hit with barely a moment of warning, and it nearly silenced Jelrik's song completely.

Was this the shadow song that Kaya spoke of? It didn't bring despair, not exactly, but a promise of emptiness. It was silence and peace, a twisted sort of order. After the last few days of chaos, running to and from the surface, she could glimpse some of its appeal. It brought an end to everything, and some days, that was exactly what she wanted.

The silence couldn't touch Kaya's song, though, and Jelrik linked his spirit to hers, and together they drove the silence away, filling the room with light and life and harmony.

Kaya's last notes lingered, clearing the air like a gust of fresh breeze down a hallway near the surface. Then she, too, went silent.

Jelrik looked even stronger than before. He lay back in his bed, not out of exhaustion, but to relax. He nodded slowly. "Thank you."

Kaya bowed. "Is there anything I should know?"

"He leaves a trail that lingers. The stronger the trail, the more recently he passed. I don't think you'll have much trouble finding him. But they have Singers, too. You've seen their work?"

Kaya nodded.

"Then there's nothing more I can say. Keep yourself safe from them, and keep the city safe from them."

Kaya turned to leave, but Jelrik stopped her. "One more thing. If you save the city, send Radyn to me. I'm not ready today, but I will be." He paused, and the next words seemed difficult to say. "It will be good to see him again."

Kaya bowed in answer, then led Nikki from the room.

Outside, once the door was closed, she met up with Radyn and they made their way towards the guest rooms. Radyn asked no questions about what had happened, but Nikki wasn't nearly so content. "What happened in there?"

"In his pursuit of the shadow song, Jelrik let some of it into his spirit, where it was festering," Kaya said.

Nikki thought back to her first meeting with Jelrik and Jyn, and Jelrik's threats to bring down the city. She'd thought Jelrik had control, but now she wasn't so sure. "Was he in danger?"

"Not immediately. He fought it well, but in time, it would have taken over. Once the spirit surrenders a foothold, there's no way to defeat it alone."

"Why wasn't he sure if he wanted your healing, and why did you say he was going to sacrifice Elora?"

Radyn's ears pricked up at that, and Nikki wondered again how long it would be until she learned the truth.

"Embracing the shadow song is a path to power, and a strength greater than many could achieve with the song of the Engine. Unfortunately, it costs everything. It devours the spirit and prevents it from reaching the gate when our bodies die. That is the true horror of the shadow song."

The casual acceptance of such esoteric ideas didn't sit well with Nikki. She believed in what she could feel, touch, and hold. She was still trying to decide what she felt about Kaya's statements when they reached the guest room and found Jyn outside the door, waiting for them with his arms crossed. Magni stood behind him.

Nikki stopped, but Radyn took another step so that he stood in front. "Magni, I was devastated to hear of your loss."

Magni bowed his head.

"It's good to see you, though, and you, too, Jyn," Radyn said.

Jyn inclined his head. "And you as well. Magni is going to join you."

Radyn looked between Magni and Jyn, considered for a moment, then agreed.

"*I'm* going to kill him, Radyn," Magni said, as though there'd be any other reason for his presence.

"And I'll help you," Radyn said.

Jyn turned and walked away without another word, and so their hunt began.

NIKKI COULDN'T REMEMBER the last time she'd felt quite so useless. She was present because she'd started on this task, and no one had thought of telling her she was no longer needed. She served no purpose, though. Kaya served as their seeker, sniffing through the long hallways like a bloodhound. Radyn and Magni served as the muscle, the men who would kill whoever was unfortunate enough to be plotting against the city. But what was she?

Nothing more than an investigator with nothing left to investigate. She'd completed the task given to her. Now they knew why Rebecca had died, and in the process, she'd solved Zak's disappearance.

She didn't think of leaving, though. Now that she'd

started this, she fully intended to see it through until the end.

For the moment, all she had to do was endure Radyn and Magni's reunion. She hadn't realized the two had known each other, but their familiarity was obvious.

"I didn't even realize you'd gotten married," Radyn said.

"I figured if you could find a woman who could put up with you, it should be easy for me," Magni answered.

Radyn grunted. "I'm sorry she's gone. I only knew her by reputation, but if she was good enough for you, she must have been an incredible woman."

Magni nodded slowly. "The best I'd ever met."

Jelrik's prediction turned out to be accurate. It didn't take Kaya long to find the lingering traces of shadow. They hadn't even reached the tavern where they'd last spotted the disciple before she caught a sense of him. She closed her eyes, lost herself in the song for a moment, then led them through the hallways.

Their journey took them to the upper levels of Firestone, toward a neighborhood designed for some of the city's largest families. It was a good area to hide. Had it been up to Nikki, it would have been one of the last places she would have searched, largely due to the inconvenience. The apartments were larger here and often crowded, meaning a search took considerable time. The larger families also tended to have many children, and as such, were intensely aware of their neighbors. Strangers weren't welcome in these hallways.

Kaya stopped outside a door and closed her eyes. "The man from the tavern is in there, but he's not alone. There are at least half a dozen others, all disciples of the shadow song."

Radyn looked at Magni. "That's too many for us to take alone, especially if they're trained."

Magni considered, and didn't look pleased by the conclusion he came to. "I'll run down to the academy and recruit more Swords. You wait here."

Radyn agreed to the plan and Magni took off at a sprint, moving much faster than Nikki would have expected.

Nikki led the others around the nearest corner, where they could keep a watch on the door without being obtrusive.

Something was bothering Kaya, though. She kept her eyes closed, listening to the song even though her work was done. Radyn noticed the same, and he shared a glance with Nikki, but she was as uncertain as him.

Kaya opened her eyes. "There's something else, too, though it's hard to be sure."

"What?" Radyn asked.

"There's something else happening here. Another shadow song, although it's hard to hear."

"Another shadow song?" Nikki didn't want to believe it.

Kaya gestured with her hands, groping for the language to explain the senses that were beyond description. "There's a shadow song in that room," she said, pointing to the door they were watching, "as well as the lingering trace of that man. He's in there. Of that, I have no doubt. But someone else is singing, I think. Somewhere else, and I think this is meant to distract us."

Radyn's eyes narrowed. "How sure are you?"

Kaya could do nothing but shrug. "The other song isn't as loud, but I sense a strength and purpose to it that isn't present here."

Radyn looked between the two women. "You two need to find the shadow Singers and put a stop to whatever they're doing. I'll keep a watch on the door, and when Magni shows up with reinforcements, we'll raid the room. You two need to stop the shadow song."

Kaya didn't hesitate. She turned and started walking down the hallway. Nikki glared. "I can't stop them even if she finds them."

"She's strong enough," Radyn assured Nikki.

Nikki swore, then chased after Kaya to put a stop to the shadow song for good.

23

Radyn leaned against the wall in the hallway, one eye locked on the door while his mind wandered. The presence of a second shadow song concerned him more than he'd allowed himself to reveal to the women. Nikki was an incredible Shield, but against the enemies he'd fought so far, her skills wouldn't take her far. Kaya he had trained himself, but she was untested.

There were no other options, though. If he was to leave with them, it opened up the possibility of this giant warrior escaping.

He took a deep breath and let it out slowly. He was only one man, and there was only so much he could do. At some point, he needed to trust others.

That was only part of his concern, though. He was back in the first place he'd considered home, but the feel of it had changed in his absence. Once, he'd considered the closeness of the hallways and his neighbors a sign of comfort, a reassurance. Now that he'd gotten used to having space to himself, though, he felt confined, as though he was trapped in a cell with a crowd of other prisoners who didn't know of their imprisonment.

The surface had changed him more than he thought. The hallways of Underhill were nearly indistinguishable from those of Firestone, but one freed him while the other trapped him.

He missed Aria, though he'd been gone for less than a day. Jyn had ordered the Singers to bring Firestone closer to Underhill, so the journey over had barely taken any time at all. Even so, he wanted to be back, unable to trust her safety to any hands but his own.

He pushed himself off the wall when Magni approached with a collection of Daggers and Swords. Radyn counted ten, and he recognized about half of them. A competent group, and enough strength to lead an assault on another city. The expression on Magni's face let him know that he understood it, too.

"Where are the others?" Magni asked.

"Kaya thought she sensed another shadow song. I told her and Nikki to go investigate. She reassured me the giant is in here, though, and there's been no movement."

Magni clearly wasn't pleased by the development, but his frustration didn't last long, not with his enemy so close. He turned to those who had followed him from the academy. "I'll go in first. If you can capture them alive, so much the better. But if not, don't lose any sleep over it."

The way that he said it made it clear to all who were listening that he couldn't care less which of their targets died.

Radyn took a position near the middle of the group, between two pairs of Swords. He and all the others lit their maniblades, filling the narrow hallway with the song of the Engine. Magni looked back to ensure all were ready, then stomped the door open. The rooms behind the door were dark, and Magni checked his advance before stepping into the unknown. Radyn squinted, trying to pierce the veil of darkness.

Something about the scene wasn't right, but it took him a moment to put the pieces together. Even after Magni had slammed open the door, the darkness within was absolute. At the very least, light from the hallway should have entered the first room, casting a hint of feeble illumination. Instead, it was as if light struck the darkness and simply surrendered the fight.

Magni jumped to the side, though Radyn wasn't sure why until he saw the shadow within the room bulge and solidify into a blade that stabbed at Magni's heart. It narrowly missed, but the blade continued to grow until a man emerged. He was an average-sized man, so Radyn assumed this wasn't the giant that had nearly killed Jelrik. He stepped calmly into the hallway and turned to face the line of Swords and Daggers prepared to enter the room. The dark blade rested comfortably in his grip, and the sight of the overwhelming force arrayed against him seemed not to frighten him in the least. He bent his legs, and that was all the warning the clan received.

Radyn connected with the shards in his body as the man leaped at the line. The first Sword in line fell to the speed of the dark blade, and his partner, a slight Sword who reminded Radyn a little of Elora, was knocked back by the force of his second strike. The man lost some of his speed, but was still quick enough to cut through the Dagger next in line.

The pair of Swords ahead of Radyn stepped forward to defend the next Dagger, and they felled the enemy with little difficulty, as he'd slowed to a speed no faster than a

Junior Dagger. Radyn frowned at the ease of the man's defeat, but didn't have time to wonder as the dark room disgorged warrior after warrior. The second to emerge from the shadows turned and attacked Magni, but the third and fourth turned toward the line Radyn was a part of, their strategy a nearly perfect echo of the first enemy's.

Both dropped into a crouch and launched themselves forward, cutting at the pair of Swords who'd killed the first disciple to step through the door. They'd lost the element of surprise, but their speed was such they still cut down the two Swords and a Dagger before they crossed blades with Radyn.

Though it was two against one in a narrow hallway, Radyn cut them down with little difficulty. The second man blocked one of Radyn's cuts with his dark sword, but Radyn's maniblade passed through it as though it were nothing more than a cloud.

The battle left Radyn at the front of the line, joined by the smaller Sword who'd been knocked to the side in the first disciple's attack. She was shaken from the force of the cut she'd blocked, but appeared otherwise unharmed. She and Radyn stood side by side, blocking the hallway, as the next wave of disciples exited the room.

At least, that was what Radyn thought was happening. He saw two dark swords emerging from the darkness, but then the darkness itself spread, leaking from the room into the hallway. The lanterns, powered by the Engine, flickered and died as shadow embraced them.

A suspicion formed in Radyn's mind, and he leaped into the shadow. The disciples he'd already fought possessed an incredible technique, but it was the same technique he'd seen in the caves down on the surface. They could summon one incredible burst of speed and strength, but time and again, they'd shown that neither lasted for more than a few moments, and once it faded, their skills weren't much better than the average Shield's. He'd bet his life that most, if not all, the disciples knew little more than the one technique.

The darkness that surrounded him was cold, leeching the warmth from his body like a parasite. His maniblade flickered, but once he focused on the song and reinforced the blade with strength from the shards within his body it glowed even in the darkness, banishing the shadow from around him. He nearly ran into the first disciple, who was striding forward, confident in the shadow's protection. The disciple's eyes went wide, but Radyn cut before the man could react.

He took another cautious step forward, but before his maniblade could reveal his next opponent, the floor shuddered and a loud, screeching cry echoed down the hallway. Radyn's stomach leaped into his throat as a distant memory became terrifyingly real. He took a step back, but the floor was no longer where it was supposed to be. His maniblade winked out of existence as he was cut off from the song of the Engine, and he was reminded once again that he was inside a floating mountain, surrounded by perfect darkness and countless tons of stone and steel.

He floated weightless for a moment, and instead of fighting, he relaxed. There was nothing to be done, and if Firestone recovered, he knew well what would come next. He sent his best wishes to Aria and their unborn child, keeping her in his mind's eye as he waited.

The lights flickered on, then burned even brighter than before, and in the brief moment between light and chaos he noticed that he was no longer enveloped by shadow.

Then the floor came rushing up to meet him, and he didn't try to fight it. His feet hit first but he let his legs and body collapse, landing in as controlled a breakfall as he could perform. He coughed as the air was driven from his lungs, but the song had returned to his shards and to his body, and he recovered quickly. Thankfully he hadn't twisted an ankle or broken a bone.

The hallway was a mess of bodies, and at a glance, he couldn't tell who was dead, who was injured, and who still posed a threat. Five disciples were before him, including one man who was nothing like the others. He was a giant, and as he came easily to his feet, Radyn saw an apex predator surveying its kingdom. He looked at Radyn, then grinned viciously and took off running down the hallway, leaping over Magni as the other man pushed himself to his feet.

Radyn cut through the other disciples as he chased after the giant, and he heard Magni breathing hard just a step behind him. They sprinted down the hallway, their legs churning, lungs burning, then up the stairs to the next level. At the top, they paused for a moment to see which way the giant had run. Radyn clipped his maniblade to his belt, then resumed the chase, Magni keeping up with his brutal pace without problem.

They'd closed the distance to about ten paces when the lights in the hallway flickered once again. Radyn cursed, but nothing happened, and he kept up the chase.

There was no other warning when the lights went out again, and Radyn took a step, but the floor wasn't there and all he heard was the cry of Firestone's steel and the cry of the people behind their doors as their home fell from the sky. The light returned and Radyn plummeted the short distance to the floor, still barreling forward. His feet hit hard, and he launched himself into a roll, returning to his feet a moment later.

Unfortunately, he hadn't gained any distance on the

giant, who seemed to have navigated the darkness without missing a pace.

The giant hit the next set of stairs at a flat sprint, leaping up three and four at a time without apparent effort. Radyn followed, Magni at his left shoulder.

They emerged on the uppermost level of Firestone, directly beneath the surface. What was the giant after? Did he think he could somehow penetrate the nest and steal a dragon? If Firestone went down, he would go down with all of them.

The giant increased his speed, forcing Radyn to give everything to keep up. Magni started to fall behind. The lights in the hallway flickered as the Engine fought its battle, and the floor began to tilt, all of Firestone leaning toward Radyn's right. The giant's pace slowed as the angle of the floor increased.

There were no apartments on this level, but plenty of supply rooms where goods crashed against one another, adding another layer of sound to the groaning of Radyn's birth city. Fortunately, the hallways were kept clear, and even as Radyn's feet slipped against the floor, he didn't have to worry about a loose rake falling over and tripping him up.

Just when he feared he would have to start running on the wall, Firestone began to right itself. Connected to the shards as he was, he heard the song battling against the darkness and recognized Kaya's efforts to help the Singers of Firestone. It wasn't his battle, though. All he could do was wish her his best and bring this giant down.

The enormous disciple reached the next set of stairs and ran up them, Radyn close behind. They came up onto the surface of Firestone, sprinting past the guards at the entrance, both of whom were on hands and knees, fingers clawing into the dirt and grass for a hold. They shouted after Radyn and the giant, but there was nothing they could do, and it would be best for them to stay away, regardless.

The giant dug a foot into the soil, and Radyn leaped to the side as the enormous man twisted around and cut with his dark blade. He missed widely, and Radyn drew his maniblade and cut down. The giant kept his distance, his feet shuffling backward quickly.

Radyn had already suspected this disciple was capable of much more than the others. He'd run at an inhuman speed since fleeing the battle and hadn't slowed like so many of his brethren. This was a man who had mastered the use of the shadow song, much as a Sword mastered the song of the Engines.

The giant held his sword in one hand, and though the blade was the length of a Sword's maniblade, it looked like nothing more than a long dagger in the man's grip. The giant's other hand was a fist, but shadow danced around it, too, protruding into short spikes that never stopped moving. That, then, had probably been what had struck Jelrik, and Radyn's stomach panged in sympathy for his old friend.

The giant struck with the sword, an almost lazy swing that Radyn had no problem parrying with his maniblade. As soon as his sword was engaged, the giant twisted and lashed out with his fist, shadow and flesh blurring with the speed of the strike. Radyn danced back and out of range, but only because he was connected to all his shards. Anything less and that would have been a killing blow.

The giant looked down at his fist as though he was confused, as though the combination had never failed to bring down an opponent. He opened his hand, and the shadow danced around both knuckles and palms, but when he closed his fist the shadow shifted, dancing only next to his knuckles.

The sight stilled Radyn's immediate response, for it looked less like the giant was controlling shadow and more like the two were some sort of cooperative pair.

Any questions he might have had about the relationship between shadow and disciple vanished as the giant closed the distance. He came in fast with his blade, wielding it more like a knife than a sword, slashing and stabbing without any pattern or purpose Radyn could discern. He attacked without concern, confident that if Radyn dared to close the distance his fist would end the fight.

As near as Radyn could tell, the disciple was right. Twice he ventured in close, and twice the giant lashed out with his fist. If Radyn turned too much attention to the fist, though, the dark sword sought his flesh. Radyn gave up ground quickly, grateful to be fighting in the open fields of Firestone.

Magni joined the fight and shifted the momentum of the duel. The defense that Radyn couldn't pierce developed holes as Magni attacked from the disciple's other side. One cut looked certain to be fatal, but the disciple opened his hand and caught Magni's maniblade, shadows dancing and protecting his palm while his massive arm struggled against Magni's incredible strength.

Firestone shifted beneath them again and Magni lost his balance. The Sword stumbled a few steps back before regaining his footing, but it was all the time the disciple needed to break from the pair and sprint toward the nest.

Radyn groaned as the song alternatively crescendoed and faded, his muscles strong one moment and exhausted the next. As soon as he felt the strength return to his body, he chased after the disciple, focusing all the strength of the song into his legs. He gained quickly over the open fields, and once again the giant realized his cause was lost and turned to fight.

Radyn only held him off for a moment before Magni struck with all the force of a dragon. The sheer power of Magni's blow knocked the disciple off balance, and the moment was all Radyn needed. He darted forward, his blade cutting across calf and tendon, bringing the giant to his knees.

Before he could protest, Magni stood before the disciple, maniblade raised for a killing blow. Radyn started to shout, but the pale blue light of the weapon arced through the disciple's neck and the fight was over. A shudder ran through Magni's body, and his maniblade dropped to the ground, followed quickly by the giant Sword collapsing to his knees. He stared up at the sky as though he was looking not just for the gate but through it, as if to ask Rebecca if she was satisfied with his revenge. Then he closed his eyes, and Radyn saw something he never thought he'd live to see.

Magni wept openly, tears trickling down the side of his cheeks.

Radyn stood awkwardly, unsure if Magni wanted space or company, forgetting, just for a moment, that the fight for Firestone wasn't yet over.

He was reminded again when the song vanished, and Firestone once again started to drop from the sky.

24

Nikki didn't know Kaya well, and didn't know how likely she was to panic in stressful situations, but she didn't like the look she was seeing on Kaya's face, nor the speed with which she rushed through the hallways, as though she was running a race against an opponent she was certain she would lose to.

Kaya's pace slowed suddenly, causing Nikki to almost run into her back. She had her eyes closed, and was holding one hand to the wall for support and another to her head, as though to tame a pounding headache.

"Are you hurt?" Nikki asked.

Kaya shook her head. "They're close to whatever they're doing. I'm not sure I can stop them."

Nikki looked up and down the hallway. A woman was carrying freshly laundered clothes about thirty paces away, oblivious to Nikki and Kaya. Behind them, two boys chased each other around their neighborhood, shouting at one another to stop cheating.

She wouldn't let them suffer. If Kaya couldn't overwhelm

the shadow song, perhaps Nikki could stop the disciples in the physical world. "Where are they? Are we close?"

Kaya grimaced and forced herself to stand straight. Her face was pale, her limbs trembled, and sweat trickled behind her ears, but she focused her gaze forward. "They're close. I think we can reach them."

Nikki squatted and positioned herself under Kaya's arm. The young woman tried to complain, but Nikki wouldn't hear any of it. "Let's go. You just tell me where."

"Down the hall, then down a level. I can't say how close, exactly, but close."

Nikki half ran with, half pulled along and supported Kaya. She barely weighed anything at all, but her strength was almost nonexistent. She wasn't well, though she hid that fact behind pursed lips.

"Are you sure you can fight them?" Nikki asked.

Kaya didn't look at Nikki. "I already am."

That slowed Nikki. "You are?"

Kaya swallowed hard. "Their first attack would have killed the Engine, but I was able to stop them. They weren't expecting that, but now they're redoubling their efforts. Firestone's Singers are trying to help, but they don't know what's happening, so they're not terribly useful. Better than nothing, though. Please, you need to hurry."

Nikki didn't need to be told twice. They found a stairwell and hurried down. Nikki shouted at a man coming up the stairs to get out of the way, that she was on official Shield business. Once they reached the landing below, Kaya stumbled toward the right.

Nikki swore she saw the lights flicker just before the hallway went dark.

She screamed, terror clutching at her heart in a way she'd hoped she would never have to experience again.

Memories struck with physical force. She'd been a promising student, excited to take the trials to become one of the clan, to bring honor to her family and serve Firestone. Her father had committed suicide by jumping off the edge of the city when she was young, and she'd grown up with her mother until she was eight, when Mother had become sick and passed away.

She'd moved in with her grandparents, both of whom she'd loved dearly, but the loss of both parents had left her unmoored, like a city floating without the guidance of the Singers. Her grandparents had done the best they could, but she was looking for something more, some greater purpose that she could shape her life around, and she thought she'd found it with the clans.

Then she'd failed the testing, and it had felt like there was nothing left. Her grandmother had taken her for a special treat, the ice cream that was only sold at one of the nearby squares, and that's where they'd been when the Little Fall had struck. One moment she'd been sitting next to grandmother, and the next she was surrounded by a darkness the like of which she'd never known.

She knew now, as an adult, that the darkness had only lasted for a moment, not much longer than the beat of a heart. But Firestone had dropped, and the bench she'd been sitting on was no more. She'd hung motionless, and when the light came back on, both she and her grandmother were in the air. She'd seen the panic in grandmother's eyes, a fear she'd never seen before.

Then they'd dropped. Nikki had landed on her rear and had escaped with nothing more than a bruise the next day. Grandmother had fallen down sideways, her head striking the bench while the rest of her body struck the ground. Nikki watched the moment of impact, had heard the crack of bones breaking. She'd seen the unnatural angle of her grandmother's head and watched the light go out of her eyes. She'd screamed then, too, like she screamed now.

And since that day, she'd never allowed herself to be in the dark.

She'd dedicated herself to finding out not just what had happened that day, but everything she could. Mystery was a darkness all its own, and she couldn't stand it in her life. She'd become a Shield, and her commendations only slightly outnumbered her disciplinary hearings. She couldn't leave anything alone, and she used her status as a Shield to dig up whatever information she could about Firestone, the clan, and the secrets both held tightly in their hearts.

Her fear in the darkness bypassed any rationality she might have possessed, running up her spinal cord and to her throat without pause.

Like before, the darkness only lasted a moment, and like before, she landed on the floor with nothing more than a bump on her rear, but her heart wouldn't stop racing, and her mind refused to send any commands to her limbs.

She looked over at Kaya, who was unhurt. The younger woman didn't even look frightened, but that was probably because she was concentrating too hard. Her eyes were scrunched shut and her lips were pressed tightly together. She was breathing hard, as though carrying a great weight.

Nikki wasn't sure how long she'd been staring when Kaya said, "I don't know how much longer I can hold them back. This—"

She stopped in mid-sentence, her eyes rolling back in her head. Nikki was certain the lights were about to go out again, but they remained on, even though they flickered.

Kaya's eyes rolled back into place as she groaned. "This

is stronger than anything I've ever known. I can't hold them for long. Two, maybe three doors down on the right. You have to finish this."

Nikki stared at Kaya, waiting for her to explain further, but she was someplace else, fighting a battle not even Firestone's Singers were prepared to win. Nikki swallowed hard and tried to convince her limbs to move, but she felt as though she were glued to Kaya's side. She couldn't leave the Singer, not now.

She looked down the hall, which grew longer as she stared at it.

Anyone but her.

The screams of people in the neighborhood jarred her out of her stupor and reminded her that her life had never been for her benefit. She lived only to banish the darkness which was far too common throughout the world. She still couldn't get her limbs to move, though.

Nikki connected with the shard she wore in the band on her wrist.

She should have done so earlier. The song of the Engine flooded her body with strength, but her proximity to Kaya's song, which she could hear as clearly as if the Singer was vocalizing it, gave her courage.

She didn't know Kaya's story, but at some point in her past, she'd known the darkness, too, and she'd refused to submit to it. Her song was defiance against destruction and despair, and Nikki wanted to sing it with her. She pushed herself to her feet and stumbled down the hall, counting the doors silently.

She tested the second door and found it unlocked. It opened on silent hinges, but the apartment was empty inside. She closed the door, grabbed her dagger, and hurried to the next door. It was locked, but she pulled the master key from her pocket and turned the lock. The handle now turned easily, but before she could throw the door open, her world was once again plunged into perfect darkness.

Holding onto the door helped. It served as an anchor, reminding her that she was still part of a city. Not only that, but her firm grip prevented her from rising too far. The scream still barreled up her throat, but she locked her lips tight and didn't let it out.

The lights returned a moment later, and Nikki glanced down the hallway to ensure that Kaya was still unharmed. The Singer looked unhurt, but it was clear the effort of fighting against the shadow song wore her down. Nikki turned back to the door, took a deep breath, and quietly opened it.

She should have known what she would find. She'd seen it often enough by this point, but the sight of the ritual in progress made the breath catch in her throat. Fortunately, those involved and still alive were so focused she had little fear of being noticed.

Blood covered the walls, the same symbols Nikki had seen far too many of over the last few weeks. Sharp and jagged lines cut through triangles, invoking forces she couldn't comprehend. She squinted and swore that the blood smoked, but when she blinked, the smoke was gone, or maybe she'd just imagined it.

The circle in the center of the living room quickly pulled her attention away from the lines. Six individuals, all about her age or a little older, lay on the ground, their heads pointing toward the center of the circle where a seventh person, an older woman, stood. Darkness danced around her. It crawled up her skin, embracing her almost like an enormous snake. Her eyes were fixed on the ceiling, staring into another world.

Those on the ground writhed in pain. Two were already dead, their struggle ended by whatever violence had exploded from their stomachs. Nikki watched from the doorway, in growing horror, as the stomachs of the other victims shifted and distended, twisting and bulging in ways flesh and organs were never meant to move. Their faces twisted in agony, but no screams broke through their lips. Despite the movement of their cores, their bodies remained perfectly still, and Nikki was left with the impression that their bodies were no longer under their control. They'd been locked in place by a force greater than human strength.

Thankfully she was still holding onto the door frame when Firestone shifted underneath her again. Her poor city cried out in agony, and a look of ecstasy passed over the older woman's face.

The sloping floor reminded Nikki that she'd come with a mission, and that Firestone's greatest threat stood in the center of the room before her. She gripped her dagger tightly, but before she could summon the courage to move, the stomach of one of the disciples burst open.

Instead of organ and blood, shadow burst from the distended stomach, stretching to the ceiling before it weakened and faded. In its final moments, though, she saw how it drifted toward the woman in the center of the circle, strengthening her for her fight against Kaya and Firestone's Singers.

The floor shifted more sharply, and if Nikki hadn't been holding onto the door frame she would have slipped to the side. The six on the floor didn't move, locked in place by the same force that prevented them from struggling. The woman, too, didn't have to move, supported by the same shadow that danced around her.

With a tortured groan, Firestone began to right itself, and Nikki felt confident in her footing. She stumbled forward, dagger in hand. The air grew colder the closer she came to the edge of the circle, her breath frosting as she advanced. The woman in the center of the circle gave no sign that she recognized how close danger had come. Nikki's heart pounded in her chest, and she feared that if it beat any faster, it would burst from her ribs the way shadow burst from the stomachs of the others.

Firestone swayed beneath her feet, and Nikki stepped into the circle. It felt as though she'd pushed aside a curtain and somehow stepped straight into a block of ice. The woman's gaze dropped from the ceiling and focused on Nikki, and she moved with inhuman speed, grasping Nikki's wrist with both her hands and pushing and twisting the tip of the dagger so that it turned towards Nikki's heart.

Nikki grabbed the woman's right wrist with her left hand and fought back, but the tip of the dagger continued to inch toward her heart.

It made no sense. Nikki was younger and stronger. She trained every day so she could protect herself. And yet this old woman, who looked so frail a mere fall might kill her, overpowered her with ease.

Nikki had no choice but to pull on the power of the shard at her wrist. It filled her muscles with fresh strength, and she barely fought the woman to a standstill, the dagger frozen between them. This close to both Kaya and the woman, she heard the battle between the song and silence as though it was being fought within her spirit.

Then, slowly, the silence surrounding the woman grew and the tip of the dagger once again inched toward Nikki's heart. Her limbs trembled under the strain, and she cursed, but her strength wasn't enough. The tip of the dagger pierced her uniform and poked into her left breast.

Nikki had never tried to connect with two shards at once, rightfully worried that to do so would kill her. But if she did nothing, she was as good as dead, anyway. She connected with the second shard that Jyn had given her, hidden against her inner thigh. The song within her banished the silence that threatened to envelop her, and with a powerful turn of her hips, she twisted away from the older woman and threw her to the ground.

She leaped after the woman, bringing the dagger down without hesitation. Somehow, the older woman got her hands up and once again caught Nikki's wrists, but the song was too strong. Nikki put her full weight and strength into the dagger, and it descended, closer and closer, to the disciple's heart. Finally, it pierced, and the woman's strength gave out the moment the tip of the dagger broke skin. Nikki fell forward, the dagger driving through the woman's heart and killing her. She breathed her last, and Nikki swore she saw the shadow leave her body, carried by that final exhalation.

Nikki slumped back, then remembered she wasn't alone in the room. She turned to look at the circle, but she didn't see a single chest rising and falling. She pushed herself to her feet and wandered over, squatting next to each of the bodies and ensuring they were dead. None of the faces were familiar, but once the threat had passed, she planned on uncovering their stories. What had led them down this path, to be willing to sacrifice their lives for this shadowy power?

She walked to the doorway and almost ran straight into Kaya. Instead of congratulations, though, Kaya's eyes were wide and her face pale. Nikki's stomach sank, for what fresh torture could be left?

"It's the Engine," Kaya said. "Whatever they did, I don't know that I can stop it. Firestone is falling."

Nikki stared blankly at Kaya. It didn't feel like they were falling, but then again, she rarely noticed when the city moved. "Are you sure?"

Kaya nodded. "Your Singers are fighting it, but they're losing. It'll be a bit yet, but I'm not sure there's anything more to be done. In an hour, maybe two, this city is going to fall from the sky."

Nikki chewed on her lower lip, wondering if this was yet another sort of trick. She didn't think so. Kaya didn't seem the type, and if Radyn trusted her, Nikki supposed she did, too. "Then let's get going. We'll need to find Jyn as quickly as we can."

Kaya nodded, and the two began their long run through the hallways toward the academy.

25

Radyn and Magni sat in the grass beside one another, looking out over the edge of Firestone and to the never-ending lands below. They'd double-checked to make sure that the disciple they'd chased was dead, and Magni had ensured the completion of his revenge by driving his maniblade into the disciple's unmoving chest. Their chase had taken them close to the edge of the city, and both could sense the conclusion of the battle between the song of the Engine and the shadow. They'd walked right to the edge and taken a seat without a word between them.

"She always loved the view," Magni said.

Radyn, not knowing how to respond, said nothing.

"I think there was a part of her that always hoped humanity would return to the surface, even though it seems impossible. I think she was called to the land, the same way she felt called to the song."

There was a long pause, then Radyn spoke softly. "If that was how she felt, I understand. I've only been on the surface for less than a year, but it's changed me. I didn't realize how much until I returned. For all that's happened to me, I still think of Firestone as my home, except it doesn't feel that way anymore. The hallways I walk every day aren't really any different than the ones here, but these feel cramped and small. There's room for everyone on the surface. We just need to fight for it."

"We've always had to fight to survive. Even the Makers."

Radyn supposed that was true enough. "What comes next, for you?"

Magni didn't answer for another long moment, but then he said, "I've asked Jyn for permission, once the threat of immediate danger has passed, to take my life. I wish to join her on the other side of the gate."

Radyn swallowed the hard lump that had suddenly appeared in his throat. "You'll be missed."

"I'm sure if you want to find someone to beat you up again, I can find someone."

"Thanks."

The corner of Magni's lip turned up in a hint of a smile. "You're stronger than you were back then. Far stronger than the shard in your maniblade. How many are you up to?"

"Enough for now."

Magni grunted. "You'll fall behind him, with that attitude."

Radyn didn't need to ask who Magni was speaking about. "Yeah? He's been pushing himself, has he?"

"Harder than ever since you went away. I think he grew a bit complacent while you were around. Think he believed he would be able to rely on you, no matter what happened with the clans. Now, though, he's taken it upon himself, and I don't know of anyone who has mastered more shards."

"I've always wondered who would win, if we had the chance to spar."

Magni actually chuckled. "I can answer that, and I'm afraid to tell you, it isn't even that close."

Radyn looked back out over the land. "Guess I'll have to train even harder, then."

"Guess so."

After another moment of silence, Radyn asked, "Is there anything I can do for you?"

"No, but thanks for asking."

Radyn nodded and leaned back on his elbows. "It's good to see you again.

"You, too." Then Magni frowned and leaned forward.

"What?" Radyn asked.

Magni pointed at the clouds, and it took Radyn a moment to realize what he meant. The clouds were closer than they had been before, and though it was difficult to be sure, it looked as though the land was closer, too. Radyn swore out loud. "We're dropping."

Magni was already on his feet. "It wasn't planned, either. Something must have happened."

They turned and ran toward the academy to find Jyn.

THEY FOUND Nikki and Kaya outside the door, arguing with the two Swords on guard. Nikki was demanding admittance, but the Swords were firm in their denials. "I'm sorry, ma'am, but he's meeting with Singers right now and ordered no admittance."

Magni strode forward, filling the hallway both with his bulk and with his presence. "It's fine, Adrian, I'll give my permission, and if the Blade wants to be angry with anyone, he can take it out on me."

Adrian looked up at Magni, glad to have someone else he could lay the responsibility on. "As you wish, sir."

There was an air of silent expectation throughout the halls of the academy, a readiness for whatever orders might soon issue from the Blade's study. Students and full-fledged Manirah alike knew something was wrong, and all they waited for was a finger to point them in the direction they needed to run.

Radyn felt the shock of his presence ripple through the halls, like a giant stone thrown into a still pond. If he hadn't walked beside Magni, he didn't know what violence he might have encountered. Years after he'd shouldered the blame for a betrayal that wasn't his, and the feelings had barely faded. The memory of the clan was long, especially when it came to the subject of traitors.

Magni knocked hard on Jyn's door, and it was Jyn himself who opened it with a snarl. The expression faded when he saw who had disturbed his meeting. "Come in."

The four of them squeezed in, Magni taking up the space of two, and they filled the tiny space until they were nearly crushed. Radyn didn't recognize the woman who had already been in the study, but her white robes marked her as a Singer.

Jyn caught them up. "The Engine is failing. Noella tells me that the Engine came under attack by forces she and the other Singers don't understand, and although the attack seems to have stopped, the Engine appears to be mortally wounded. They're doing everything they can to keep Firestone in the air, but they aren't optimistic."

Magni spoke for himself and Radyn. "We found the giant who attacked Jelrik. Radyn and I were able to kill him and all his fellow disciples."

The giant gestured to Kaya. "But she said she felt the shadow song somewhere else in the city."

Noella turned in her chair to look at Kaya. "Are you the other Singer we felt?"

Kaya nodded, and Noella's eyes widened. When she turned back to Jyn, she said, "If not for her, I fear the attack would have succeeded. I don't know who she is, but she saved us, sir."

Nikki took over after the Singer finished her praise. "Kaya and I pursued the source of the other shadow song and interrupted some sort of ritual. Kaya fought against the shadow song itself while I dealt with those in the ritual. We killed the shadow singer and ended the ritual, but I'm afraid it wasn't before they were able to do an incredible amount of damage. I'm sorry, sir."

Jyn grunted. "Doesn't sound like you have anything to be sorry for. If not for you and Kaya, Firestone might already be a smoking ruin on the surface." He turned his stare to Noella. "What are my options?"

"I don't know that you have any, sir. We're trying to sing to the Engine, but the best we've been able to do is slow the descent. At our current rate of descent, I think we'll be grounded within two or three hours."

A heavy silence fell over the group. In two or three hours they could save a handful, maybe, but it wasn't nearly enough time, and they all knew it.

Kaya was the one who spoke into the silence. "Sir, with your permission, and with the aid of your Singers, I'd like to study your Engine. There is a possibility, although it is slim, that I might be able to heal it."

Noella scoffed. "You can't heal an Engine, girl. Don't speak to the Blade with such nonsense."

Radyn spoke in Kaya's defense. "It's true, Jyn. Over time,

she's been able to heal Underhill's Engine. She's even been able to grow new shards organically. If she says there's a possibility, there's a possibility."

Jyn stared at Kaya with an intensity that would have caused most people to flinch away, but Kaya stood tall under his gaze. Radyn kept his smile to himself. Kaya was young yet, and still suffered from some of the overconfidence that came with youth, but she was as fearless as they came. Jyn would like her, if they got the chance to know each other better.

Jyn spoke carefully. "When you say there's a possibility, what do you mean? Are you talking the flip of a coin? The roll of a dice?"

"Worse than that. Your Engine has been hurt badly, and I'm not entirely sure what effects the shadow song had on it. A possibility is just that. Maybe one chance in ten, if you forced me to put a number to it, but even that's uncertain."

Radyn wondered if anyone else saw the way Jyn's hands reflexively tightened into fists. He kept his face still, but Radyn knew him too well. He didn't blame the Blade. If their positions were reversed, Radyn didn't think he'd handle the situation nearly as well.

Without warning, Jyn cursed, causing everyone else in the small study to flinch back. He looked like a caged animal who wanted to stand and pace, but there was no room in the crowded study. "I won't be the Blade that oversees the end of this city!"

He said it with such force, Radyn almost believed it, as though Jyn's sheer force of will would be enough to bend the laws of physics and keep Firestone in the air. He would become a Maker reborn, capable of feats beyond their imagination.

He blinked at the thought of the Makers, then swore

softly to himself. In the stunned silence that followed Jyn's declaration, everyone heard, and every eye turned to him.

"You have something to add?" Jyn asked.

Radyn's mind raced, considering the alternatives and the risks. It was a gamble. An incredible gamble, but at this point, what did they have to lose? Firestone was falling, and not even Kaya thought she could save it.

Jyn waited expectantly, and finally, Radyn said, "Jyn, I recently discovered something down on the surface. It might—*might*—be able to help us."

"What?"

"I discovered one of the Maker sites where they built the cities. Or at least, a place capable of serving as a landing spot for the city. It's only a few dozen miles west of Underhill, in the hills."

"You've done *what*?"

"It's a long story, and one I can tell you later. But it's a Maker structure, designed for cities. Kaya's seen it, too."

"Are you saying we could land there?"

Radyn shrugged, feeling hopeless. "Maybe? There were warriors using it as their base, at least, and maybe their home. A people I've never met before, but they've mastered the shadow song, much like the disciple Magni and I just fought in the hallways. I don't know if they're still there, but we'd have to act as though we're certain that they are."

Jyn crossed his muscular arms in front of his chest. "You've got a plan."

"*Plan* might be a strong word, but an idea, yes. What if Magni and I led an assault against the Maker structure? If we can defeat the warriors there and figure out a way to turn it on, it's possible we can land Firestone safely."

"That's an awful lot of ifs, even for one of your typical harebrained schemes."

Radyn shrugged again. He knew it as well as any of them, but he had to at least present the plan to Jyn.

Noella was shaking her head. "Sir, that's madness. Even if all this comes to pass and we do somehow land Firestone, all it means is we're going to attract all the dangers on the surface."

"Perhaps, but that's still farther away than if we didn't." Jyn sat for what felt like a long time, though it probably wasn't more than a few minutes. Then he turned to Magni and Radyn. "We'll do it. I'm only making one change to your plan. I'm going down to the surface instead of Magni. Radyn, do you have coordinates?"

Radyn needed a moment to gather his thoughts. He hadn't expected Jyn's company, and he wasn't sure it was wise, but the look on Jyn's face made it clear he wasn't about to accept any debate. "A rough idea, yes."

"Give them to Noella."

Jyn looked around the room. "Is there anything else?"

Kaya held up her hand, and Jyn stared at her until she spoke. "What do you want me to do, sir? I can try to help keep Firestone afloat, but you'll need someone to activate the Maker city, and I suspect I'm the one most qualified for that."

Noella, to Radyn's surprise, didn't argue.

Jyn considered, then decided with a resigned sigh. "I suppose I need you more on the surface, so you'll join me and Radyn. Anyone else?"

There wasn't anything. Jyn stood. "I'll issue the orders around the academy. Magni, the city is yours until I return."

Magni's eyes went wide. "Sir?"

"Get Firestone to Radyn's coordinates. It's the last order I'll give you, if you choose, but make it happen. There's no one I trust more."

Magni wrestled with the weight of his newfound responsibilities for a moment, then bowed deeply. "We'll make it, sir."

Noella shot a demanding glance at Jyn. "Sir?"

Jyn stopped, then realized he'd forgotten something. He looked around the room quickly, then pointed at Nikki. "Tell her. She'll take care of it. The rest of us have bigger problems."

Then Jyn was pulling Radyn out of the room to lead an assault on a Maker city.

26

Noella pulled Nikki aside as the various warriors and Kaya hurried down the hall, pulling every Manirah behind them. Noella grasped Nikki's shoulders and forced Nikki's attention on her face. "Who are you?" the Singer asked.

"Senior Shield Nikki, ma'am."

A flash of recognition passed across Noella's face. "You're the one the Blade calls whenever he has a problem, aren't you?"

"I am."

"Good, because we have a problem. Jelrik has gone missing."

Nikki blinked, not sure she'd heard the woman correctly. "Missing? He was with the healers the last time I saw him."

"And that would be a logical place to find him now, but he isn't there. None of the healers saw him leave, and none of the Singers can sense his presence. If there's anyone who can help keep this city in the air long enough to reach these coordinates, it's him."

"Do you have any clues at all?"

Noella shook her head. "We didn't even realize he was missing until we were dealing with the aftermath of the strike against the Engine. We checked on all our Singers, and he was missing."

"I'll find him," Nikki said.

Noella kept a firm grip on her shoulders. "You understand, don't you, what this means?" She held up the slip of paper Radyn had written his precious coordinates upon. "These coordinates are closer than I would have expected, but they're still hours away. If we don't find Jelrik, and soon, none of Jyn's efforts are going to matter. We won't make it."

"I'll find him," Nikki repeated.

Noella nodded, then let her go. Nikki raced through the halls of the academy toward the healers.

It had been a bit of a stretch to think she'd end her search so quickly, but she figured the best place to start the search was the place he'd disappeared from. The story she got from the healers was very much the same one she'd heard from Noella. Jelrik had been resting in his bed when the attacks had struck. When everything had ended, one of the healers had checked on their most important patient, but he hadn't suffered so much as a scratch. The healer hadn't thought about it, besides thanking the fates their Master Singer possessed such luck.

That was the last anyone had seen of him. Nikki checked with a handful of the other healers, but their story was the same.

She asked her questions quickly, sacrificing some of her customary thoroughness for speed. Once she was reasonably certain she wouldn't learn anything useful, she ran up the stairs toward the Singer's neighborhood. His home was the next logical place to check, though she somehow felt she wouldn't be likely to find him there.

The Dagger standing guard at the main entrance frowned at Nikki's questioning. "The Master Singer, ma'am? No, he hasn't been through in days. He's been in the healing quarters, though no one will say why. Are you looking for him?"

Nikki dodged the question and convinced the guard to grant her access, an argument that wasted several precious minutes. She ran through the Singers' neighborhood, and it was as though she ran through an abandoned city. She imagined every Singer in the city was making their way down toward the Engine room, but that was only her best guess.

Her master key opened the door to Jelrik's apartment.

"Jelrik?" she called.

She needn't have bothered. As soon as she stepped in, she knew the apartment was abandoned. She turned on the lights, and her breath caught.

Perhaps Jelrik hadn't been here, but someone had. The place was torn up. The paintings of Jelrik and Elora were scattered around the floor, ripped from their frames and then trampled upon. Books had been grabbed from the small library and thrown haphazardly across the room. Most of the spines were bent and broken.

She drew her dagger and connected with one of her shards, then advanced through the rest of the apartment. The first bedroom was in similar shambles. Someone had taken a blade to the bed and searched through the debris, and the study was in even worse condition.

No sign of Jelrik, though, and if the Singers couldn't sense him, there wasn't any way of tracking him through the song.

Nikki sheathed her dagger and wondered if there was any point in searching through the debris. Either the person searching the room had found whatever they were looking for, in which case Nikki would likely never know what they sought, or they hadn't, and given the thoroughness of their search, Nikki wasn't like to find it either, whatever it was. Either way, she didn't see how searching the room would help her find Jelrik.

As she looked around the room, she developed the sense that something was off. She forced herself to focus on her breath. A long inhale, a short hold, followed by a long exhale. A slow breath led to a slow mind, and hers stopped racing in circles. She let her gaze travel around the room, not searching for anything in particular, allowing whatever she'd noticed to rise from the depths of her awareness to the front of her thoughts.

The process took several long minutes, minutes that she worried were wasted. But as soon as it struck, it seemed so blindingly obvious. She swore to herself. She couldn't be sure it was the right answer, but it felt right. The longer she turned the idea over in her head, the more pieces fell into place. It answered questions she didn't even know to ask.

She left Jelrik's rooms, only then realizing that the door had been locked when she'd tried to enter. She'd needed her key. Another small clue that made her think that her intuition was correct.

The hallways of the Singers' neighborhood remained as quiet as though it was the middle of the night. Nikki ran through the halls, only to stop when she reached the gate to the neighborhood. As soon as she opened the door, she stepped into a scene of madness. Citizens were running through the hallways, many of them carrying packs and boxes. They jostled and shouted with one another, the communal behavior that Nikki had so often respected thrown to the winds. She stared, wide-eyed, for a moment. There was only one explanation.

She'd wondered if Magni would announce the trouble publicly or attempt to keep Firestone's predicament a secret. As of late, it seemed that Jyn had trended more toward secrecy, but his chosen replacement apparently felt differently. She couldn't see any of the Shields trying to maintain order, but she could hear their whistles as they desperately fought for the crowd's attention. It was a losing battle, but she didn't have the time or inclination to tell them.

She turned to the lone Dagger still standing guard over the empty neighborhood. The space around the gate was quiet. The only reason to enter this hallway was to visit the Singers, and everyone had bigger problems on their mind at the moment. The Dagger observed the chaos in the nearest intersection with wide eyes. He looked as though he'd just graduated from the academy within the past year, and none of his lessons had prepared him for this. She ended up shaking his shoulder to get his attention.

His eyes turned to her, saw her uniform, then recognized her face. A spark of hope glimmered in his eyes. He saw her only as a source of authority, someone whose orders he could follow. "Yes, Ma'am?"

"Who was the Sword responsible for guarding the Master Singer today?"

He thought for a moment, his remembrance disturbed

by a quarrel that broke out in the intersection. He shook his head, focused, and said, "I don't know, ma'am. The Master Singer has been in the healer's quarters for days now, so I'm not sure who was on rotation."

Nikki cursed. She was going to need Magni, and from the look of it, fighting her way to him was going to be a challenge. She looked back at the Dagger. "Are you looking for a way to contribute?"

The Dagger swallowed hard and nodded. "Yes, Ma'am. I heard the Shields with the announcement, but I haven't received any other orders. Seems pointless to be here, given that all the Singers are down by the Engine."

"Then come with me. I need you to help me clear a path through the crowd. I need to find Magni, and quick. It's possible all of Firestone depends upon it."

The Dagger barely needed to be told. He nodded and left his post without any further persuasion. Nikki stayed right behind him as he hit the crowd. She couldn't remember a time when the hallways had been quite so crowded, not even after the Little Fall.

But back then, the citizens had never known the full extent of their danger. They'd believed, and rightfully so, in hindsight, that if they hadn't needed immediate assistance, they were better off in their rooms, allowing those that needed the hallways to travel without hindrance. No such understanding existed today, though, and everyone was fighting their way to wherever they thought they were safest. Most pushed toward the surface, but a few had other destinations in mind.

Nikki was immediately grateful she'd asked the Dagger for his help. He was strong on his own, but even in times of crisis, his uniform demanded respect, and once people realized they were bumping up against a Dagger, they found some way to make him space. So long as Nikki remained close behind him, she could travel in his wake before the press of bodies closed behind her. The academy was several levels below them, and with most people pushing toward the surface, they were fighting against the currents.

They bypassed one of the busier stairwells in favor of a maintenance ladder that was empty, dropping down several levels before coming to the bottom. This level was as chaotic as the one they'd come from, but there was an entrance to the academy here, and the Dagger pushed them through the crowd.

Nikki wanted to shout at everyone in their way. She understood well enough their desire to reach the surface, but it wouldn't do them any good. Even if Magni ordered the dragons to start ferrying citizens down to the surface, what would it matter? The surface was just as deadly as the sky. Underhill was a potential option, but Radyn had said they were already low on food.

She snorted when she realized the whole line of thoughts was pointless. Jyn had taken all the dragons with him on the raid. He'd gambled everything on Radyn's plan. All a trip to the surface was good for was to get a better view of Firestone's end.

The guards at the academy door let Nikki in after a brief fight, but she kept the Dagger with her. His name was Jona, and if they'd forgotten about him, then she'd use him as protection. There was a very real chance she was going to need it, if her guess was correct.

The hallways within the academy were busy, but not nearly as chaotic as the mess outside. Students, Daggers, and Swords moved with a focused determination, and Nikki took it as a testament to Jyn's leadership that they didn't break at the first sign of trouble.

The flow of people in and out of Jyn's study was constant, and few looked pleased to see a mere Shield trying to insert herself in the queue. Unfortunately for them, she was no stranger to angry looks, and soon found herself in front of Magni.

He frowned at the sight of her. "What do you want?"

"I need to know who was guarding Jelrik today."

Magni had appeared composed when she entered, but her question pushed him over the edge. He rose to his full height and slammed his palms against Jyn's desk. "Are you serious?"

She stepped forward until they were almost nose to nose over the desk. It didn't intimidate him, but it at least interrupted him. "Jelrik was taken after the fight earlier today, and now he's missing. But there's no dead guard in the healing quarters."

Magni's mind leaped to the conclusion it had taken her too long to reach. "You think the guard is involved with the disciples?"

"I'm thinking so, yes. But I won't know for sure until I ask him."

Magni swore, then shuffled through a pile of papers on Jyn's desk until he found a duty roster. "Josiah. He's the same Sword that was with you when you came across that disciple that almost killed Jelrik."

Nikki had wondered as much, and was now more certain of her guess than ever. "The same Sword that survived the attack without a scratch, despite the disciple's skill?"

Magni's eyes widened as he made the same connection.

"Where does he live?" Nikki asked.

Magni listed off an apartment number from memory, and Nikki frowned. "He's not in the academy?"

Magni shook his head. "He had a family and chose to

put some space between the clan and them. His wife's been sick for the past few years, and he wanted to be closer to the healers."

"That's where he'll be, then. It would have been a simple matter to smuggle Jelrik out of the healers' quarters in the chaos following the attack, and no one will check his home. Do you have anyone else you can spare?"

Magni cursed again. "Jyn took all the Swords with him on his assault. All I have is Daggers, and most of them are occupied. Pull open the door."

Nikki did, and Magni called the next Dagger in the queue in. The Dagger who entered looked even younger than Jona. She bowed quickly and gave Nikki a questioning look. "Give me your report, and quick," Magni said.

She told him of problems around one of the dining halls on the sixth floor. Magni nodded, then said, "I'll take care of it. For now, you're with her. Whatever she says, you do. Is that clear?"

The girl nodded and Magni dismissed them.

Nikki introduced herself, and the girl said that her name was Ralynne. As Nikki had feared, she was a child who had graduated from the academy and become a Junior Dagger just a few weeks ago. They met up with Jona, and Nikki led them through the academy's halls.

If she was being optimistic, she figured that between her and the two young Daggers, they would stand against the Sword for all of a minute, if they were lucky. If they were even luckier, that minute would give Jelrik enough time to escape whatever predicament he was in and save the city.

There was nothing for it, though. Nikki gave Jona the address, and after they exited the academy, he led them to the appropriate apartment, pushing against the crowd once again.

Nikki could only hope they arrived in time. The rogue Sword hadn't killed Jelrik, which frightened Nikki more than a murder would have. He wanted something from the Master Singer, and she couldn't help but fear what that meant for the future of Firestone.

27

Radyn glanced backward, still not quite able to believe what he saw. He was connected with Tanwen, but he was hardly alone on the dragon's back. Six of Firestone's strongest warriors sat behind him, studying the surface with cold, studious eyes. Behind them flew a dozen other dragons, nearly the full complement of Firestone's allies, each following Radyn toward Underhill.

Had it been up to Radyn alone, they'd be flying straight toward the Maker base, but he wasn't in command, and Jyn had argued otherwise.

Radyn had lost the argument, and it still burned in his stomach. Despite his efforts to think of anything else, the memory of it came to him, as vivid as when it had happened. They'd been standing in the nest as the Swords ran back and forth, preparing both themselves and the dragons for the assault.

"We're going to need her," Kaya said.

"I'm not putting her at risk!" Radyn said.

Jyn watched the exchange, uninvolved for now, but

Radyn could guess his position easily enough. Not that it mattered. Jyn no longer commanded him.

Kaya tried to reason with him. "I can sing to the Engine, but it's going to take everything I have, even with the help Firestone is providing. No one understands the creations of the Makers better than Aria, so we'll need her to figure out how to actually control the city."

"Find someone else. Anyone else. I'm not putting her in danger." Radyn understood he was being stubborn, but he'd almost lost her once already this week, and he'd let himself be cursed before he willingly put her at risk again.

"Why not?" Jyn asked, as though he couldn't understand why a man wouldn't want to escort his wife into a battle.

Kaya answered for Radyn. "She's pregnant."

The news cracked Jyn's stony expression, and he grinned. "Truly? Congratulations."

"Thank you, but I'm not going to risk her or the child," Radyn said.

"You can either risk their lives today or you can risk their futures," Jyn said. There was sympathy in his gaze but steel in his voice. "You understand this, so don't pretend to be a fool."

It wasn't Jyn's words that bent Radyn's refusal to cooperate. It was instead in the manner in which he addressed Radyn, knowing that Radyn knew the correct way forward and that his refusal was nothing but cowardice.

And so here they were, on the back of their dragons, flying not toward the Maker city, not yet, but toward his second home, his true home.

They landed outside the main gates, and while everyone dismounted and stretched their limbs, it was Jyn, Kaya, and Radyn that walked toward the ruin. The gates stood tall and looked exactly as Radyn had left them, which eased some of his worry. They opened wide as he approached, and those standing guard on the other side recognized him and Jyn. Radyn let Jyn speak with his Swords standing guard, catching them up on all that had happened in the short time they'd been on the surface, while he hurried through Underhill toward his apartment. It was late enough in the day that Aria should be there.

She looked up when he entered, and he walked straight to her and held her in his arms. She wrapped her own arms around him in response, holding him as tightly as he held her. "Something's wrong?" she asked.

"A long story, but Firestone is bleeding altitude and can't be fixed. We're going to assault the Maker city Kaya and I found, and hopefully land Firestone there."

Each of his sentences deserved a long explanation, but there wasn't time. Aria didn't need the details, not now. She heard his words and heard the message behind them, jumping ahead to the inevitable conclusion. "You want me to come with, to see if I can understand the Maker's machinery."

"I want you to stay safe, but yes, we need you."

"I'll grab what I need."

She hurried to their study and quickly rummaged through the various tools she'd collected over the years, tossing a handful into a small pack she slung over her shoulders. Radyn watched from the doorway, amazed at the ease with which she adapted to changes. She'd always been that way, ever since the first day he'd met her, rescuing her from Whitehawk's crash.

The thought made him grimace. He forgot, sometimes, all that she'd already survived. If she knew that he'd wanted to hide her away while another city fell from the sky, one she could have helped save, she would have been disappointed in him. How many times had she told him that she hoped no one else would ever have to experience the same suffering that she had?

Once she was ready, they made their way back to the main gates, where Jyn was waiting for them. Jyn bowed toward Aria. "It is good to see you again," he said.

She returned the bow. "And you as well."

The Blade of Firestone wasn't as polite to Radyn. "I'm pulling the Singers and the Swords from Underhill to help us. It's not open for negotiation."

Radyn had expected something of the sort, and though he wasn't pleased, there seemed little point in arguing. Underhill would likely be fine through their absence, and Radyn felt better having as much help as possible with the assault. He nodded, and they returned to their dragons and circled up.

Jyn asked Radyn to give the clan warriors as much information as he could, and he quickly detailed the nature of the Maker city, as well as the warriors they'd found there. He described the abilities he'd witnessed, both down on the surface and against the disciples in Firestone. There were a few questions, and then they mounted the dragons and took to the sky.

Jyn had decided, and Radyn had agreed, that they would launch the assault from the hidden hatch Radyn had discovered. There were too many questions surrounding the machines Kaya and Radyn had first taken in, and though the long ladder represented a terrible choke point, it was a guaranteed entrance into the city. It was worth the risk.

Radyn kept his eyes on the ground below, but he didn't see any evidence the unusual warriors were advancing on Underhill. The flight was quick and uneventful, but the sun kissed the horizon by the time they landed on the hillside

Radyn and Kaya had once emerged from. A short search revealed the hatch. The groups of Swords gathered round, and Kaya searched for any sign of the warriors with her song. After a moment, she said, "I don't think they're anywhere close."

"But they're within?" Radyn had dared to hope they might have left the area, but Kaya's expression made him think that he had been overly optimistic.

"They are. I can sense them near the Engine."

There was nothing for it, then, but Radyn was more than happy to lead the way down the ladder and into the hallways below. As Kaya had predicted, there was no one nearby, and soon the hallway was filled with Swords, maniblades at the ready.

Radyn, Aria, Kaya, and Jyn took position near the center of the column, and Kaya directed the group toward the center of the Maker city. They quietly stepped down silent stairwells and crept down empty hallways, their path well-lit and clean. Radyn didn't miss the way Aria studied her surroundings, and he had the feeling that if they survived the next few days without a catastrophe, and if they cleared this city of the dark-eyed warriors, she'd be sleeping here within the week. She couldn't resist any mystery the Makers had left behind.

Radyn didn't think he would mind. Philosophers, researchers, and builders had plundered the cities for generations to recover the secrets of the Makers, and while there was no doubt plenty that remained undiscovered, the path to finding it wasn't obvious. This city represented another way forward, and he'd be pleased to stand by Aria's side as she interrogated every piece of machinery for its secrets.

He focused his attention as they reached the lower levels

of the city and made their way closer to the cavernous center.

Kaya slowed, and the entire column, more than forty of Firestone's best warriors, stopped around her. She appeared to be looking off into the distance, though there was nothing but blank wall for her to see. Then she said, "We've been noticed. Their Singers have begun the shadow song. We should move quickly, before it gets much stronger."

Jyn fell into step beside her. "What does that mean for us?"

"It means that you should be ready for a fight when we arrive. Your Singers need to connect with their shards, now, too, to help me protect the group from any attacks."

Jyn did one better, and asked the Singers to follow Kaya's orders. Then he took command of the Swords, and every maniblade came to life in the column. They resumed their march through the city, only having to detour once because of a dead end. They backtracked a bit, took a different route at the last intersection, then finally came upon a hallway that led to the center.

At least, it looked as though it led into the center. The space at the end of the hallway had the feeling of an enormous cavern, but that was precious little to go on. Light ended at the same place the tunnel did.

Though the darkness was nearly perfect, Radyn swore he saw it moving, bulging in places and running like a waterfall in others. It was alive in ways mundane darkness was not, seeking release from the prison created for it, but unable to escape.

Radyn held out his hand, and Jyn ordered a halt. "That's the same darkness we encountered when we fought the disciples in Firestone."

"The darkness you can't see though, but they can?"

Radyn nodded.

Jyn looked to Kaya. "Is there a way for you to dispel it?"

"Not unless you want to bear the brunt of the force the shadow singers are already attacking us with," Kaya said.

Radyn hadn't sensed a hint of the attack, and from the expression on his face, Jyn hadn't either. "It's that bad already?" the Blade asked.

"It would be best if you could hurry. The power they're hitting us with is considerable."

Jyn looked to Radyn for confirmation.

"If she says we're under attack, I believe her."

Jyn turned back to the cavernous room. "If what you've said is true, we'll get slaughtered if we go in there."

Radyn thought back to his last fight in the darkness. "Maniblades dispel the darkness, at least for a few paces. It's not ideal, but if we move forward as a group, we might be able to keep the surroundings lit enough to defend ourselves."

Jyn just shook his head, as though he didn't believe he allowed Radyn to keep talking him deeper into madness. Then he said, "Junior Swords, you'll form the outer perimeter, one pace ahead of the Senior Swords. Leave yourselves gaps so you aren't getting in each other's way or the Senior Swords. If you can't see far enough ahead, back up half a step."

The Swords shuffled into position, forming two rough rings, with Jyn, Radyn, the Singers, and Aria in the center. Jyn took up position closer to the front of the formation, and Radyn protected the Singers and Aria from the rear.

Jyn took one last look around, then broke from his position and joined the Junior Swords near the front edge of the circle. Radyn grunted. It was a foolish risk, but he saw the way the Swords' shoulders straightened at the presence of the Blade. Whatever he and Jyn might disagree about, there was no doubt he was among the greatest of Blades Firestone had ever known.

"Be on your guard. When they attack, they'll attack quickly," Jyn said.

Then he led them into the darkness, the pale blue of his maniblade piercing the veil and pushing forward.

28

After what felt like a trek that had taken half a day, Nikki found Josiah's apartment. She silently thanked Jona and Ralynne, whose uniforms and sometimes forceful presence had cleared the worst of the mob from their path. It was better than cursing herself for knowledge she couldn't have had. Josiah's apartment wasn't merely near the healing quarters, it was only one level down and a few hundred paces away. If Josiah had made away with Jelrik, as Nikki feared, it would have been an easy journey. And if she'd somehow figured out Josiah was responsible earlier, and somehow known where he'd lived, she could have cut nearly an hour off her chase.

It was impossible for her to know, of course, but when she envisioned Jelrik alone with his captor for an hour, she started to fear what she might find when they opened the door.

The hallways in this area were busy, but it seemed that most of the families who lived nearby had either already left for the surface or decided to wait out the chaos in their homes, spending what might be their last hours together.

They reached the door and Nikki tested the handle. It was locked, but that came as no surprise. She pulled out her master key and slid it into the lock, grateful that the noise from the hallway would be enough to prevent the sound of the key from being heard. A few curious passersby slowed as they neared Nikki and the Daggers, but the danger of Firestone's descent and some glares from Jona and Ralynne were more than enough to keep most mindful of the fact they had other places to be.

Nikki twisted the key gently and the door unlocked. Now the noise of the hallway was a detriment rather than a help. If she cracked open the door, sound would pour through the crack and alert Josiah. She spoke quickly with the two Daggers, planning out their assault. "If it comes to a fight, go for the kill. Seize any advantage you have, because he won't give you many chances."

Both the young Daggers nodded, but neither went for their maniblades until Nikki reminded them they couldn't fight empty-handed. She ignored the sinking feeling in her stomach by twisting the door handle and leading the way in. The door opened into a living area filled with furniture and paintings. Nikki noted the paintings, one of which was of a happy family, painted on the surface of Firestone. Josiah stood as the proud father over two young girls and a beautiful wife, and it looked to have been painted in better times.

None of the women in the painting appeared to be in the apartment. Josiah looked up, surprise written on his face as he recognized Nikki. Jelrik was here, too, though in substantially worse condition than when Nikki had seen him last. His left eye was swollen shut, and his right didn't look like it was far behind. Blood streamed from a broken nose and dripped onto his white robes.

He was tied, hand and foot, to a chair, and it looked like at least one of his fingers had been broken, and another was gone completely.

Nikki saw it all, but she never stopped moving. She pulled her dagger from the sheath on her hip, woefully unprepared for the fight she had no choice but to attempt. Pale blue light shone from behind her, and Ralynne and Jona charged Josiah at the same time.

Their surprise almost lasted long enough, but Josiah recovered as Ralynne brought her maniblade up. He took two steps back and reached for his hip. His eyes went wide, though, when he didn't find anything there. His gaze darted around the room before they landed on the dining room table in an adjacent corner. His maniblade, coated in blood that had to be Jelrik's, rested there.

Ralynne cut down, and though she was every bit as quick as a clan-trained Dagger should be, Josiah was faster. He stepped closer, sweeping aside her arms with one forearm and driving a fist at her stomach with the other arm. Ralynne twisted her hip and torso away from the fist, turning what might have been a devastating blow into nothing more than a glancing one.

It still let Josiah escape past her, though. Nikki desperately lunged at him with her dagger, but she didn't have the reach or the speed. He was outside her reach by the time she stabbed at him. Jona might have been quick enough to intercept the Sword, but the Dagger stood rooted in place, maniblade in hand and still as a carved stone.

Josiah reached the maniblade and woke it in time to intercept Ralynne's next cut. Nikki connected with the shard at her wrist and leaped to help the Dagger, approaching Josiah from a different angle. He shifted to keep them both in sight, but Nikki didn't dare get too close with her shorter weapon and slower speed. She placed herself just beyond the edge of his reach and kept to his side, a constant threat he had to adjust for as he battled Ralynne. Even with the distraction, Ralynne couldn't land a single cut on him.

Josiah quickly tired of the game. He deflected Ralynne's maniblade away with a strong swipe of his weapon, then leaped at Nikki. She retreated, but he was too fast. He cut at her with the maniblade and like a fool, she tried to block with her dagger. The maniblade went through the steel like it was silk and sliced through her cheek as she pulled her head away.

Jona joined the fight in time to save Nikki from Josiah's next cut, which gave Ralynne enough time to rejoin the battle. Maniblades filled the living room, and Nikki backed away from the fight, knowing her presence would only hinder the Daggers. She ran to Jelrik and cut at the ropes holding him with what remained of her steel dagger. She accidentally cut him, too, but after the injuries he'd already suffered, she didn't think he'd notice. He barely seemed aware of his surroundings as it was.

Josiah roared, and Nikki turned her head to judge the progress of the battle. Ralynne and Jona seemed to be holding their ground, but she couldn't tell if they were pressuring Josiah or if he had the upper hand. The fight was beyond her skill to judge.

Did she try to take Jelrik out of here while the other three fought, or did she stay and help in whatever way she could? It would have been an easy decision if she'd known how the fight was likely to turn out, but she couldn't tell.

Then Josiah broke through Jona's guard and cut across the side of his neck. Blood sprayed from the cut, and Jona dropped to his knees, clutching his hand to the side of his neck in a futile effort to stop the bleeding.

Ralynne, who'd fought so well until that point, froze as Jona fell, and in the blink of an eye had a maniblade thrust through her torso. Josiah pulled the blade out and Ralynne stared, wide-eyed, at the hole just above her stomach.

Nikki couldn't fight Josiah on her own, so she did the only thing she could think of. She grabbed Jelrik, connected with the shard on her wrist, and tried to pull him out of the chair and out of the living room. She'd made it all of a step when a maniblade appeared in front of her throat, slowing her to a stop.

"Put him back," Josiah demanded, voice cold as ice.

She turned her head to him and saw black flecks floating in his eyes, something she was sure hadn't been there before. She would have noticed. Moreso, she would have seen the hint of madness lurking behind those flecks. Or maybe not madness, but another force that simply looked like madness. She didn't know. She only knew that she'd spent time with Josiah, had looked him in the eye before, and she hadn't seen anything like this.

Her mind raced even as she obeyed. It was, she believed, a wise practice to obey any Sword holding a maniblade to your throat, for few arguments were more persuasive than the threat of force issued by one more than capable of following through. Jelrik's condition and the bodies on the floor left no doubt as to Josiah's ability.

How had it happened? Had Josiah always been a traitor, as she'd initially thought, or had he been corrupted by the shadow song? Both? And perhaps most importantly, did any of it matter? He was here, and he was her enemy. At the moment, explanations seemed superfluous.

Nikki placed Jelrik back in the chair, trying to be gentle, but he groaned anyway, and she wondered how much of the abuse he'd endured was hidden beneath his stained white robes.

"Get away from him."

She took a step back and held up her hands to show she was no threat.

"Take off the shard," he ordered.

She obeyed, taking off the wristband and dropping it in front of her.

"Now kick it to me."

She did, watching as one of her most valuable weapons skidded and rolled to his feet. Then she blinked, and he was in front of her. She took a step back, but his free hand closed around her throat, cutting off her air and locking her in place. She clawed at his wrist, but it might as well have been made from steel. He leaned in close, his breath smelling of decay.

"How did you find me? Do you know where it is?"

She tried to explain, but couldn't get the words past her constricted throat. Josiah snarled and loosened his grip, and with that first intake of air, Nikki silently thanked Jyn for his abundance of caution. She connected with the shard tied tightly to her thigh and formed a blade in her hand. Every instructor she'd ever had would have been disappointed in the quality of the weapon, but it had a sharp point and was formed from the song itself. She drove the blade up and under his chin, the pale blue glow piercing the soft skin underneath, traveling through his mouth, open in surprise, and up to his brain, where it killed him instantly.

He fell, and she fell beside him, still gasping for air. After a few deep, shuddering breaths, her lungs recovered, and she pushed herself to her feet. She grabbed the band that she'd kicked at Josiah and strapped it again around her wrist. Then she picked up his maniblade, ripped the clip off his belt and put it on hers. As a mere Shield, she wasn't allowed possession of a maniblade, but they'd forgive her today.

Jelrik groaned in his chair and Nikki hurried over to him. "How bad is it?" she asked.

"Nothing fatal, and nothing a healer won't be able to fix when we have the time. But now is not the time. He was trying to force me to bring the city down. He believed I had a corrupted shard, something from when you had captured Branden."

Nikki helped Jelrik from the chair and supported as much of his weight as she could. "What happened to him?"

"Not sure. I think he'd been a disciple for a while, but today was the first day I felt the shadow song within him. Something had changed, and it got hold of him. I think something might have happened to his family, but he never said."

"Should we get you to a healer?"

Jelrik vehemently shook his head. "We need to go to the Engine room. The other Singers need my help if we're ever going to land Firestone without a disaster."

Nikki looked around the room and wished there was something more she could do, but the Daggers were dead, and so was Josiah. The only way to honor their sacrifice was to save Firestone. "If that's what it takes, I'll get you to the Engine room," she promised.

29

The pitch darkness that existed beyond the glow of their maniblades made it nearly impossible to know how far they had traveled into the bowels of the cavernous space. Their footsteps sounded dully against the stone floor, and any noise they made was devoured by the unnatural darkness that tried to swallow them whole. Radyn guessed that they had advanced maybe a third of the way into the room when the shadow warriors attacked.

Their attack demonstrated either their absolute confidence in their superiority or a complete lack of battlefield tactics. Three warriors emerged from the shadows at the head of the circle, moving with that unnatural speed Radyn was becoming all too familiar with.

The Swords' concentration hadn't faltered, though, and they reacted as quickly and professionally as Radyn had come to expect from Jyn's warriors. Maniblade met shadow as the battle was joined. Two Swords fell before Jyn joined the fight, flowing like water as his maniblade cut down one of the shadow warriors.

Radyn watched Jyn with undisguised interest. He'd never seen the Blade of Firestone so much as spar, and though rumors of his skill were plentiful, it was the first time Radyn had an opportunity to weigh the truth of the rumors with his own eyes.

Jyn's confident cuts left no doubt as to the baseline of his skill. Radyn didn't think he was connected with more than two shards, but he moved with a flowing grace that effortlessly connected one action to the next. He didn't seem that fast, and yet the second shadow warrior fell back before Jyn and died before he reached the safety of the darkness.

Radyn wasn't just witnessing Jyn's ability with the shards; he was watching a martial master, strengthened by more shards than any human in living memory had endured before.

Before the third shadow warrior fell to the focused efforts of several Swords, another pair of shadow warriors attacked from behind the group, their arrival more devastating than the first, as many Swords were at least partially distracted by the fighting on the first front.

Radyn counted himself among the distracted, and by the time he realized the danger, four Swords already lay dead. The shadow warriors' advance stalled as they met more Swords, and Radyn rushed to lend his strength to the circle's defenses.

He joined the fight in time to prevent one of the shadow swords from striking down an exposed clan member. Radyn and the Sword retaliated together, and the Sword landed the killing blow. Radyn looked around the circle, but there were no further enemies.

"Tighten up the formation. We keep moving," Jyn ordered.

Radyn returned to his place in the smaller circle, and they continued their walk through the darkness. The bodies drifted away from the pool of light, and Radyn was possessed by an uncomfortable certainty that he'd never see the bodies again, as though the darkness was hungry and would devour flesh and bone alike.

They stopped again when the Singers started falling to their knees, one after the other, until only Kaya was standing. It was all the warning they received before the darkness tried once again to close in around them.

Primal screams erupted from the darkness, surrounding them and deafening them to all else. The sounds chilled his blood, unlike any noise he'd heard before. Then they attacked from all directions, and Radyn couldn't count them. It felt like fewer warriors than Jyn had brought, but they had the shadow song on their side, and Kaya and her fellow Singers were on the brink of their own defeat. Connected to his own shards, Radyn felt the pressure of the silence squeezing the last of the light from the room.

He held himself back for a long moment as he observed the clash of Manirah and shadow warrior. The warriors, whom he'd only seen down on the surface, were far superior to the men and women Radyn and Magni had fought in Firestone's hallways. They weren't limited to a single technique, but used the shadow song much as the Swords used the song of the Engines.

More Swords than shadow warriors fell in those first moments. The shadow warriors weren't just strong and fast; they fought like a people whose home was about to be taken away, rushing into fights heedless of any risk to life or limb. They died, but almost always at a cost higher than Firestone's clan could bear.

Jyn's light burned brighter than ever. He held fully a

quarter of the circle on his own, and none of the shadow warriors could stand before him.

Radyn defended in the opposite direction, reinforcing a group of Swords who were close to breaking. His appearance shifted the momentum of the battle in that part of the circle, tipping the scales in the clan's favor. Swords who had been slowly giving ground stopped, and Radyn's maniblade helped them regain a few precious paces. The clan still had numbers, and Radyn kept the shadow warriors' dark blades from pruning those numbers more than they already had. More than once, he deflected a shadow blade long enough for a Sword to land a deep cut on the offending shadow warrior, and together they pushed their assailants back.

Radyn's thoughts of victory were dashed as one Singer's stomach distended and burst open. The darkness that waited beyond the boundary of the battles rushed in, and Radyn and the other Swords retreated several paces, only stopping once the combined strength of the Singers and their maniblades could keep the darkness at bay and their enemies in sight.

Radyn took another step back, disengaging from the fight and studying the battle. Victory for either side still balanced precariously, like a coin standing on edge that could fall either way, but if it went on for much longer, he feared it would fall on the side of the shadow warriors. The strength of the shadow song was too much for Kaya and her small group to handle, and it would decide the battle if it was allowed.

He retreated farther, to where Kaya had also fallen to her knees. "Where?" he asked.

She pointed in a direction that was slightly downhill. Radyn oriented himself that way.

He felt Aria come beside him. "You're going?" she asked.

"I'll be back soon. I love you."

"Love you too." She didn't try to convince him to stay, didn't try to do anything but support him.

He waited for an opening in the battle, and once it appeared, he sprinted into the darkness.

NIKKI STRUGGLED with Jelrik against the crowds. His Singer's robes were too bloodied to be instantly recognizable, and she had no more Daggers to clear the way for her. They were jostled, pushed, and shoved, each unexpected motion causing Jelrik to groan in pain. Once, she glanced back and saw that they left a trail of blood drops behind them, and she was glad she didn't think anyone else was tracking them.

One rude shove knocked her up against another body, and the impact was such it almost dislodged the maniblade from its clip. She repositioned it with her free hand, then gripped it tighter. She pulled it free from the clip and connected with the shard within.

Her body and mind were already tired from the fights she'd endured, and despite her affinity with the shards, she wasn't clan and hadn't trained with them nearly enough. She feared, as her heart raced and fresh strength flooded through exhausted limbs, that it might be too much for her body to handle. But she held the maniblade in the air as it lit, and the sight of it cleared the hallway faster than even the Daggers had.

She and Jelrik made good time after that, and it wasn't long before they'd worked their way through the rest of the crowds. They were going down toward the Engine room as everyone else was escaping up. She released her connection to the shard and slipped the maniblade back into the clip at her hip.

"You're stronger than you give yourself credit for," Jelrik said between wheezing breaths. Under any other circumstances, Nikki would have rushed him to a healer. It was clear the wounds he'd suffered were worse than she could see. Perhaps he'd punctured a lung, or maybe it was just some broken ribs. When she'd connected with the song, she heard him Singing, strengthening himself with power that wasn't his own.

"You can compliment me after this is over," Nikki replied, "until then, let's focus on conserving your strength for what's to come."

He gave her a knowing smile, but she couldn't say exactly what it was he thought she knew. She could guess, but she pushed the possibility out of her mind.

Jelrik got them through the various protections around the Engine, and before long Nikki found herself again in the heart of Firestone. The Engine was nothing like she'd seen it the last time. It flickered, then brightened, then weakened, its glow anything but constant. Perhaps a dozen Singers stood on the catwalk around the Engine, and Nikki felt the song in her bones, even though she wasn't connected to her shard.

He spoke to Noella, who was so glad to see him she didn't ask any questions about how he'd come to them in the condition he had. She caught him up on their goal, and on the rough coordinates Radyn had given them.

Nikki meant to leave him in the Engine room and retreat to the hallways beyond, with some half-formed idea of guarding against any last attempts to sabotage the Engine, but Jelrik gripped her wrist with a bloody hand, surprising her with his remaining strength. "Connect with your shards and join me."

"I can't sing!"

"You don't have to. Just join your strength to mine. You have three shards of the Engine on your body, and I can draw on them while I sing. Your presence is all I ask for."

What he didn't say, but what was easily understood, was what joining him meant for her. If she connected with all three shards, it was more than likely the power would destroy her body. Only a Senior Sword could handle so many, and that, she most certainly was not. Jelrik would draw the strength from her, but even so, it didn't mean her future was guaranteed.

Still, it was an easy decision. She'd be a part of the song, no matter how small, and that was an honor afforded to very few. The song was a mystery she'd never thought to solve, and here was her chance. Besides, she'd long ago sworn to protect Firestone with her life. That decision had been made long ago, and now all that remained was to stay true to her word. If it sent her to the gate, well, so be it.

She helped Jelrik to sit, as he lacked the strength to both stand and sing. Then she sat beside him and took his hand. She waited until he began, and then she closed her eyes, possibly for the last time, and connected with her shards, pulled by him into the song.

RADYN COULD BARELY SEE in front of him. The maniblade's glow banished the immediate darkness, but never for more than a pace or two. He trusted his footsteps to the Makers' smooth, uniform floors and rushed forward. If anyone chased him, he didn't know. If anyone waited ahead for him, he'd soon find out. His stomach was lodged in his throat, and he didn't think he'd even been so scared the day he'd been working in the fields of Firestone and he and Father had been attacked.

He saw nothing, heard nothing, and sensed nothing, but he plunged forward, maniblade ahead, trusting in Kaya's direction. Darkness continued to part until he sensed the difference through his shards, a silence deeper than the rest, angled slightly farther down the slope of the floor. He shifted that way until the light of his maniblade revealed the first limbs of the shadow Singers.

They were sitting in a circle, and as near as he could tell, they were undefended. His stomach churned at the thought of striking down unarmed enemies, but they fought with powers not visible to the naked eye. He cut two down and the darkness that surrounded him weakened noticeably, bringing into view a guard racing back from the main battle.

Radyn cut twice more, and two more bodies slumped to the side, but the last woman, who'd been in the center of the circle, opened her eyes and froze him in place. They were purely black, with no trace of iris or bloodshot veins. Her gaze wrapped him in the shadow song, as though he'd been encased in Makers' steel. The darkness around him faded more, and in the corner of his vision he could see the clan Swords, led by Jyn, retaking the ground they'd lost.

Their advance would do him little good. He strained and struggled against the invisible force holding him in place, but all he earned for his efforts was the feeling of darkness seeking a grip on his own core, as though it wanted to reach in and pull his insides out.

Radyn connected with all the shards in his body, and the woman with the pitch-black eyes shrank back from him, as though he was a fire she might get burned by if she came too close. He moved his arm an inch, and could start to wiggle, but the bonds around him remained tight. The warrior was almost on him, and he could do nothing but watch as the shadow blade came up to take his life.

He reached for the song with his spirit, searching for an extra burst of strength that would help him break through his bonds, but there was nothing but the beauty of the song, which he could hear but not use.

Lacking any better options, he gave himself to the song, allowed himself to fall deeply into it, letting his spirit wander through its endless beauty. If he was to die, at least let it be like this, close to what he loved almost as much as Aria.

In his surrender, the song surrounded him and held him close. It took away his pain and fear, and it was only then, when his heart stopped racing, that he felt that he wasn't alone.

The spirit was familiar, and yet impossible, but he reached out his spirit to it, missing her guidance more than he would have thought possible. He'd always felt lost since, though he'd charged ahead anyway, for what else could one do with a life? She gave him strength beyond what he was capable of summoning from the Engine, greater than he could control with his shards.

The shadow blade fell on the back of his neck and cracked. Light and song that weren't his own burst his bonds, and he cut the last of the shadow Singers down even as she tried to scramble away. Only then did he turn back to the warrior who'd come so close to killing him, and that duel was won in the beat of a heart.

To Nikki, the song of the Engine occupied a unique place in her thoughts. She believed in it because it was what kept her city in the air, and when she was in touch with the shards, she sensed its presence and basked in its power. Despite that, it was never real to her the way that food, steel knives, and other people were. It existed in a world that overlapped hers, but in such a way she barely touched it.

Taking part in Jelrik's song was no different than learning firsthand that the gate was real and waiting for her on the other side of her body's death. He pulled strength from her body and spirit even as the song wrapped itself around her and held her in an everlasting embrace.

The song was beyond her ability to describe it. It was music, yes, with harmonies that built on top of one another like layers in a cake, but it was so much more. It was the stuff of the world, the order that rested beneath the surface of all things. Even Jelrik, she sensed, didn't understand it, not really. He'd only learned how to interact with it, and only crudely at that. If one were to truly understand it, they'd have the power of gods.

The song closest to her, though, was no longer beautiful. It bled silence like a wounded animal, stumbling toward a hiding place where it might die. Singers coaxed, encouraged, and threatened, but they needed more to give, and they were already giving everything they knew how.

Song and silence battled, and Nikki gave her spirit to Jelrik to use as he needed. He pulled, but she sensed his reticence to pull too much. She would have complained, but she understood the truth behind his decision. He could pull enough to kill her easily, but it wouldn't make the slightest difference in the outcome. Her shards were nothing more than a drop of water in a bottomless well.

The Engine was dying, and it seemed as though there

was nothing they could do. Jelrik and the others sang louder, putting all of their spirits into the song, just to keep Firestone in the air, but body and spirit were only so strong, and over time their efforts weakened, and the city fell faster. Though she was locked within the city, there were times when Nikki swore she could feel the acceleration, a failure the Singers never permitted themselves.

Jelrik was loudest among the Singers despite his injuries, leaving nothing of himself separate. In the realm of the song, he stood tallest and shone brightest, but even his light dimmed as the silence reached out to engulf him. He kept singing, though his voice grew more distant. She willed more of her spirit and strength to him, but couldn't tell if it made a difference.

Another voice joined the chorus of Singers, different than all the rest. Jelrik and the others differed in strength, but their song was mostly the same, rougher and harsher to the ear than the song of the Engines. The voice that joined them wasn't an Engine, but it was closer to the Engines' song than Firestone's Singers. Its tune was ethereal, lighter than a feather, but stronger than the edge of any maniblade.

Jelrik's song faltered when he heard the new voice, as though all he wanted was to listen. The pause was only for a moment, though, and then the two songs rushed together, like friends reunited after a long time apart. The new song joined Jelrik's, which had itself become stronger than before. They became inseparable, and far greater than the sum of their individual songs.

For the briefest of moments Nikki felt the weight of her body and knew that Firestone had stopped falling. It still wouldn't be enough to save the city. At this point, Nikki wasn't sure such a feat was even possible. But they'd stopped losing altitude, and maybe, just maybe, that gave them a chance.

Except now they faced another problem, one Nikki only became gradually aware of as she listened to the Singers begin to sing against one another, not out of any maliciousness, but out of ignorance. She heard them calling to one another, not through the song, but using their voices.

"Where to?" one asked.

"A few degrees north," another answered.

"Hold steady!" came Jelrik's command.

It was all they could do to simply keep Firestone in the air. If they started fighting one another about small changes, the whole city would drop.

Nikki understood the problem, remembered well what Radyn had said when he'd given Jyn the coordinates. They had only been a rough guess as to their destination. Now that they were close, they needed something or someone to guide them the rest of the way. Otherwise, all their sacrifices would be for nothing, and Firestone would crash into the side of a hill.

THE SUDDEN ABSENCE of shadow almost made Radyn lose his balance. He swayed like a drunk, then spread his feet and stood straight. With the shadow gone, Firestone's Swords made short work of the remaining defenders. Radyn glanced down at the circle of shadow Singers and shuddered. A hand to his stomach assured him he remained in one piece.

He ran back to the others, sharing a nod with Jyn as he helped Kaya to her feet. The city's Engine lay cold and dark at the center of the room. Kaya looked to it, then at the surviving Swords. "I think it's best if you stay here. I don't know how much resistance you'll have to the song right now."

Jyn nodded. "We'll wait here. Hurry."

Kaya ran toward the Engine with the other Singers, and Radyn stood beside Jyn. "Don't you think someone should protect them?"

"There's no one else here. Even if someone were to attack from the opposite side of the room, we'd reach the Singers before they were in trouble. And she's right. I'm not even confident of my own ability to resist the song. That shadow, it leeches our spirit if we're even close. It's more dangerous than any Sword I've ever fought."

Radyn agreed. "I wish we could have left at least one alive, to see what we might learn from them."

"I think this was far from the last we'll see of them, don't you?"

"Unfortunately, I agree."

After so much struggle, the stillness of the moment made him feel antsy. He connected with the shard in his maniblade and listened to Kaya begin her song to the Engine. It was familiar to him, now, but that didn't mean it wasn't beautiful. Without training, she'd found her own, better path. "You should connect to at least one of your shards and listen to her. She's like nothing you've ever heard before."

Jyn glanced down at him, then back to Kaya. His eyes widened slightly, then closed as he let her song wash over him. The lines of tension on his face eased and his shoulders relaxed. He took a deep breath. "She should have been with us. None of this might have come to pass."

"She needed an Engine of her own, one she could do with as she pleased. What you're hearing wouldn't have been possible if she'd remained on Firestone. And you would have made even more enemies than you already have."

Jyn grunted. "Most people don't casually tell me when I'm wrong."

"Your loss. There is one thing you were right about, though, as much as it pains me to admit it."

"What's that?"

"If we were to fight, I couldn't beat you."

Jyn smiled at that. "Are you going to keep trying to surpass me?"

"Of course."

Jyn smiled wider. "Good."

"How many shards are you up to?"

The grin turned mischievous. "At least six."

Radyn snorted and shook his head, and then there was nothing else to speak about as the Engine came to life with a pale blue glow, another song to add to the beautiful web of harmonies sung by the Engines across the land.

Kaya shouted for Aria, who ran toward the Singers. They conferred briefly, with Kaya pointing north. Aria nodded and ran that way.

"I'm going to protect my wife," Radyn told Jyn.

"By all means. I'll keep an eye on the Singers. If you need any reinforcements, just shout."

Radyn ran after Aria and caught up to her with ease. He asked no questions, more than content to stay by her side. She ran into the hallway Kaya had pointed out, then stopped at the first door on the left. She tried to open it, but it refused to budge. Aria stepped back and gestured to the door. "If you could do the honors," she said.

"With pleasure." Radyn woke his maniblade and cut down the left side of the door, slicing through the locking mechanism. He put his shoulder to the door, and it cracked open without much resistance. He bowed and let Aria pass.

The room lit as soon as they entered, and Aria looked around. A flat, angled surface that appeared to be made of glass stood near the center of the room, and Aria made for it. "Kaya said that a considerable amount of power from the Engine was flowing into this room. Hopefully this works."

Before Radyn could even issue a warning, Aria pressed her hands against the glass and closed her eyes. Nothing physical happened, but Aria was squeezing her eyes tight and leaning forward, connected with the Makers' machinery. Time stretched, and he imagined Firestone coming close, crashing into a hill while Aria tried to understand the Makers' methods. He kept his lips pressed tightly together, knowing, too, that anything he said would serve as nothing more than a distraction.

He was startled when what he thought was a wall flickered and disappeared, revealing the cavernous room on the other side. He took a few tentative steps toward the wall, holding out his hand, until it pressed against something solid. It wasn't Makers' steel, but it was something smooth that could either become transparent or show what was on the other side of the wall.

"Figured you would want to see what happens," Aria said.

He turned, his perspective shifting yet again. She believed she had time to give him a view, and she knew well the stakes of the moment. Though her eyes were closed, she was grinning from ear to ear, as happy as he'd ever seen her. She'd learned more about the Makers' machinery than he'd suspected.

"Draining the water above," she said.

As soon as she spoke, it became true. Holes opened in

the floor of the cavern, covered by grates, and a moment later, an enormous amount of water poured from holes in the ceiling, falling through the cavern into the drains below. They were protected by the walls of the room, but even so, Radyn could hear the roar of the water as though he was standing next to a waterfall. For those in the room, it must have been nearly deafening. He looked, and sure enough, the Swords were covering their ears, looking around as though in a daze.

Draining the pond above took less time than Radyn would have imagined, and soon the water was no more than a steady trickle, and Aria moved to the next stage. "Opening the doors," she said.

Radyn didn't realize what doors she meant until he saw cracks appearing in the cavern ceiling. He almost screamed for the others to run, but his voice wouldn't reach them in time. "Will they be safe?" he asked.

"They will," Aria said. "It's a marvel of construction unlike anything I've seen before."

Radyn waited for stone or soil to fall from the sky and crush either the warriors or Kaya and her singers, but none came. Some dirt fell, and water dripped down, but nothing large enough to be fatal. He could do nothing but watch, jaw hanging open, as the doors retracted, revealing the night sky above. Even the size and strength of dragons paled in comparison.

"Turning on the landing pad," Aria said.

The giant machines in the cavern started to move, as silent as anything the Makers had ever built, their enormous arms rising to the sky. Beside the machines, the Swords looked like ants, and Radyn reminded himself to breathe.

"Ready," Aria said.

The words had barely left her lips when a light shone

straight up from the Engine, defiantly piercing the darkness of the night sky.

JELRIK WAS STILL SURROUNDED by the other presence that Aria didn't dare name, but even their combined efforts were beginning to fail. Silence spread to other parts of the Engine, killing it slowly, much like having one's air choked off. Nikki's neck still felt raw from where Josiah's hand had tried to wring answers out of her.

Nikki's own body was weakening, reaching the absolute end of its strength. She didn't know how much longer they needed to last, but she hoped it wouldn't be long. Jelrik and the other presence were all that was keeping the Singers together, and even they were fading fast.

She felt the beacon as clear as day, promising refuge, and it was so very close.

She heard the smile on Jelrik's face as he said, "There it is."

"YOU SHOULD STEP BACK into the room. You're not going to want to miss this," Aria said.

He glanced back at her. His wife's eyes were still closed, but he had the feeling she was seeing everything and more. "You'll be safe?"

"I will."

"I won't be far."

Her grin grew a bit wider, the smile of a wife confident in her husband. "I know."

He stepped out of the room and walked down the

hallway. In a moment, he saw what she hoped he'd see. The edge of Firestone moved into view, crawling forward until it hung over the hole above his head. The light from the Engine below shone straight up, onto the very bottom of Firestone, and he could see the observation deck on the bottommost level.

A family stood there, and Radyn couldn't help but wonder what their story had been. Had one of them thought of finding refuge from the disaster near the bottom of the city? Had they thought they could somehow jump or climb off as the city neared the ground? Or had they just wanted the best seat in the city as their inevitable demise approached?

Whatever the reason, they'd walked into the most spectacular view of them all. Firestone shuddered to a stop, the Singers' control over their precious city failing even as they neared their destination. The city began to drop, and Aria, controlling the enormous arms, reached out to catch it.

Radyn briefly connected with one of his shards, then immediately regretted it. The song surrounded him, and to his untrained ear, it was a chaotic mess as the Makers' machinery, the two Engines, and a handful of Singers all worked to bring Firestone to a stop. He imagined that if they were a bit more knowledgeable, the songs would have harmonized with one another, but they weren't, and it sounded as though if Firestone survived, it would be in spite of their lack of knowledge. He disconnected and let himself watch.

The giant arms that Aria reached up with ended in enormous platforms that angled to match the slope of Firestone's base, but as Firestone settled, it never quite touched the platforms. Incredible energies kept the city in balance as the arms caught the city and guided it lower.

Finally, they groaned as they took the weight Firestone's dying Engine could no longer bear. The arms flexed, and Radyn held his breath as he waited for the arms to crack or shatter, but this was why they'd been made. They held the city above Radyn's head, and Firestone and its citizens were safe, at least for now.

30

Nikki slumped down, fighting just to stay upright. If she let herself lie down, she'd be asleep in a moment, much like many of the other Singers. They'd given everything they had, and now they rested, drawn to sleep by an exhaustion they couldn't resist. She knew well how they felt, felt it very much herself.

The Engine was dead, dark and grey, lifeless for the first time since Firestone had been launched into the sky by the Makers. The only light came from the hallway through the open door, where the lanterns still flickered dimly, casting just enough light to see by. Nikki didn't know how the lanterns burned. The Engine was dead, but power still trickled through Firestone. From the Makers' city, perhaps? She was too tired to care. Just so long as there was a little bit of light, she could keep going.

She crawled across the catwalk to where Jelrik lay. There was a smile on his face, easier than she could remember seeing from him. "It's over. We did it."

She lay down next to him, catching her breath from the effort of crawling a few mere steps. She stared up at the dark ceiling, refusing to ask the question of what came next. That problem would still be there in the morning. No need to worry about it now. For now, they were alive. On the surface, sure, but alive.

She took a few deep breaths to gather her strength. She connected with her shards, but there was no strength there to claim. They'd come from Firestone's Engine, and it was dead. She cursed softly, then pushed herself back to hands and knees. "Come on, let's get you to a healer," she said, wondering how effective healers would be without shards to aid the process.

There was no response, and a sudden fear seized her. She stared at Jelrik, and only then realized that his chest wasn't moving. Now that she thought about it, he hadn't been breathing since she lay down next to him, but she'd been too consumed by her own exhaustion to notice.

He was peaceful, though, so much so that he almost seemed like a different person. The lines on his face that existed when he frowned were gone, and the smile made him look several years younger than he had been. In his other hand, the one that hadn't been in Nikki's, he clutched his wedding ring. Nikki swallowed hard and had to look away for a moment.

He'd given everything to save Firestone. She would always remember the last few moments, when Singers had started collapsing all around them. Near the very end, it had just been her, Jelrik, and the presence, and right before the end, he'd pushed her away, then removed his ring and held it tightly in his hands. When she'd looked up at him, he'd been kissing the ring, smiling just as he was now, the other presence wrapped around him in an embrace.

Then they'd landed, and there'd been a blinding flash of light, and everything had gone dark.

She'd heard it said, often, that no Singer dared sing to the Engine alone, that its power was always too much for a lone individual.

Jelrik, at the end of his life, had proven that wrong. Although, upon reflection, she wasn't so sure he'd been entirely alone.

She closed his unswollen eye and commended his spirit to the gate, thanking him for all he'd given. Hopefully his spirit's journey was an easier one from here on out.

She groaned as she stood. Firestone was safe, and for now, that was all that mattered.

THE SEER GROANED as shadow vibrated in pain. He couldn't tell what, exactly, had happened. News was slow to travel in this world, and he could only guess so much from what he sensed.

On one hand, shadow was wounded. He'd lost some of his most talented disciples, their darkness wiped out by the light like they were bugs crawling across a table. His closest friend in the cities was dead, too, a void where shadow should have been. He thought he'd known the strength of his enemies, but they had surprised him, stronger even than his most generous estimates.

Although it wasn't strength alone that had saved them. He'd felt the movement in the song of the Engines, the presence of songs that didn't belong. As always, this world was deeper and more mysterious than he knew, and his enemies had discovered secrets he hadn't even considered possible. Light itself conspired against him, as it should if it wanted to survive.

It wasn't just his own allies in the cities that had suffered losses, though. His allies below, who were still a mystery despite all he'd learned about them, were also reeling from the blows they'd taken. It wasn't all bad, though. They'd become too confident as of late, too convinced their strength was effortlessly superior. He hardly blamed them, but Firestone had shown them that humanity of the skies still had strength to spare.

It would be in his favor, though. Now they'd flock to his cause, angry at their defeat, and no one would be able to stand against him.

At the same time, he'd dealt a crippling blow to Light and to Firestone. He no longer sensed Firestone's Engine, and though the cost had been one of his closest friends, it would all be worth it, for once Firestone fell, the rest would soon follow.

It hadn't been the victory that he'd imagined, and the cost had been so much higher than he'd planned for, but it was still a victory.

Darkness would spread, with him leading the way.

There was much to do, and little time in which to act. He rolled from his bed and went to his desk, where he'd start writing the missives that would eventually bring humanity to its knees.

THE REST of the night passed in a blur as Jyn, Radyn, and the other Swords did what they could to protect Firestone. The surface of the city was chaos, but Radyn and Tanwen started patrolling the skies, ensuring no other threats approached from the surface. Kaya and Aria worked in the Makers' city below, sealing its entrances as well as they could.

In time, Jyn got Firestone under a semblance of control, though true order would doubtless be days in coming. There were hundreds of new problems to solve, and the clan had suffered severe losses. They'd already been stretched thin, but these next few months would push them to their limits, and that was assuming no other disasters loomed.

Radyn had once dreamed of becoming the Blade of Firestone, but now he was grateful he wasn't. If Firestone had been commanded by anyone less than Jyn, he wouldn't have rated their chances highly. With Jyn, he supposed their odds were even.

As the sun rose on the eastern horizon, Radyn spotted a lone figure hiking up one of the hills. He flew closer and was surprised when he recognized the dark form. Of course, of all the people in Firestone, he was one of the most recognizable. Radyn waited until he was certain of the giant's destination, and then he asked Tanwen to land him at the appropriate summit. By the time Magni reached it, Radyn was sitting there, waiting for him.

Magni stared at him for a long moment, the hint of violence in his eyes, but then he sighed and sat down next to Radyn. "I'd hoped to be alone."

"I can leave, if you like. But there's something I wanted you to know before it was too late."

Magni's gaze traveled over Firestone, the surface of which was just a little lower than the summit of this hill. The surface was empty now, exhausted families having finally been herded back to their dimly lit apartments. "Yes?"

"When I was down there, fighting the shadow Singers, there was a moment when I thought I was dead. A moment when the shadow felt as though it had worked its way inside me. A song saved me, but it was one I didn't think I'd ever hear again."

Magni's eyes were dead inside, but he kept his peace, waiting for Radyn to get to the point.

"Magni, it was Elora. I'm sure of it."

Radyn kept his own gaze locked on Magni, and the giant slowly turned his head and fixed him with a stare. He swore he saw a hint of light in Magni's eyes, but it was quickly snuffed out. "You're either a liar or deceived," he finally said.

Radyn didn't flinch away from Magni's judgment. "Have you ever known me to be either?"

Magni looked away. "So what?"

Radyn fought the urge to lean over and put his hand on the giant's shoulder. He'd likely lose the whole arm, and that was if he was lucky. "I won't sit here and tell you that Firestone needs you. That's Jyn's duty. I just wanted you to know that there is something more happening here, something even beyond the forces of shadow we've uncovered. Elora should be on the other side of the gate, but she was here. She died saving the Engine on her own. It sounds familiar, doesn't it?"

Radyn expected more of a reaction from Magni, and he was surprised he didn't get one. The giant deflated, as though somehow disappointed. "Nikki reported something similar to Jyn. Said that there was another presence in the Engine room with them. It gave Jelrik a strength beyond what he should have been capable of. Said Jelrik died clutching his ring, a smile on his face."

A tear sprang from Radyn's eye, and he quickly wiped it away. He hadn't heard Jelrik had died, and now his last chance for forgiveness was gone. But if what Magni reported was true—it meant he'd truly sensed Elora, and his life wasn't the only one she'd saved last night.

But right now, that didn't matter as much as Magni's decision. "Will you stay with us?" Radyn asked.

Magni sighed again, and Radyn was reminded of Tanwen, when Radyn asked him to fly again after he'd already been in the air for hours. "I suppose I will. I think she'd want me to, anyway."

Radyn bowed, glad that he wouldn't have to lose another friend he respected today, then shifted his weight so he could stand.

"Will you sit with me?" Magni asked.

Radyn let his seat drop back down to the hillside and brushed off his hands. "Of course."

The sunrise found the two Swords sitting silently on the hillside together, waiting for the dawn of a new day.

THE ADVENTURES CONTINUE!

Top of the morning!

I hope that wherever you are in the world, this finds you doing well. Thanks for reading, and I hope you enjoyed the story. In an age of endless entertainment options, the choice to spend your time in these pages means the world to me.

The Song of Rising Shadow was an absolute pleasure to write, and I'm excited to share more of Radyn's journey and his world with you in 2025!

Before you go, I'd encourage you to sign up for my newsletter. In a world where everybody seems to be spamming people every 20 minutes to make a dime, I'm trying to do something different. I email every two to three weeks, usually on a Friday, and I do everything I can to make the newsletter something you'll look forward to reading. Free short stories that expand the worlds. Special offers. Fun conversations with fans. It would mean the world to me if you came over and took a look. You can sign up here:

https://ryankirkauthor.com/pages/newsletter-sign-up

And once again, thank you for being here. You're awesome.

Ryan

December 2024

ACKNOWLEDGMENTS

No author works alone, and I'm reminded of that every time I go through the process of releasing a new book. From the team of editors that helps clean up my words to the graphic designers who turn my scribbles into cover art, what you hold in your hands is the work of a team of dedicated professionals. To all of you, thank you.

As always, a tremendous thanks to my family. None of this would be possible without them, and all of this is for them.

And finally, a very special thanks to those readers who are part of my ARC team - picking through these books for errors and being willing to leave reviews to bring new readers in. If I miss anyone, I'm sorry - the fault is my own.

Thanks in this book, especially to:

Chuck

Chris

Chester

Terry

Terry F

Alexina

Neil

Floyd

Karen

Greg

Sarah

and

Kate

And one final, very special thank you to all of you reading. I couldn't do this without you.

Sincerely,

Ryan

Relentless Souls

Heart of Defiance

Their Spirit Unbroken

The Nightblade Series

Nightblade

World's Edge

The Wind and the Void

Blades of the Fallen

Nightblade's Vengeance

Nightblade's Honor

Nightblade's End

Standalone Novels

Blades of Shadow

The Last Fang of God

The Primal Series

Primal Dawn

Primal Darkness

Primal Destiny

ABOUT THE AUTHOR

Ryan Kirk is the award-winning and internationally bestselling author of over forty fantasy novels spanning nearly a dozen worlds. He lives in Minnesota with his family, where he enjoys long, meandering walks outside even when the snow is high enough to cover his legs. When he isn't glued to his keyboard, he's usually in the woods, either on foot or on a bike.

RyanKirkAuthor.com
contact@waterstonemedia.net

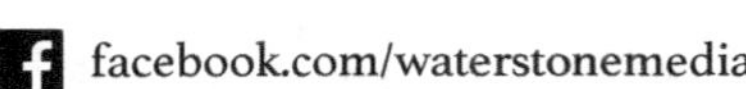 facebook.com/waterstonemedia
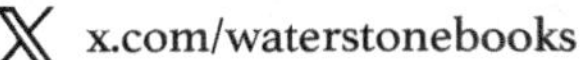 x.com/waterstonebooks
instagram.com/waterstonebooks